A New Arrival

CW01508785

Sasha Morgan lives in a village by the coast in Lancashire with her husband and has one grown up son. She writes mainly contemporary fiction, her previous series having a touch of 'spice', probably due to all the Jilly Cooper novels she read as a teenager! Besides writing, Sasha loves drinking wine, country walks and curling up with a good book.

Also by Sasha Morgan

Lilacwell Village

Escape to Lilacwell
Return to Lilacwell
Together in Lilacwell

Samphire Bay Village

Second Chances at Samphire Bay
A New Arrival at Samphire Bay

Sasha Morgan

A New Arrival *at* Samphire Bay

1₵ CANELO

Penguin
Random
House

First published in the United Kingdom in 2025 by

Canelo, an imprint of
Canelo Digital Publishing Limited,
20 Vauxhall Bridge Road,
London SW1V 2SA
United Kingdom

A Penguin Random House Company
The authorised representative in the EEA is Dorling Kindersley Verlag GmbH.
Arnulfstr. 124, 80636 Munich, Germany

A CIP catalogue record for this book is available from the British Library.

Print ISBN 978 1 80436 838 1
Ebook ISBN 978 1 80436 839 8

Cover design by Diane Meacham

Cover images © Shutterstock

Printed and bound in Great Britain by Clays Ltd, Elcograf S.p.A.

Look for more great books at
www.canelo.co | www.dk.com

1

For my brother and sister, Paul and Clare.

Chapter 1

'Found it.'

'Really? Where?' replied an excited voice.

'In Lancashire, a place called Samphire Bay. A huge Art Deco house on a peninsula. It's perfect,' stated the man, sounding very pleased with himself. He lifted his shades to look out onto the bay before him, then back again at the property he was discussing: a white Art Deco house built in 1939 sat high on a large piece of land that showed off the architecture perfectly. It showcased all the character features from the era – the modernist curvature of the bow windows, Art Deco motifs and parapets on the exterior.

As a director, he and his location manager had been scouting for months, not only to find the ideal spot, but property too, for their new drama, '*Lady Scarlett Investigates*'. Nowhere until now had fit the bill. They needed the period house as the drama was set in the 1920s, which had opened a few possibilities, but the locations hadn't been right. They were either too crowded, closely surrounded by other modern buildings or in poor condition. One house had come close to their requirements but the respective owners had proved to be a nightmare in negotiating a contract. Too many hours of discussion and planning had been poured into a deal that never went through, which had wasted valuable time and set back the production. Hence the location manager's next question.

'Have you spoken to the owners?' he asked warily, ever mindful of the previous hindrance.

'No need.'

'Why?'

'I've just bought it,' came the smug reply.

Registering an interest in the house a week ago, under his real name – Adam. F. Sinclair – had proved extremely advantageous. It had given him a degree of anonymity, which is exactly what he desired. As a relatively well-known actor, he went by the stage name of Felix Paschal, Felix being his second name and Pascal his French mother's maiden name. Now, after years of treading the boards in theatres up and down the country and starring in various TV series and films, Felix had decided to go into directing. He'd often envied the directors' role on shoots, their ability to lead and manage. That's what he'd craved, a bit of control. Gone for him the early morning starts, unsociable hours and monotonous slog of memorising lines. Plus, there was the intrusion that acting inevitably brought, as well as the copious amount of fan mail. Not that he didn't appreciate his fans, he did, but when he couldn't leave the studios for fear of being followed, or when one or two had taken to stalking, the alarm bells started to ring.

However, the biggest drawback to being a successful actor had been the complete invasion of his personal life. He had recently split up from a long-term girlfriend, supermodel Anika Genness. With both of them being in the public eye, their separation had been hot news and was just about plastered over every tabloid going. For Felix, it was a bridge too far. For Anika, it was welcomed publicity. She loved to be the centre of attention and relished being the focus of the paparazzi. She could work it. Boy, could she work it, turning on the tears at the drop of a hat or a sniff of a camera. Anika had played the victim, the 'wronged woman' to the heartbreaker Felix Paschal. It was far from the truth – they both knew it, but she wasn't going to let that get in the way of a good story. And a good story was exactly what she was spinning, for all the world to see.

All the media interest had evidently been fruitful for Anika, so much so, her agent positively encouraged it. Several modelling contracts had appeared as a result of her very public break up with the heartthrob actor. She had also been approached to be the face of a make-up advertising campaign, which offered a very lucrative fee. So for Anika Genness, she was the 'It Girl', forever in the news and with plenty of work coming in – happy days.

For Felix, it meant even more attention and a further invasion of privacy and he *hated* it. He wanted out. Out of London where it seemed the world and his wife knew where he was, constantly having to look over his shoulder. He'd grown tired of having to disguise himself. Felix wanted space, to be able to just be himself.

'You need to get away, *mon chéri*,' his mother had sighed down the phone.

Yes, he agreed, he *did* need to get away.

When he'd been offered the director's job for a new BBC drama, Felix had seized the opportunity. At last, he was able to fulfil his dream. He'd still be in show business, but on a more private level, behind the scenes and not in front of a camera. He'd also be in charge, not at the beck and call of others. As a director, he would be making the decisions; casting the actors, interpreting the scripts, co-ordinating with the film crew and, best of all, identifying set locations. This was just what he had yearned for – a new location, a change of scenery.

Felix had joined forces with Andy White, the location manager, and their quest had become personal. They had both been searching for suitable sites for some time. But when Felix had spotted a new property on the market, the phrase '*killing two birds with one stone*' came to mind. His eyes had narrowed when seeing the magnificent Art Deco house on the Grand & Country estate agent website.

> This stunning property sits in an equally dramatic setting. Standing on the peninsula of Lancashire's picturesque Samphire Bay, this spectacular period property, influenced by the Art Deco movement, boasts much character and charm...

Felix scoured each and every photograph, loving what he saw. From the marbled hall with its high, cherry yellow ceiling with glamorous lighting in gold leaf and chrome finishing to the full-length fan wall mirror and the sweeping staircase. The rooms leading off the hall had the typical Art Deco sunburst mantels above the door frames, and the light switches had the original brass cases. It was all so captivating and very fitting of the era it had been built.

The drawing room had high dusty pink walls covered with two elaborate mirrors and various water-coloured paintings with gold ornate frames. There was also a retro glass drinks cabinet. The bedrooms featured geometric patterned walls, double beds with huge plush velvet head-boards, matching velvet scalloped shell chairs, mirrored dressing tables, cut-glass chandeliers and Burr Walnut wardrobes.

It was indeed an impressive house and just what they wanted. It was ideal, ticking all the right boxes and very in-keeping for their drama. What made it even more appealing were the fixtures, fittings and furniture all included in the price. The property came ready-made and the main character, Lady Scarlett, would look so at home in it. But what's more, the location was picture-perfect. Cut off from the tide twice a day, the house was secluded on the peninsula of a remote coastal village, away from prying eyes. No being pestered by the public or having to work round the locals, and above all peace and quiet. Privacy, precisely what Felix sought. And for that reason he bought it.

He'd basically already made his mind up before attending the scheduled open house day. The scenic journey further enforced his decision. Samphire Bay was an absolute dream of a place with its turquoise, glittering shore and sandy coves. It made complete sense to him, especially after the debacle with the owners of the previous property they'd selected. This way the whole crew could get moving, making up for lost time. If he was the owner, it would save on any negotiations and time scales. Felix and his team would have free range. He would also have the isolation and freedom he wanted.

Chapter 2

'Miss Scholar, you look like you're miles away.'

If only, thought Emma. She was bored and tired in equal amounts and this team meeting wasn't helping much. She'd had a late night, gigging with her band in a local pub, and really was not in the mood for her manager's glib remarks. Cursing herself for not ringing in sick, she quickly stifled a yawn and sat up straight.

'Sorry, Mr Butterworth,' she said, and forced her eyes to stay open.

'As I was saying,' he continued, giving her a reprimanding look, 'we are looking to reduce numbers, therefore voluntary redundancy will be an option—'

Emma's ears suddenly pricked up. *Voluntary redundancy?* Since when had this been an option? Sitting forward, eagerly listening now, Mr Butterworth had her full attention.

'Latimer Bank realise this may come as a shock to you all, but loyal employees will be rewarded, you can be assured of that…'

Don't know about shock, more like a golden ticket out of here, thought Emma.

'So, you will all receive an email with the details, giving you time to mull over your choices,' Mr Butterworth finished with what he hoped looked like a genuine, regretful smile.

Emma's hand immediately reached for the mouse on her desk to click on her email inbox. She hoped beyond hope she would qualify for voluntary redundancy. She was a loyal employee, wasn't she? Having worked there since leaving college, surely she'd be considered. Her sick record was good, well, good*ish*, she corrected herself, conscious of pulling the odd sickie, like when she'd been too knackered to get up in the morning after a gig, like last night. But other than the occasional day off, Emma believed herself to be an honest, hardworking member of the team and had often deputised to the grade above hers when requested.

Loyal she may be, but Emma's heart had never been in the job. At first, she'd been keen to just get any job after leaving college. She'd welcomed the admin position at Latimer Bank. Her dad had been super proud of her when announcing she'd got the post. Although it had swiftly been backed up with, 'It's only for a year though, Dad, until the band makes it big, then I'll be off,' she had warned.

Without wanting to dash his daughter's hopes, Perry Scholar had simply nodded, pretending to understand.

Now, seven years later, Emma had finally succumbed to the realisation that the band was never going to 'make it big'. They were good, but maybe just not good enough, she'd sadly accepted. Still, the gigs were a nice little earner and locally they *were* big. Equinox – their band – often sold out tickets at various venues, including Lancaster's music festival. A few times she'd been recognised and stopped whilst out and about. It had totally made her day once

8

when a shy teenager had asked her to sign his festival programme.

So, whilst Emma was enjoying her time with the band, she also had to keep the day job in the bank as security. The extra gig money was nicely saving up and the wages from the bank helped at home with just her and Dad. Not that Perry actually took any rent off Emma. Unbeknown to his daughter, he was putting the money she gave him aside into a separate savings account for her.

However, redundancy money would be an absolute godsend to Emma, who was constantly moaning about working for the bank and threatening to quit. Only that morning, when her head was pounding from the previous late night – and also the tequila shots the band had downed after a great gig – had she complained.

'My head's killing. I really can't be bothered going into work today,' she'd whined.

'Perhaps cut down on the drinking then, Emma?' suggested her dad.

'It's customary for the band to celebrate with tequila shots!' Emma countered, then, when seeing his raised eyebrow, added, 'It's how we roll, Dad.'

Perry's mouth twitched. Despite trying to act the strict parent, he half envied her devil-may-care attitude. Emma was young, free, single and full of joie de vivre. She had everything to live for and he felt blessed to have such a doting daughter.

Technically, he was her stepdad. Perry had married her mother, Valerie, when Emma was eight years old. Then, when Emma was just thirteen, Valerie had tragically died of breast cancer, leaving the pair of them in their quaint, stone cottage in Lancaster. Perry couldn't have loved his stepdaughter any more had he been her natural father. The two were quite alike in many ways, both free spirits. Perry owned a narrowboat, aptly named *The Merry Perry* and, up until marrying Valerie, he had lived a rather transient life, chugging along the waterways, cherishing the beauty of nature and the freedom. He still kept the narrowboat, although only used for day trips or minibreaks with his newly found lady companion, Bunty, an old flame from the past.

He and Emma both had a quirky sense of dress too. Emma loved vintage, retro style clothing and often bought from charity shops and pre-loved websites. Whereas Perry always looked dapper in neckerchiefs, paisley shirts and colourful waistcoats. His thick, grey hair was cut into long layers. Emma joked that he had a David Essex vibe about him, while he teased her for her freckles and copious chestnut curls.

Emma had a natural beauty, a real girl-next-door look, but because she compared herself to the sleek, long blonde-haired, sassy Sophie in the band, who got most of the attention, she didn't appreciate her own worth. Often Perry would remind his daughter just how pretty she was, only to be waved away in dismissal. He also pressed how talented she was too. On the occasions he'd seen the band, it was blatantly obvious who was the most gifted. And it wasn't Sassy Sophie. She may look the part with her golden, flowing locks and svelte figure in skin-tight leather pants, but her voice wasn't a patch on Emma's. Fact.

Finishing up her shift at the bank, Emma hurried home that evening, bursting through the door, urgently needing to tell her dad of the news.

'Guess what?' she gasped.

For Perry, this could be anything. The band could have landed a super gig, she could have met a new boyfriend, she could have been promoted, she could—

'I'm leaving the bank!' Emma declared with glee.

Perry blinked.

'Well, say something, Dad,' said Emma, hands on hips.

He frowned. 'But... why?'

'I'm taking voluntary redundancy. Well, hopefully. I've applied, so fingers crossed it'll be accepted. Then,' her eyes danced with joy, 'I'll be off!'

'Off? Off where?' Perry began to worry now.

'I don't know, wherever the mood takes me,' she trilled, hands raised in the air.

Even though this was the happiest he'd seen Emma for a while, Perry forced her to calm down and tell him all the facts. He dearly hoped that his daughter's impetuous nature hadn't got the better of her. It was all well and good ditching a job she'd grown bored of, but what was the alternative? What on earth was going on inside that scatty brain of hers?

Chapter 3

Bunty's eyes flickered open. The morning sun was shining through the skylight, waking her. She was still getting used to her new home. The stone-flint cottage overlooking the bay was in an idyllic location, but then Bunty was accustomed to panoramic views.

Being the previous owner of the Art Deco house on the peninsula, she was still adjusting to living in a smaller home, albeit beautifully renovated. The huge benefit to downsizing had been the next-door neighbour, her young friend, Jasmine. It was through her friendship with Jasmine and her boyfriend, Robin, that had made Bunty realise just how vulnerable she'd been, living alone in a huge house, stuck out on a headland. The magnificent house had been a family home all her life and a wrench to leave, but she knew it was for the best to sell. The time had come to say goodbye. Luckily Jasmine, Robin, plus his best friend, Jack, and Perry, her gentleman friend and his daughter, Emma, had all helped with the move, making it as painless and stress-free as possible.

She still smiled to herself remembering the open house day which her estate agents had insisted upon. Bunty had never heard of such a thing until she'd been convinced that 'dressing' the house and allowing a selective cliental to browse it was indeed the way forward. They'd been proved right. The current owner hadn't long stepped into the place before declaring he'd 'take it', like it was a second-hand car or a puppy for adoption.

The sale had been pretty seamless and straightforward as he was a cash buyer, with no chain and, apparently, in a rush to get in. Well, good for him, thought Bunty, but tittered to herself when thinking about the worn-out old boiler this bigshot had been saddled with.

Looking back, the past few months had been a bit of a whirlwind. All thanks to Jasmine, for it was she who had managed to trace Perry. Jasmine and her late husband, Tom, had lived on a narrowboat. They had had contact with Perry through a marina Facebook group, after buying an old pump from him. A few years later, after Tom had been tragically killed in a hit-and-run accident, Jasmine had moved to Samphire Bay for a new start. After befriending Bunty, she became aware of an old flame of hers by the name of Perry, who had owned a boat. By remarkable coincidence it was the very same Perry and Jasmine had managed to obtain his whereabouts from the registration details of his boat.

Perry had been a rock for Bunty. He had reappeared in her life at just the right time. Selling the beloved family home had been quite traumatic for her, especially the open day. Bunty had had to witness strangers enter the marbled hall and wander round at will. It was such an invasion of privacy, but, as the estate agents had advised, she had valiantly tried to distance herself and not take any overheard comments personally. After all, she did want to sell the place. Perry had been there as moral support, along with Emma, who had ended up saving the day.

In an attempt to create the perfect ambiance, the estate agent had arranged for a grand piano to be installed in the hall. However, the pianist didn't show up, so Emma had stood in and played instead. When a late arrival came to view the house, he had been rather taken with Emma's playing, going so far as to make a request. Emma had accompanied his chosen piece with her singing and the whole place had stood still in awe. By the time the applause had finished, to the estate agent's delight, the late arriver had offered the asking price, in cash. Every estate agent's dream. The only condition had been that the grand piano was left. And that was it. Done and dusted. The big, white house standing proudly on the peninsula no longer belonged to a Deville. It had a new owner. A 'Mystery Man' to all at Samphire Bay, because nobody knew anything about him. He'd turned up at the open day wearing dark sunglasses and had pretty much kept himself to himself. Various inhabitants had quizzed Bunty about him, thinking she'd know something, but she was as clueless as the rest. Emma had mentioned that his voice had struck a chord with her, but couldn't explain why. She, Jasmine and Bunty had all remarked on how tall, dark and handsome he'd appeared (much to Robin's disgruntlement) which had only made everybody all the more curious.

It was all so intriguing for Samphire Bay, who were not at all used to such newcomers. The small village tended to be inhabited by the same people who had always lived there. Once settled, it was hard to find anywhere else to match it, hence property on Samphire Bay was like gold dust.

Jasmine had been lucky. Not only had she managed to purchase a cottage in such a stunning spot, but she'd been well and truly accepted by the locals. She had set tongues wagging from the start, especially Trish from the corner shop, a well-known gossip, and it hadn't taken long before the tragic background of her late husband's death had filtered through the community. Even more commotion was caused when news struck that his killers, who had been driving the van that ploughed into him, were actually from Samphire Bay.

It had been Robin who had helped the police with the investigation. He had also helped Jasmine renovate her cottage and so their relationship formed. Now, thankfully, Jasmine had been given a second chance at Samphire Bay. After the loss and pain of her husband's death, she was now happy and content with Robin. He was her anchor and she was his.

So, all in all, Samphire Bay was a cheery place. Nestled just beneath the border to Cumbria, it offered sheltered walks along limestone paths and amongst woodland, leading to open views of sandy beaches and glittering water. A place where people once found, never left. But who was its mystery newcomer? That was the question on everyone's lips.

Jennifer Paige sat at her desk and ticked off another two jobs on the list of things to do. She liked lists. It was the way she operated – steadily, methodically and thoroughly. Which was precisely why Felix had employed her. From the moment he'd interviewed Jennifer as his personal assistant, he knew she'd fit the bill perfectly.

Being a middle-aged, no-nonsense kind of lady, she very much reminded Felix of his mother and, in many ways, she *was* his second mother, managing his busy diary, sorting his mail and making sure he kept his appointments. Of course, the fact Jennifer was a mother figure also meant she could keep him in check. Something his real one encouraged her to do.

'Keep him on a tight rein,' she'd gently warned in that smooth French voice, peppered with humour.

And Jennifer did just that, but with a clever technique so that Felix didn't realise it.

Needless to say, Felix couldn't cope without the sturdy guidance of his PA. It was down to Jennifer's efficiency that his life ran in such order. He'd be forever in her debt at the way she had handled the fiasco with Anika; fielding his calls, blocking unwanted messages and telling the press where to go. Jennifer had been an absolute star and now, with his latest venture, she was coming up trumps again.

Initially, when telling her of his purchase of the house in Lancashire, she'd been puzzled.

'Why?' Jennifer had bluntly asked.

'A few reasons,' Felix replied, having fully anticipated this reaction.

'Them being?'

'It's the exact property we need for the drama being the main one, but also its location. It's both beautiful and secluded, overlooking a gorgeous bay and on a peninsula,' he explained with enthusiasm.

'Hmm, could be a little inconvenient though,' she remarked, her mind automatically pondering the impracticalities. 'Is there a strong internet connection there?'

Her question was answered with a broad smile. 'That's where you come in, Jennifer.'

'I walked straight into that one, didn't I?' She gave him a wry grin.

'Yep. But with your skills and tenacity, I'm sure you'll soon have the broadband up and running in no time. Oh, and whilst we're on it, can you make sure security cameras are installed too?'

'Of course,' she nodded. Jennifer, more than anybody, knew how important Felix's privacy was to him. Especially after the farce with Anika Genness.

'Here's the specs of the house.' He passed her the glossy Grand & Country brochure containing all the property details.

Jennifer gasped at the covering photograph of the property, understanding what prompted Felix to buy it. He was right – the period house was perfect and the location was incredible.

'Well, what do you think?' he asked, already knowing the answer, but wanting to hear her say it out loud.

'It's amazing.' She looked up, almost dazed.

This, coming from Jennifer, was high praise indeed.

So, here she was, having overseen the installation of broadband and the security cameras meant another two ticks could be marked off her list. Now to tackle the rest, she sighed to herself before answering the ringing phone.

'Jennifer, what are you doing this weekend?' asked Felix.

Taken off guard at the question, she stalled before replying. 'Nothing too important, why?'

'I need you to come to the new house. We're holding a pre-production meeting.'

'And you need me?' Jennifer frowned.

'If you could, I'd be eternally grateful. We'll be casting and I'd prefer a note-taker, plus help with looking after everyone.'

'Everyone?' she questioned.

'Yeah, me, the location manager, the casting director and the associate producer, we'll be stopping over for the night.'

Jennifer's mind was quickly ticking over. If he and his team were staying over it would require clean bedding, toiletries, catering—

'And, Jennifer,' Felix interrupted her thoughts, 'there's a tidal road to the peninsula which is cut off twice a day by the sea.'

'What?' she blurted, eyes widening.

'I'll leave it with you, OK? Gotta go.'

Then off he rang, leaving Jennifer staring into the distance. At what stage had she actually agreed to give up her weekend to go to Lancashire? The cheek of the boy!

Felix was on a roll. Since exchanging contracts on the house, he'd gone into overdrive. He was keen for Andy, the location manager, to explore the house. Obviously he'd seen plenty of photos and footage that Felix had sent, but he was desperate for Andy to explore for himself.

He was also anxious to get on with the casting. Felix had his own ideas on who he wanted, but it had to be a group decision. The casting director, Mel Nichols, was very experienced and this was Felix's first role as a director. He didn't want to ruffle any feathers, but equally his opinions had to be taken onboard. Hopefully the fact he'd bought the house would be taken as a sign of how committed he was to the project. Budget-wise, he'd saved a lot of money not having to pay any house owners for however long it took to film, plus he'd pulled back precious time they'd lost on the previous house they'd located.

As the director, Felix was determined all the filming would be done entirely on location, rather than some scenes in a studio. The result of studio-based filming to Felix always looked slightly forced and, as he owned the house where the majority of the drama was to be set, it meant they wouldn't be restricted or dictated to by deadlines. It gave him freedom, which for his first hack as a director was invaluable.

Not only that, he was truly proud of his house. It was an amazing place. Once all the filming and drama was over, he'd still have his own oasis to retreat to. Just the thought of a haven to relax in and have the peace and quiet he so badly needed filled his soul. Then, as if on cue, his phone bleeped. He took it out of his pocket and opened the text message:

> You'll never be free from me. No matter where you hide.

His stomach contracted. All the harmony he was beginning to feel fled in an instant. Would she *ever* leave him alone?

Chapter 4

Emma braced herself before pushing through the heavy glass doors into Latimer Bank. It had been a week since she'd submitted her application for voluntary redundancy, and she was waiting with bated breath for some kind of response. From discreetly asking round her colleagues, she knew that there were only two others who had done the same, both in their late fifties with good pensions no doubt to rely on. What did she have? Her savings for a start, but they wouldn't last forever, then what? Initially, when Emma had heard of voluntary redundancy, she'd been elated. Now, having had time to reflect on the matter, she was more rational than excited. Although adamant she still wanted to leave Latimer Bank, it had opened up a whole new can of worms.

Emma was a big believer in fate. She truly trusted things happened for a reason. Look how her mum and Perry had met. They were *meant* to visit the Maritime Museum that day. Perry had worked there as a volunteer and they had got chatting. Then, when Emma and Valerie had gone into the café, he'd been there too on his coffee break and little Emma had run over to sit at his table. The rest was history. Perry had wowed them both with his canal boat, taking them on day trips and weekend aways. A year later Perry and Valerie had married and he'd moved into their cottage in Lancaster. Perry had been the best thing to have happened to them – and all because Emma had pestered her mum to take her to the museum. It was inconceivable to think what they could have missed out on had they not. Emma would have been an orphan at the tender age of thirteen.

Then there was the band. Emma had just happened to be stood by the bar in a crowded pub when she overhead a conversation between two guys. They were forming a group and needed a singer. Emma, being Emma, turned round and introduced herself. She could sing, she told them with gusto. One of the boys gave a lobsided grin.

'Go on then,' he coaxed, looking her up and down.

Not to be put off, she lifted a provocative eyebrow.

'What do you want me to sing?' she replied, determined to stand her ground and not be intimidated.

'You pick,' said the other boy, narrowing his eyes in assessment. It would be interesting to see what she chose. She certainly looked confident enough to head a band, with her self-assurance and style. He took in her tie-dyed fitted dress, biker jacket and laced boots. She wore amber jewellery which matched her eyes and those chestnut curls ran wild. Very rock-chic. But did she have the voice?

'How about *Respect*?' she suggested, holding his gaze.

He gave a wry grin. She'd obviously clocked him giving her the once-over. Hmm, feisty too, he thought, warming to the girl.

'Go ahead,' he nodded.

Emma sang the famous opening line and soon the people around them stopped mid-drink and turned to see who was singing. Once Emma had finished, they all cheered, put down their glasses and clapped. She gave a small bow and grinned at the two boys.

'Well, am I in?'

'You're in,' they replied in unison.

That had been seven years ago, and she'd made friends for life with Gaz and Mitch. When Mitch's girlfriend, Sophie, had later joined the band, Emma had played the keyboard as well as sang. Sophie tended to be the lead singer, as she didn't play any instrument. Together they'd all got on well and it had been a successful venture.

If Emma hadn't been stood at the bar that night eavesdropping on Gaz and Mitch she wouldn't have joined the band. Fate again, in her eyes.

So, according to Emma, voluntary redundancy had reared its head for a reason. It was her opportunity to seize the moment. Or so she thought. Now, after she'd just entered the bank, taken off her coat, sat at her desk and opened her inbox, it was all too real. There sat the email she'd so, so wanted. Latimer Bank were offering her voluntary redundancy. Emma blinked and re-read the message with all the terms and conditions attached. She was leaving.

Gulping, she grabbed her bag and rose from the chair. She went straight to the Ladies'. Once alone, she pulled out her mobile, sat in a cubicle and rang her dad.

'Dad,' she whispered, 'I've got it.'

'Voluntary redundancy?' asked Perry.

'Yes,' she hissed.

'I'm pleased for you, if that's what you really want,' he replied calmly.

'It is…' she said, her chin wobbling slightly, suddenly feeling emotional.

'Well then, time to start a new chapter,' Perry stated assertively, sensing her unease.

'Yes, time for a fresh start,' replied Emma with conviction. She always felt better after talking to her dad.

Later that night, after a celebratory supper of fish, chips and prosecco, Perry sat back and eyed his daughter. He could read her like a book.

'Having second thoughts?' he asked.

'Not really, but I do need to start looking for another job. I know I've savings and a lump sum from the bank, but—'

'There's also the money I've kept aside for you,' Perry gently interrupted.

Emma frowned. 'Sorry?'

'The rent you insisted on giving me, I kept it in a separate account for you.'

'But…that's years of—'

'Yes, I know,' he cut in, 'and I've been saving it to give back, plus the interest, when the time was right. Now is the time,' he said with a kind smile.

'Oh, Dad!' She ran and wrapped her arms round him.

At least it would help to give her a bit of breathing space, until she decided on what to do next.

'Have faith in yourself,' whispered Perry.

'It's freezing!' wailed Jasmine as her feet entered the sea. Robin had already braved the cold and dived straight in.

'Come on! It's not so bad when you get used to it,' he called back laughing, then ducked his head under the waves. Swimming underwater, he made his way to the edge where his girlfriend was hesitantly wading in with a grimace on her face. Eventually he coaxed her in further.

'This has got to be the last time this year we do this,' she shivered, treading water.

When Jasmine had first moved to Samphire Bay it had been a glorious summer. She had soon developed the routine of an early morning dip, leaving her invigorated to start the day. And she'd certainly needed the kick start, ploughing all her energy into the work on her cottage. It was more than just good luck she'd had Robin as a next-door neighbour, renovating the adjoining cottage as his next building project. Now, the two of them were enjoying a new romance, which had developed over that summer.

'Come on, I'll race you!' cheered Robin, laughing at her reluctance to get swimming.

'No, you always cheat.' She shivered, hugging herself.

'No, I won't, promise.' He smiled, admiring her shapely, tanned arms. 'Ready, steady, go!'

Off they set, splashing along the waves. For once, he deliberately slowed down and let Jasmine overtake him. She turned a few moments later, noticing the distance.

'You let me win!' she shouted.

'I never,' he replied in mock indignation.

'Yes, you did,' she chuckled, making her way over to him.

He reached out and embraced her cold body. Then kissed her shoulder, which was covered in goosebumps.

'Let's get back,' he said, giving her a quick squeeze.

Once back at Jasmine's cottage, Robin soon got the wood burner blasting out warmth. They sat by it, drinking tea and munching toast. Robin looked at the clock.

'Best get going soon, Jack'll be wondering where I've got to.'

Jack was his best friend and business partner. Together they renovated properties, and when they had finished working on the cottage next door to Jasmine's, Robin had at first considered keeping it for himself instead of selling it. In the end, he had decided against it, admitting the main reason for keeping it was to be near to Jasmine. Once their feelings for each other had eventually come out in the open, he was happy for Bunty to buy the cottage.

For now, he was quite happy living in his apartment which sat sheltered behind a small wood near to the bay. Converted from a large Victorian property, the place had served him well, giving him splendid views of the coastline and friendly neighbours. It was just the right size for a single person, easy to maintain and, best of all, it was in Samphire Bay. For now, he was content in living between his apartment and stopping the odd night at Jasmine's cottage. It suited them both, giving them each space as well as time together.

'I think Jack will have an idea where you are,' grinned Jasmine, 'and no doubt have some quick remark to make.'

Robin laughed. 'Probably.'

Jack wasn't exactly known for his subtlety. He was quite the opposite to Robin, not just in looks, but personality too. Whereas Robin was dark haired and rather shy, Jack was blond and full-on with his teasing. It had taken a while for Jasmine to warm to him, initially being put off with his sense of humour. Now, she just accepted who Jack was and that he was probably better for knowing.

'Maybe it's time we try to find Jack a girlfriend, see if that'll stop his teasing?'

Robin considered the idea before shaking his head dolefully. 'I'm not sure if he'll ever be ready to settle down.'

'Oh, I don't know,' Jasmine said with a small smirk. 'My mum always jokes that there's something in the water here at Samphire Bay.' She wrapped her arms around Robin's waist and leant her head against his chest. 'Just look at us.'

Perhaps there was some truth in that? Jasmine and Robin's broken hearts weren't the only ones to be healed at Samphire Bay. Bunty and Perry, after years of separation, had also been reunited, mending their hearts too. So maybe there was something in the water?

Felix was pacing the marbled hall like a caged tiger.

'Jennifer!' he bellowed anxiously.

In she came, looking her usual calm and efficient self.

'Yes, Felix?' she said, straining to keep the impatience out of her voice. It had been a very long and tiring journey from London up to Lancashire and she hadn't stopped since her arrival.

'Is everything in place? They'll be arriving any minute,' he asked, lines of worry furrowed on his forehead. The pressure of holding the pre-production meeting was getting to him. Not only was it his first as a director, but he was host too. Although he had to concede his PA had done a sterling job so far in preparation, and the cameras dotted about the house and grounds meant they were secure. She'd even contacted a local catering company and the kitchen was full of buffet food, ready to be displayed in the dining room, though Jennifer had made a comment on lack of assistance in carrying all the plates and dishes up the stairs from the lower ground floor. Not to mention she'd made up all the beds, stocked the fridge and cleaned the place – the poor woman was shattered. And, as she kept reminding Felix, she was 'no spring chicken'.

'Yes, Felix,' Jennifer sighed, 'the bedrooms are ready, as are the refreshments, and the library is set up for the meeting.'

'Brilliant, thanks, Jennifer, you're a star.' He gave her one of his winning smiles, only this time it didn't win Jennifer over. This time, quite frankly, he'd taken liberties.

Jennifer was still smarting over having to give up her weekend. She hadn't particularly enjoyed driving for five hours down the motorway. It left her tired and anxious. When she had finally arrived at Samphire Bay the tide was in, rendering the road unfit to drive. She'd had to sit and wait for bloody hours for the passageway to clear. Time that could have been well spent elsewhere.

Finally pulling into the gravel driveway and seeing the place up close, instead of being impressed with its grandeur and beauty, all she could do was wince at the size of it and the dreaded task of cleaning it. All down to her. It was ridiculous. She was expected to not only do her proper job of administrating the meeting, but also act as scullery maid, butler and housekeeper. And for how long? Would Felix be expecting this level of service in future? Supposing he made a habit of entertaining in this spectacular home he'd acquired? She sincerely hoped this pre-production get together was a one-off, all part of the novelty of buying his new house.

Despite Jennifer already looking dog-tired before the weekend had even begun, Felix didn't notice. He was way too wrapped up with the impending meeting. A lot was hinging on it. He was out to impress. Secretly, he was also brooding over Anika's latest malicious text message.

His head turned sharply at hearing the screech of brakes on gravel.

'They're here!' he shouted unnecessarily, as Jennifer was inches away from him.

She jumped in shock then rolled her eyes. 'Yes, Felix,' she said witheringly.

Andy was the first to arrive.

Felix threw the front doors open. 'Andy! Good to see you.' He pumped the man's hand then ushered him inside. Keen to gauge his reaction, he examined Andy's face, which appeared to be suitably impressed.

'Some place you got here, Felix,' he whistled, eyes darting around the hall.

This was exactly the response Felix wanted.

'Right location then?' he asked.

'Absolutely.' Andy homed in on the sweeping staircase, the grand piano, then to the huge chandelier above them, casting its glass shadows on the high ceiling. 'Perfect. Exactly what we want,' he affirmed with a nod, making Felix's shoulders relax.

'Wait till you see the rest of the house.'

'And grounds,' Jennifer chipped in, determined that her efforts of hiring a gardener were acknowledged.

'Yes, of course, the gardens are pretty amazing, even if I say so myself,' agreed Felix, then upon seeing Jennifer's stern look quickly added, 'all thanks to my wonderful PA who had the foresight to get them tended to asap.' He gave her another winning beam. This time she at least acknowledged it with a stiff smile in return.

'Shall I take Andy's coat while you give him the guided tour?' she asked.

'Yes, marvellous, thank you, Jennifer,' replied Felix.

Just then the doorbell chimed.

'I'll get it,' said Jennifer coolly, hiding a sigh.

The casting director, Mel, arrived with the associate producer, a rather timid looking lady introduced as just 'Flo'. Mel flounced in wearing a grey woollen pashmina and felt hat.

'Good Lord, Felix, we're in the back of beyond here!' he announced, whilst taking his hat off and arrogantly giving it Flo to carry.

Felix froze, not sure how to answer. Jennifer, as ever, came to the rescue.

'Yes, that's its charm. Out of view, enabling you all to get on with the job.' She chuckled softly, taking the edge off any awkwardness.

'It's a lovely spot,' murmured Flo, then put her head down, clutching Mel's hat tightly.

'It certainly is,' gushed Andy.

His approval seemed to resonate with Mel, who tipped his head to one side in consideration.

'Hmm, let's see the rest,' he suggested, then looked directly at Jennifer, 'after drinkypoos.' He smiled, showing a set of pure white dentures.

Jennifer took a deep breath. Clearly she was to play waitress too.

'Of course,' she replied between gritted teeth.

After a full guided tour of the house and grounds were given, Felix directed them all into the library. Jennifer had set up a long table running down the middle of the room. She herself was sat next to Felix at the top of it, pen poised, ready to make notes. Felix had handouts which Jennifer had prepared to pass round. The first one contained suggestions for the leading role, Lady Scarlett.

Felix had his heart set on Polly Andrews, a young up-and-coming actress who had impressed him with her rendition of Eliza Doolittle in the West End play *Pygmalion*. On seeing her name, Mel raised an eyebrow.

'Not my first choice, must admit.'

Felix's heart sank. Trying desperately to sound impartial, he replied, 'Who did you have in mind, Mel?'

'I was thinking... Alicia Davenport!' he proclaimed with his hands raised dramatically in the air.

The old queen, thought Felix, and remained as calm as he could muster.

'Maybe a tad predictable? Bearing in mind she's already played a lady sleuth in the past?' he questioned as diplomatically as possible.

'Oh.' Mel frowned, obviously not expecting that response. Not to be outdone, he had another name to throw into the ring. 'How about Selina McKenna?' he suggested with a sly grin.

That was a curveball, thought Felix, considering Selina McKenna was originally a model and, fully known to Mel, a good friend of his ex-girlfriend Anika. Was the old ham deliberately provoking him?

There was a difficult pause round the table. Jennifer, knowing how challenging this could potentially be, gave a cough.

'I believe she's currently been taken ill, if that needs to be considered,' she spoke quietly.

Felix turned to her in surprise. How did she know that?

'Yes, it does,' replied Flo. 'If we're to crack on with these scripts,' she patted the huge pile of papers in front of her, 'then we need our main role to start immediately.'

'Here, here,' agreed Andy, ever mindful of the time lost already due to the problem with the first location.

Felix seized the moment. 'Polly showed her capability as Eliza Doolittle. She'll pique people's interest, not being a big name already. This drama would catapult her career and help promote our production at the same time,' he reasoned.

'Plus she'll be eternally grateful for the part, as opposed to some demanding prima donna,' Andy added. Flo was vigorously nodding in agreement.

Mel narrowed his eyes in contemplation. 'OK then, let's give her an audition,' he said.

Felix inwardly sighed with relief. Mel might be a touch temperamental and a little stagey, but he was a team player, not stuck in his own opinions.

'I'll get on to her agent prompto,' said Flo.

The rest of the meeting was held quite amicably, with everyone agreeing on the rest of the cast. When all was done Mel turned to Jennifer, but before he could open his mouth she pre-empted him.

'Drinkypoos?' she curtly asked, raising an eyebrow.

'You're an angel.' He smiled, his dentures dazzling.

After a weekend full of entertaining, Felix waved his guests off and closed the front doors with relish. Thank goodness that was over with. Turning to an equally relieved Jennifer he looked quizzically at her.

'Jennifer, how did you know about Selina McKenna being ill?' he asked, head tilted to one side.

'I didn't,' she stated flatly.

He paused, then broke into a smile once the penny dropped.

'Where would I be without you?' he said with genuine affection.

'Well, unless you hire a housekeeper, Felix, without me *you will be.*' She stared him full in the face.

'But…' He frowned, perplexed at her words.

'I have given up my weekend, played waitress, cleaner, cook and scullery maid, on top of minute taker and assistant host. It's too much, Felix,' she said with force.

Felix closed his eyes in shame. Now, once the meeting was all over, he had time to take stock and realise just how hard Jennifer had worked.

'I'm so sorry, Jennifer. I'll pay you double,' he tried to appease.

She shook her head. 'It's not about the money.'

'Right… sorry… I'll—'

'Hire a housekeeper?' cut in Jennifer directly.

'Yes, I'll—'

'Good. I'll advertise for one tomorrow,' she replied in that no-nonsense tone he was accustomed to.

Chapter 5

Felix stretched his limbs out and rested his head on the plush velvet headboard. This was the life. He stared out of the large window facing the bay and took in the view, just like he had shortly before sleeping the night before. Not wanting to block out the setting, he'd left the curtains open, and it felt so good to be able to do so, not having to worry about anyone seeing inside his home. How different it was from his apartment in London. Although he lived in the penthouse at the top, everyone else living in the tower knew where to find him. He was easily access-ible and sharing the lift had on occasions made him a little uncomfortable, especially when being blatantly gawped at or asked for his autograph. If it wasn't for his work, Felix would have cheerfully sold his Knightsbridge apartment. It had served its purpose up to now as a handy base when he'd been acting and needed to get to the studios. Hopefully now though, he wouldn't be needing it for a long while.

He'd been pleased with the way the pre-production meeting had gone. It pleased him more that his first choice of leading lady had been agreed on. All he needed now was to see the audition takes, but that didn't concern him, as he felt sure Polly Andrews was the right actress for the role.

Felix looked at the clock on the bedside table. He hadn't set his alarm, choosing to have a well-deserved and rare lie in. Jennifer had returned to London the day before, not without replenishing his fridge and kitchen cupboards, bless her. She'd also left him with a stern reminder about the housekeeper and told him she was most definitely on the case. He didn't doubt it, not for one moment. Jennifer had dutifully advertised the position and was no doubt sifting through applications already.

With that in mind Felix sighed and closed his eyes. How was having a housekeeper going to pan out? Obviously they'd have their own room, but what about other boundaries? Would they be expected to share the drawing room, for example? Or would she (or he, as corrected by Jennifer) stay boxed up in their own room of an evening, watching a portable TV?

Another thing worrying Felix was his privacy. Jennifer had assured him that nobody would initially know whose house it was. She absolutely guaranteed him that, when interviewing, honesty and discretion would be the key elements. The last thing he needed was some star-struck girl (or boy) to be goggling him in his own home. Neither did he want some wannabe actor seizing opportunities with him.

Felix groaned. How could he not have considered all this in the first place? Because he'd fallen in love with the house and the idea of working in it, that's why. Only now was he having to think about the practicalities of living in such a huge house, with little or no idea on how to run it. His apartment had been easy, with the concierge service readily available 24/7. All he had to do there was ring down to reception and all his needs were taken care of, from running out of toothpaste to a lightbulb change. It was all too convenient for him in London. Jennifer was there, seeing to all his admin, his busy schedules, running his diary like clockwork. He'd miss the likes of her in Lancashire. Let's hope that whoever his new housekeeper was, they'd be as efficient and capable as his PA. He reflected on just how much Jennifer did for him and how lucky he was to have her. Shame still ate inside him at her efforts over the weekend. He genuinely had let his anxiety of the meeting take over him instead of being more aware of poor Jennifer and how hard she worked. He was going to treat her, he decided, pay for a mini break for her and her husband to enjoy. He could just imagine what his mother would say to all this.

'You've been spoiled, *mon chéri*,' she'd tell him with a warm, knowing smile.

Perhaps he *had* been pampered, just a touch. But certainly not by his ex, Anika. If anything, it had been him who had given her the attention she'd demanded. He shuddered at the memory of her petulant temper. Anika might be easy on the eye but not on the soul. She had well and truly sapped him of any spirit he had. And those fucking texts she kept sending him were draining him further. He never reacted to them, no matter how threatening or disturbing they were. He thought by ignoring her messages she'd soon grow bored and give up. No such luck. As if reading his mind, his phone bleeped. With a sense of dread, he reached for it.

All settled? Maybe it's time for a visit?

He stared at the message. What worried him the most was that she knew he'd bought the house and of its where-abouts. *How* did she know? To his knowledge there were only a few close people who knew about it. He had thought of barring her name from his phone, but knowing how Anika worked, this would only antagonise her more so and he really didn't want to do that. God knows what she might be capable of doing. He deleted her message and pulled back the bedsheets. He was in need of a nice, hot, soothing soak.

He made his way to the bathroom and turned the gold taps. A splutter of water came bursting out, then halted, followed by a clang from the pipes. Don't say there was a problem with the waterworks, thought Felix, beginning to feel more dismay. Thankfully the pipes made a hissing noise and water began to flow steadily. Good. The last thing he needed right now was any domestic problems. The sooner he got his housekeeper, the better.

Bunty poured a cup of Earl Grey and sat back contently. Although autumn had set in, the October sun was still glimmering. Eager to make the most of it, Bunty was enjoying an afternoon tea in the garden and was expecting Perry to join her any minute. Simple pleasures, she contemplated, always appreciative of them nowadays. This time last year she would have been hitting the gin and gazing melancholily out of the huge bow window, musing on the past and regretting choices made – not anymore. Perry was back in her life and she simply couldn't imagine being without him now. Not only had she Perry, but his daughter too.

Bunty's life had changed dramatically in the space of such a short time. She'd always known Robin and Jack, as they were locals and had done many a manual job for her over the years, and Trish from the shop as well as various other members of Samphire Bay from the church committee. However, coming to know Jasmine had created a treasured friendship, and one she'd never expected to find so late in life.

Despite the obvious age gap the two of them had forged a deep bond. In many ways, Jasmine reminded Bunty of her younger self; she was gutsy, knew her own mind. Bunty would always admire Jasmine's spirit and strength of courage at moving to Samphire Bay, alone and still mourning the loss of her late husband. To start again, in an unknown place, solo, was indeed commendable in Bunty's eyes. And she, in turn, was like a mother to Jasmine, offering sound advice and comfort. It had been through Bunty's efforts that she and Robin were now a couple; her ability to play cupid knew no bounds.

Often Bunty would sit out in her garden and see Jasmine in her studio over the hedge. There she'd be, working away, absorbed in her latest project. Jasmine was a freelance graphic designer and Bunty was often left speechless when shown her artwork. Jasmine was rather modest about her talent. The latest book cover she'd designed included a beautiful bay with golden sand dunes and colourful surrounding flora.

'It's exquisite!' Bunty had raved.

With a shrug Jasmine had replied, 'I've been inspired by this place.'

Bunty stole another glance at her neighbour's studio, then noticed Perry come through the garden gate.

'Hello, you.' She smiled and poured him a cup of tea.

'Afternoon tea, very civilised,' remarked Perry, sitting down to join her.

'How's Emma?' asked Bunty.

'Hmm, a bit bored I think,' he replied. Now that the novelty of no longer working for the bank had worn off, Emma was beginning to become a tad restless. Perry, being honest, was feeling the agitation. He was used to his own space and not having his daughter around all day, every day. Thankfully he always had his boat to retreat to, and Bunty's cottage. This afternoon's invitation had been most welcome. 'The sooner she finds a job the better, I reckon,' he added.

'So nothing's taken her eye then?' enquired Bunty.

'Not really. There are a few office jobs about, but she's dead-set against working behind a desk again.'

'Don't blame her. Emma's far too talented to do that,' she replied with force.

'But that's just it,' sighed Perry, 'she's always wanted that band of hers to make it big, but it's not going to happen.' He gave Bunty a sad smile. 'It hurts to say it, but I think she now realises it's time to live in the real world.'

'Yes, but she could still find something that suits her creativity,' retorted Bunty, remembering how well Emma had played and sang at the open day at her old house. She pictured the man who'd bought it, propped up at the grand piano, enjoying her performance. So much so, he'd offered the asking price. That thought triggered her memory. 'There is a job advertised in the local paper. A housekeeper for my old place.'

'Really?' frowned Perry.

'Apparently, so Trish was telling me. In fact,' Bunty got up, 'I'll just go and get the paper and have a look.' She soon returned with a folded newspaper and passed it to Perry to read. There in the job advertisements read:

> Housekeeper wanted for a large period property in a secluded area in Samphire Bay. It is a live-in post and will require a person without dependants. Duties include cleaning, cooking and organisational skills. Honesty and discretion are key qualities required. To apply contact: JPaige@ sinclairestate.co.uk

Perry read it with interest, knowing how much his daughter had wanted to see inside the house. She'd practically begged him to take her with him when he'd first reacquainted with Bunty. When Emma had been asked to step in for the pianist who had let them down on the open day, she'd accepted with elation and had been captivated by the place. With this in mind, would she fancy becoming its housekeeper? She could cook, he'd vouch for that, and clean for that matter. But would Emma want to be responsible for such a big house? And what was the owner like? The 'Mystery Man' who'd bought it they knew nothing about.

Bunty assessed him with narrowed eyes, knowing how protective he was over his daughter.

'Well, what do you think?' she asked.

'I could always run it past her...' He rubbed his chin thoughtfully.

'Yes, let her make her own mind up,' she replied. 'It'd give her some independence. She is twenty-five years old after all Perry.'

The tone in her voice wasn't lost on Perry. It irked him a touch.

'Hmm, because the last thing I want to be is an over-protective, controlling father, isn't it?' he challenged. He was of course referring to Bunty's father, who had been *exactly* that.

Touché, thought Bunty. She well and truly earned that response. Their eyes met and she gave a grin.

'You're a brilliant dad,' she said, covering her hand with his.

'I am,' he smiled back. 'I'll let Emma know about the position this evening.'

However, there was no need. Emma had already seen the advert for herself after hunting through the job advert-isement column. The only thing putting her off was that it was a live-in post. Would her dad be OK with her leaving home? It had to happen one day, she wasn't going to stay living with her dad forever, was she?

With determination, Emma contacted the email address given and received an automated message reply, asking for her to complete an attached application form. She glanced over it. Besides the expected personal details requested, she gave particular attention to the remaining questions.

> Did she consider herself a prompt time-keeper?

Err… well… ish. But then, she'd be living there, so what did that matter? she thought.

> Was her cleaning to a high standard?

Probably, her dad never complained... apart from when she accidently kicked a full bucket of soapy water all over the kitchen floor when mopping up.

What would she call her signature dish?

That was easy, her spaghetti bolognaise was legendary. But would that be a bit basic? Should she be giving a fancier dish, like duck a l'orange, or what about a traditional Sunday roast, she could cook that too?

The last question on the application form filled her with more optimism.

What, if any, further qualities could she offer
to the position of housekeeper?

How about her talent of singing and playing the piano? She knew that grand piano was still in the hall, it had been the only condition the guy buying the house had had, that the sale included the piano. Emma felt cheered when completing the application form, after all, how many of the other applicants could offer entertainment like that? She imagined some stuffy, middle-aged matron type figure applying for the job and chuckled to herself at the comparison. Then again, they would probably have far mor experience than her at running such a house. Oh well, nothing ventured, nothing gained she told herself and pressed the 'send' button with hope.

Jennifer was busy sifting through the application forms. She had received fifteen in total, ten of which she'd dismissed outright after reading them. Fancy asking if they could smoke in the house? A definite no-no for Jennifer, who called it a filthy habit. Another application form was full of spelling mistakes and grammatical errors, another bugbear for Jennifer. Knowing the size of Felix's house and the amount of energy it would need to clean it meant that the two older applicants were perhaps not suitable; such a vast house would need a young pair of legs to get about it, someone full of oomph to run up and down all those stairs. Then there was the personality side to consider. Whoever was employed had to get on with Felix, they would be living together under the same roof after all. After much deliberation she had narrowed it down to three applicants to interview.

As agreed with Felix, they would be held next week. She would be doing the interviewing, but Felix would be present from a distance. They only wanted to disclose who he was, once a candidate had been selected. It was vital to get the right person, especially before the filming started. The house would need strong, steady organisation, given that it would soon be filled with a whole production team and cast of actors. Jennifer cringed. Whoever the new housekeeper was going to be, she didn't envy them.

Chapter 6

Robin's alarm woke him early morning. Quickly turning to switch if off, so as not to wake Jasmine, he saw that she had already risen. He'd stayed over after a take-away and couple of bottles of wine and it always amazed him how Jasmine managed to get up so promptly, even after a heavy night's drinking. He dressed and went downstairs to join her.

Jasmine was by the cooker, busy filling a frying pan. 'Hi,' she smiled as he came into the kitchen. 'Fancy a cooked breakfast?'

It amazed him how well she looked in the morning too, all fresh-faced and energetic.

'Sounds good, thanks,' he replied, rubbing his eyes.

Despite it being Saturday, he and Jack were supposed to be looking at another possible building project. It was an old warehouse which had planning permission to turn into apartments in Lancaster by the quayside. A lot of money was to be made, especially in that location. Although at the moment, Robin was more interested in spending the weekend with his girlfriend rather than having to work. He wouldn't normally mind as he did enjoy his job – helped by the fact he worked with his best mate – but lately he craved just a little more time to relax with Jasmine. It had been a long while since he'd been in a relationship and he wanted to relish the new one he'd just found.

He watched her cooking their breakfasts with ease, looking a million dollars in his eyes. Her silky blonde hair sat on elegant shoulders, her toned arms effortlessly moving from chopping board to frying pan. Jasmine must have sensed him watching her because she turned round to face him.

'What are you staring at?' she laughed.

'You,' Robin replied and got up to hug her from behind. He kissed the top of her head and sighed. 'I wish I didn't have to go to Lancaster with Jack today.'

'I know, but it's a good opportunity, isn't it?' said Jasmine.

'Yeah, but if we do take the warehouse conversion on, we'll not be starting it straight away.'

'Oh, why?' she asked, surprised to hear this.

'Because, my lovely,' he gently turned her round to face him, 'we are going away on a mini break.' He'd decided there and then they were due some quality time together.

'Are we?' she sounded even more surprised now.

'Oh yes,' he nodded resolutely and kissed her full on the lips.

Jasmine smiled, liking the sound of this. 'Where to?'

'I was thinking a city break?'

Jasmine bobbed her head in agreement. She quite liked the idea of bustling streets and bright lights. It would be a change to the quiet, costal countryside of Samphire Bay.

'London?' she suggested.

'Good idea,' Robin replied. Already he was filled with anticipation. He imagined the pair of them taking in the sights, hitting the shops and enjoying romantic evening meals. Yes, that was just what they needed.

What Emma needed was a stiff drink to steady her nerves. Looking in the full-length mirror, she grimaced at her reflexion. The person staring back just wasn't her. The navy suit her dad insisted she bought for the interview looked hideous and the curls she'd tried to tame just made her hair flat and straight as cardboard. Even the 'sensible' court shoes that she'd picked up in a charity shop appeared old womanish.

'I look like a Tory MP,' she complained as her dad popped his head round the door.

Moving further into her bedroom he too gazed at his daughter and found it difficult to disagree.

'I do, don't I?'

Perry tipped his head thoughtfully to one side, hesitating to give his answer.

'Just admit it, Dad, I look ridiculous,' Emma sighed.

'Well, there's nothing wrong in looking smart for an interview,' he tried to appease. It didn't work.

'Oh, sod it. I'm going as *me*,' Emma said in exasperation then proceeded to kick off the sensible shoes and open her wardrobe in defiance.

Her eyes scanned the rail packed with all sorts of colourful garments, from tie-dyed dresses, embroidered shirts, tassel hemmed skirts, patched denims, leather jackets, all manner of boots and trainers, the storage rammed full. In an attempt to compromise, she pulled out a black dress.

'How about this?' She held it up against her for Perry to see.

It was the right colour and length, he thought, but a halter neck? Wouldn't that be a little too revealing for an interview?

As if reading his thoughts, Emma delved inside the wardrobe again and fished out her silver biker jacket.

'With this?' she asked.

'Yes,' said Perry with a thumbs up.

'And how about these to match?' Emma had dug out a pair of silver ankle boots.

'Yes. Original, yet classy.' Perry winked.

'That's me, Dad,' replied Emma, laughing. Then she looked back into the mirror. 'But this hair style definitely isn't.'

On that Perry couldn't agree more. He loved his daughter's wild, chestnut hair.

'I much prefer your curls,' he granted, then left her to it.

'So do I,' called Emma and reached for her water spray. She dowsed her head until the flat, lifeless hair bounced back into its natural springy self, and she contained it with a thick, black ribbon.

The finished effect hit the mark.

'There, that's better,' she nodded with more confidence when assessing her reflexion for the second time and marched downstairs.

'Go knock 'em dead,' Perry cheered in support. He was giving Emma a lift to the interview and was feeling nervous for her. Driving to Samphire Bay, he kept stealing side glances at his daughter. She seemed calm enough, now that she'd changed her appearance. Although he'd suggested the navy suit, he was glad Emma had had the conviction to wear her own choice of clothes. She was right, she had to be *herself*. And if that wasn't good enough, they were the fools.

As Emma walked up the steps to the house she was greeted by Jennifer at the front entrance.

'Hello, you must be Emma?' she welcomed with a smile.

'Yes,' replied Emma, holding her hand out.

Jennifer shook it and showed her inside. Emma was once more in awe of the marbled hall and her eyes homed in on the grand piano she had previously played at the open day. Jennifer noticed.

'Do you play?' she asked.

'Yes, I've actually played that one.' Her head nodded towards the instrument.

'Really?' Jennifer said in surprise.

Emma gave her a quick explanation. As she did so, she heard a door creak open. Turning towards it, Jennifer quickly hurried her along the hall and into the library where the interviews were taking place.

'Please, take a seat,' Jennifer sat behind a desk and signalled Emma to sit opposite her.

All the time Emma was taking in her surroundings. The library was amazing with floor-to-ceiling shelving crammed with colourful books. It even had a ladder that ran across a wooden rail to access the top. She was enchanted by the place. Again, this wasn't lost on Jennifer who smiled to herself. It was good to see that the girl was impressed. The previous interviewee seemed a touch underwhelmed, stating that the manor house where she had previously worked was far bigger. Unfortunately, the other remaining applicant had cancelled, saying she had decided to take another position overseas. This Emma looked like she appreciated her environment, which was a positive thing for Jennifer.

'So, Emma, tell me a little bit about yourself,' she started, and sat back in her chair.

'Well, up to now I've worked in a bank and have just taken voluntary redundancy,' replied Emma. She gave an outline of all the duties she had covered, keen to emphasise her organisational skills, honesty and time keeping, plus how she had been deputised to section manager on occasions. Then not wanting to sound too boring, added, 'but my passion lies with the band I'm in,' and went on to give a potted history of how she joined it and the gigs they performed.

Jennifer listened with interest, thinking how different this girl was, even her dress sense was a touch quirky. The one thing bothering her was if she would soon tire of housework. It was all well and good living inside a marvellous Art Deco house, but having to clean it was another matter. When she voiced her concern Emma shrugged.

'It's what I do at home, at least I'd be getting paid to do it here,' she reasoned, before she went on to tell Jennifer about the circumstances at home, of how her mum had died when she was thirteen years old and that it was just her and her dad now.

Jennifer sat and listened with compassion, definitely warming to the girl. She had a natural confidence, no airs or graces, but appeared comfortable in her own skin. So far, so good. Now to outline all the duties that would be expected of her, including the cooking aspect.

'The owner of the house lives alone, although he does entertain and you could be catering for large numbers at times,' warned Jennifer, closely observing Emma's reaction. 'Sometimes at short notice,' she threw in to really test her.

Emma remained unfazed. If anything, the question had sparked curiosity within. What did the owner do? Her mind cast back to the house open day and she tried to picture his face again. He'd worn dark sunglasses which had obscured his features. Had that been deliberate? She also remembered that his deep, smooth voice had resonated with her. She'd definitely heard it before. Her curiosity started to build momentum. Deciding to dig for information, Emma considered her reply before answering.

'What kind of hosting are we looking at? Social gatherings or business?'

'Would that make any difference?' replied Jennifer.

'Just considering whether the gatherings be a formal, sit-down dinner or… a party buffet for example?'

'Both,' said Jennifer, staring directly at her, not giving anything away.

'I see. Well, as long as I was given clear instruction as to what exactly was required, then yes, I'm sure I could manage that.'

'Good,' nodded Jennifer.

'I could even throw in the entertainment!' Emma exclaimed, struck by the idea. She was of course referring to her singing and playing the piano but realised what she'd just blurted out could be misconstrued. She blushed as her head turned sharply towards a slightly open door coming off from the library. She could have sworn she'd heard a faint chuckle of laughter. Jennifer coughed.

'Yes,' she smiled, 'very good,' then shuffled some papers in front of her.

Emma's eyes narrowed. She got the distinct impression that they weren't alone. Someone was listening in to their interview, she could feel it.

Felix was indeed stood behind the adjourning door, eavesdropping on every word being spoken. He'd seen Jennifer greet Emma when she arrived, hidden behind a door off the hall, and had overheard her say she'd played the piano on the open day, instantly remembering who she was. He also recalled how she had drawn her audience in when singing *Champagne Problems*, including himself. Peeping discretely through the gap in the door, he found himself attracted to her again. She had a calm way about her, an effortless quality. He loved that mass of chestnut curls and found his lips quirking at the silver ankle boots she wore. A real sense of style. Then he stopped himself. Did it matter what his housekeeper wore? Of course it didn't, he told himself, and concentrated on the job in hand. He had to admit, though, Jennifer seemed rather taken with her, he could tell. He also knew Jennifer hadn't been overly impressed with the previous woman she'd interviewed. Neither had he, to be honest. They both found her a touch pompous. Emma was a breath of fresh air in comparison.

As agreed, if he approved of the applicant then he'd let Jennifer know. He rang the phone on the desk in the library. Within seconds Jennifer picked it up.

'This is the one,' he said.

'Yes, of course,' replied Jennifer in a formal voice. Inside she was pleased of his choice, fully agreeing with him. She put the phone down and turned to face Emma. Now for the clincher. 'How discreet are you?' she asked directly. There was a slight pause.

'Very,' replied Emma, then deciding she'd had enough of all the secrecy asked, 'Why?'

'Because the owner of this house is in the public eye. His privacy is extremely important to him.'

'I see,' nodded Emma. Her curiosity was absolutely ablaze.

'If he were to offer you the job of his housekeeper, then he would expect nothing but loyalty and commitment.'

'And he'd get it,' came her instant reply.

The adjourning door opened, and both Emma and Jennifer turned towards it. In stepped a tall, dark, handsome man.

'Then welcome onboard, Emma,' said Felix with a broad smile.

Emma sat and stared at him, gobsmacked. She knew that voice now, fully seeing his face. It was Felix Paschal!

Chapter 7

The next few days were a blur for Emma. After getting over the initial shock of working for the actor-come-director Felix Paschal, she just about managed to drop back down to earth. As promised she had to be discreet, so had only told her dad and Bunty, under sworn secrecy, who her new employer was. It was generally accepted that word would eventually get out, Felix more than anyone knew that. However, Emma had agreed that she would remain tight-lipped.

When Jennifer and Felix had informed her fully of the house being the location for a new TV drama series, Emma just couldn't contain her excitement.

'O-M-G!' she'd cried, eyes wide as saucers.

At this Felix and Jennifer exchanged an amused glance. It was hard not to be endeared by her reaction. And, as Jennifer pointed out, what young woman wouldn't be overwhelmed by such news. It *was* exciting, of course it was, especially given that Emma had had no idea in the first place.

Considering that Emma had turned up to be interviewed with no knowledge of who her employer actually was, she had handled the whole situation remarkably well. Yes, she'd been in awe of the place and astounded at seeing Felix, but once accustomed to the idea, Emma had taken it all in her stride. She'd been far too busy to be star-struck. Not only did she have to get to grips with moving in, but she had to familiarise herself with the place.

Emma had been in her element, discovering every nook and cranny of the beautiful, grand house, plus the grounds.

'I can see why you chose this as the location,' she'd said to Felix as he walked her through the gardens. They came to a stop, facing the bay.

'I know. It's an amazing spot, ideal for the drama,' replied Felix, turning back to face the house. 'I couldn't believe my luck when I first saw it on the market.'

'What's the drama about?' asked Emma.

'It's called *Lady Scarlett Investigates* and set in the 1920s. The house is a perfect backdrop.'

'So, Lady Scarlett's a super-sleuth, is she? Like a younger, glamorous Miss Marple?'

'Exactly,' nodded Felix with a smile, liking her interest.

'Who's playing the role?' she enquired, then swiftly added, 'If you don't mind me asking.' The last thing she wanted was to appear nosey or too intrusive. She was just the housekeeper after all.

There was a delay before he answered.

Felix found it very easy talking to her, but he had to be careful. He didn't know Emma yet and there had to be trust before divulging too much. Although all the cast had now been confirmed and contracts drawn up, nothing had been leaked to the press yet. Looking at Emma's innocent face told him her question had been out of genuine interest, but still, he couldn't afford to take any chances.

'The roles haven't quite been decided yet,' he lied.

'Ah, right,' replied Emma, unconvinced of his answer, sensing she'd over-stepped the mark by asking. Note to self, she inwardly reprimanded – just get on with the job.

Emma had been more than happy with her living quarters, having moved in a few days earlier. She had the Blue room, which was at the far end of the landing and had its own en-suite. It was big enough to have a small seating area and TV by the window as well as a large double bed. Once more she'd been wowed by the Art Deco flair and style of furnishings with mirrored furniture, a big plush headboard crowning the bed and velvet, scalloped chairs in the seating area. The bathroom had a black and white patterned tiled floor, white bathroom suite and a large vintage mirror which hung over the sink. It was all a far cry from what Emma had been used to in the cosy cottage she'd shared with her dad. There, she had occupied the tiny box room. It took some getting accustomed to the sheer volume of space. It also took some getting used to living with someone other than her dad. Knowing he wasn't far away helped, but being so occupied meant she'd had very little time to feel any home sickness.

What had proved to be the most challenging was that bloody boiler! It truly had a mind of its own. One minute it worked splendidly, the next it rumbled and groaned like a banshee. She made a note to get it looked at. The other thing she struggled with was the aga. Luckily Bunty was on hand at the end of the phone to guide her. Having explained its workings, Emma was still getting to grips with it. Fortunately, there was a microwave in the kitchen as back-up.

All in all, Emma was adapting to her surroundings and new position of housekeeper very well. Thankfully she only had Felix to look after and he hadn't planned any entertaining yet, or for the foreseeable future. She did wonder how it would all be when the place was full of actors and the production team. Would she be expected to wait on all of them too? Still, the anticipation of being around on set when filming was taking place filled her with a sheer thrill. It was hard not to be euphoric. Who knew who might be here!

Jennifer had returned to London with a clear conscience knowing Felix was in safe hands. Finally, she could heave a sigh of relief. No more trips up to Lancashire and playing hostess with the mostess. No, she was back safely in London and fully intended it to stay that way.

She couldn't help but smile to herself at Emma. The girl had a real warmth to her. For someone in her mid-twenties she was pretty level-headed too, all things considered. Perhaps it was because the poor thing had had to grow up fast, with her mum dying when she was so young. Professionally, she thought Felix had absolutely made the right choice, though a small part of her also suspected that maybe something else, more personal, had helped him decide on Emma. The girl was attractive in both looks, with her quirky, flamboyant style, and in personality. She appeared open and honest. Jennifer presumed what you saw was what you got. 'Does what it says on the tin,' her pragmatic husband would say. What she most liked about Emma was how she behaved around Felix. Apart from the obvious first shock of seeing him, she had soon treated him like the ordinary person he basic-ally was deep down. And that was just what he needed, someone to handle him in a down-to-earth way.

All this sat well with Jennifer. If she was a betting woman, she'd have a wager on the relationship as employer and housekeeper *overlapping*, perhaps? She laughed softly. So what? As long as that awful Anika was well out of the picture.

Jasmine was deep in concentration, working on the graphics of a holiday brochure, when Bunty tapped on the garden studio patio door.

'Busy?' she mouthed through the glass.

Jasmine smiled and motioned her to come in. She got up from her desk and went to put the kettle on.

'Hi, Bunty, fancy a cuppa?'

'Oh yes, thanks,' she replied.

Ever since Emma had told her and Perry about who her employer was, Bunty had been dying to tell Jasmine. Although she'd been told on strict instructions not to tell a soul, she knew that Jasmine wouldn't pass the information on. It was just too juicy to keep to herself. Both she and Perry had been astounded to learn that not only was Felix Paschal the new owner of her childhood home, but it was to be the location of a new TV drama series. It was all so much to take in. She simply *had* to tell her friend.

'So, how's Emma getting on with her new job?' said Jasmine, passing Bunty a cup of tea.

'Well, now there's a story.' She gave a secretive grin.

Jasmine frowned and waited for her to elaborate. It didn't take long; it was blatantly clear that Bunty was itching to tell her something. However, nothing could have prepared Jasmine for what she revealed. She stopped mid-drink and blinked.

'*Felix Paschal* has bought your old house?'

'Yes, he has,' confirmed Bunty with a chuckle. 'It's incredible, isn't it? Apparently his real name is Adam Felix Sinclair.'

'And he's filming a TV series there?'

'Yes, he is.' Bunty nodded with glee. 'How exciting's that?' she squealed, clapping her hands. Who would have thought her old home, the set of a drama series!

'I can't believe it,' said Jasmine, shaking her head.

'Oh, but you mustn't tell anyone,' Bunty urged. 'We promised Emma we'd keep it quiet.'

'Yes, of course,' replied Jasmine.

Later that evening, after dinner, Jasmine and Robin were relaxing with a bottle of wine, snuggled up together on the sofa. Jasmine was feeling suitably laid-back and couldn't help but mention her news. Robin would be discreet.

'Guess who's bought Bunty's old house?'

Robin turned to face her with a look of surprise.

'How come you know?' he asked. It had been a much talked about mystery on Samphire Bay, who the new owner of the big, white house on the peninsula was.

'You'll never guess,' teased Jasmine.

Robin laughed. 'Just tell me then.'

'Felix Paschal.'

There was a stunned silence.

'Felix Paschal?' replied Robin.

'Yea,' said Jasmine.

'You mean *the* Felix Paschal, the actor?'

'Yes,' chuckled Jasmine, 'and what's more, there's a new drama going to be filmed there. Apparently he bought the house because it's the perfect location.'

'Blimey.' Robin was still absorbing all the newfound information.

'Oh, but you must keep it to yourself,' Jasmine quickly told him. 'It's top secret.' She mimed pulling a zip across her mouth.

'Right, OK,' replied Robin.

As soon as Robin got back to his apartment he texted Jack, knowing he'd keep quiet.

Felix Paschal has bought Bunty's old house.

No way?

Straight up. And he's filming there too.

You sure?

Deffo. Keep schtum.

Will do.

The next morning Jack called in at the grocery shop to get some milk and a newspaper. As he picked up a copy, he quickly scanned the headlines, wondering if there was any news of Felix Paschal buying a local property. He couldn't see any mention of it on the front pages.

Trish, the shop keeper and well-known gossip, saw him studying the papers.

'Looking for anything in particular, Jack?' she asked.

'Only about our new resident,' he replied, still squinting along the shelf.

'Our new resident? Who's that then?' asked Trish.

'Only Felix Paschal,' muttered Jack, still straining to see if there was any mention of him, then stopped. Should he have just said that?

'Felix Paschal!' shrieked Trish.

Oh well, too late now, thought Jack. The word was well and truly out. If Trish knew then all of Samphire Bay would know before the day was over.

Chapter 8

Perry sat back in his armchair, turned the TV off and sighed. He listened to the sound of silence and hated it. Normally Emma would be stomping about upstairs or calling him from the kitchen that tea was ready. Now there was only the tick of the clock to keep him company. He homed in on it. Tick, tick, tick, reminding him of the long evening that lay ahead.

Time had never passed so slowly since his daughter left home. He'd even taken to popping his head into her bedroom, just to feel a bit closer to her. There were all her cuddly toys, lined up on an empty bed. The little box room had never been so neat and tidy. Spotless in fact, since she'd last slept there. Perry swallowed. So, this was what empty nest syndrome feels like, he supposed with despondency.

Deciding to pull himself together, he reached for his mobile and sent Emma a cheery text, just to let her know he was thinking of her. Truth be told he'd thought of little else.

Hi there, still OK? Hope he's treating you well!

That was another thing which had concerned Perry, the fact his daughter was living under the same roof as a total stranger. Well, not a stranger exactly, he conceded, her employer, but still… After waiting for a reply which never came, he decided to ring Bunty – she always cheered him up.

'Hello, you,' she answered.

Just hearing her voice was a comfort.

'Hi, Bunty, what are you up to?' he asked.

'I've poured myself a large gin and tonic and I'm about to put the TV on. My favourite film's on tonight,' she said cheerily, clearly feeling upbeat. The opposite to him. How he wished he could inject a touch of Bunty's enthusiasm and joie de vivre into his own life.

'*Dirty Dancing*?' He smiled, knowing she loved that.

'Absolutely!' gushed Bunty, then detecting his mood asked, 'Are you all right Perry?'

'Yeah… it's just…' he stumbled, trying to find the words. To his horror his eyes began to fill.

'Perry?' Bunty sounded worried now.

'I'm OK, just missing Emma,' he managed to reply in a choked voice.

'Oh, Perry, it's only natural that you should miss her,' she consoled, 'you're so close, it's inevitable.'

Although Bunty was trying to comfort Perry she was in fact making him feel worse.

'I know, why don't you come here and join me?' she suggested.

'Watch *Dirty Dancing*?'

'Yes! It'll be fun. We can even try a bit ourselves,' she said mischievously.

'What, dirty dancing?' he chuckled.

'And why not?' Bunty retorted with mock indignance. 'As I recall you could make some pretty hot shapes in your day,' she teased.

'Yeah, in my day,' Perry replied dryly, but still couldn't help feel brighter by her invitation.

'Oh, come on! There's life in the old dog yet.' She was openly laughing now.

'Right, you're on,' he said in a decisive tone.

'Good. I'll pour you a stiff gin then.'

'Sounds like I'm gonna need it.'

Perry put down his phone with a smirk. Bunty really was just the tonic he needed.

She was in high spirits when he arrived at her cottage, opening the door with a drink clutched firmly in hand, a playful light sparkling in her eyes.

'Come in, Snakey Hips,' she giggled.

Perry shook his head. Just how many of those gins had the old girl had?

'Quick, it's the bit where Patrick's teaching her to dance!' Bunty ushered him to sit down in front of the TV. He noticed his drink was ready and waiting for him on the coffee table. He took a gulp and winced at its strength. Oh well, if you can't beat 'em, join 'em.

Later that evening a very tired Emma was stepping into a hot bubble bath. She was exhausted, having spent most of the day cleaning. Felix had been in London and was stopping overnight so, having the house to herself, she thought it a good opportunity to hoover throughout. It would be better to do the noisy jobs when he wasn't around. She also didn't fancy interrupting him when he was busy in the library.

Often she would overhear snippets of telephone or Zoom calls. From what she'd gleaned, the filming was about to commence very shortly. After having asked Felix who the leading lady was, Emma was reluctant to make any further enquires, working on a need-to-know basis only. What she had learnt was that the production team was ready and keen to start. Emma had also become aware of another caller, just the once, but one which she suspected was unwanted due to Felix's clenched jaw when answering. His voice had become quiet and flat and he quickly ended the call. Emma wondered who it had been, but soon reminded herself it wasn't her business.

After hoovering the whole house, which had taken hours given the surface area, Emma had mopped the marbled hall floor and kitchen slate floor. It really was tiring. Her body was used to sitting behind a desk all day, not constant physical work. Her back ached. Her muscles ached. *Every* part of her ached! Never had her limbs cried out to be soaked in a hot bath so badly. She lay, soaking her body and relaxing for a good half hour, then got out and slipped on a dressing gown and wrapped her wet hair into a towel. Her mass of curls would take ages to dry but she didn't like using a hair dryer as it caused it to frizz. Padding out in slippers to her bedroom, she noticed her mobile on the bedside cabinet flashing. One missed call from Felix and a text from her dad. Felix had left a voice message.

'Hi, Emma, I'll be back tomorrow as planned. I'll be bringing a guest with me, so could you make up a bedroom please?'

Hmm, thought Emma, wondering who Felix's guest was. Then she opened her dad's text.

> Hi there, still okay? Hope he's treating you well!

Oh, Dad! Things had been so hectic she'd hardly had a chance to think about him. She quickly replied.

> I'm fine dad. How are you? Been mega busy but hope to see you soon, yea?

She sent the text, gave her hair another rub down, then climbed into bed, desperately needing her sleep.

Robin was on his laptop searching for the right hotel in London. He was at pains to make their upcoming trip extra special for Jasmine. Not only was it a well-earned break for both of them, it was also their first time away together as a couple and – most importantly – Robin planned to go when it was Jasmine's birthday.

He'd been thinking of what to do for her thirtieth birthday, which was looming. Jasmine's birthday was on Bonfire Night, 5 November. She'd told Robin how most of her birthdays had been spent around a fire, watching fireworks light up the sky, so he was determined for this birthday to be different. On the quiet, he'd contacted her parents to run the idea of whisking Jasmine away on a city break. This had been met with gleeful approval.

'Good idea, Robin. It'll do you both the world of good,' her mother had told him.

So all he had to do now was pick the perfect, romantic hotel and put an exciting itinerary together for them. He, personally, hadn't ever been on the London Eye so was

67

keen to book them a pod to themselves, with an accompanying bottle of champagne. The rest of the planning he'd discuss with Jasmine.

As for the hotel, well there was so much choice, but Robin wanted somewhere relatively quiet, not completely in the buzz of the centre. Maybe a hotel near to a park? He scanned the internet and finally saw just the right place.

> Nestled in the charming borough of Richmond, 'The Old Coach House' offers an ideal hideaway from the hustle and bustle of Central London. Located a stone's throw from Kew Gardens and Richmond Park, this quaint former coaching inn is an absolute haven after a busy day's site seeing in the city.

Perfect, thought Robin, and proceeded to book it. For once he wasn't going to consult Jack about taking time off work. Not that Jack would have minded, far from it, but usually they informed each other first before arranging a holiday. Lately though Robin had started to resent the amount of time they both poured into the business. And the latest project they'd looked at in Lancaster was definitely going to take up a colossal amount of time.

At first, when he saw the size of the warehouse, Robin felt daunted. It was far bigger than he'd expected. Jack, on the other hand, appeared excited by the prospect of renovating the huge building into apartments.

'It's an amazing opportunity, Rob. Just think what each apartment could fetch!' His eyes almost flashed with pound signs.

But for Robin, it wasn't just about the money any more. He'd found that there were more important things in life. Love, for one. Meeting Jasmine had changed him. He wasn't the same as Jack since Jasmine had come into his life. He realised there was more to it than making a profit. The trouble was Jack didn't see that, simply because he hadn't yet met the right girl. But Robin had. He knew it and had done from the moment he'd clapped eyes on Jasmine. That said, he was also level-headed and knew he had a livelihood and living to make.

Feeling torn knowing how much time, effort and hard slog the project would take had left him undecided. He really did not want to jeopardise his relationship with Jasmine. His mind cast back to his ex-girlfriend and how she'd royally dumped him because of his demanding workload. But, he quickly acknowledged, Jasmine was a whole lot different to his venomous ex.

As these thoughts were being processed in his head, he had Jack in his ear, full of enthusiasm for the development.

'This could set us up for life, mate,' he'd said, rubbing his hands.

'But we haven't the full funds to buy it,' Robin countered.

'So? We borrow it,' shrugged Jack, refusing to be put off. 'We've a sound business, the bank won't have a problem, especially when we outline the proposition.'

'Hmm, I'm not sure, Jack.' Robin was trying his best to be practical. He didn't want to miss out on what could be a fantastic chance, yet was uncomfortable about racking up debt.

Jack was on fire for the venture but could see Robin's hesitancy.

'Look, Robin, just envisage yourself a year or two from now. This warehouse could fit six apartments easily. Once they're all sold, we can sit back and take things easy for a while. We wouldn't have to rush into another development for ages, if ever.'

Now this, Robin *did* like the sound of. Realising this job could potentially provide for his long-term future settled him. It was risky, of course it was, but thinking about Jasmine and the life he could provide for them both, it was a risk he was willing to take. He puffed his cheeks out.

'OK, let's go for it,' he said, and they shook on it.

So, knowing what busy times lay ahead of him, Robin was determined to make his mini break with Jasmine all the more special.

Felix had had a lot to contemplate too. His mind was a quagmire. Just when the production was making progress – after the cast was selected, scripts handed out and a date set for the start of filming – Anika had thrown a spanner in the works. She'd upped the ante and the nasty texts had now been replaced with phone calls. He'd finally taken Jennifer's stern advice and blocked her number on his phone. Felix had honestly thought Anika would have grown bored by now and it staggered him how she was behaving. Did she truly not have anything better to do than keep pestering him? The woman was gorgeous (even if a touch unhinged) and could have anyone she wanted. So why not find someone else? It wasn't as if they'd been deliriously happy in the first place.

The early days had been fun, but that had soon worn off when Felix had witnessed first-hand her vile temper. The trouble was, Anika could switch in a second. One minute she was all smiles for the catwalk and camera, the next a raging diva in the dressing room. Within the industry she was renowned for her tantrums, having reduced young makeup artists to experienced designers to tears with her brand of humiliating annihilation.

At first, Felix had been flattered by the attention the great beauty was showing him. They'd met at a film premier, where he'd played a supporting role. She'd eyed him from the bar at the after-show party and summoned him over. Felix couldn't believe she'd even noticed him. But notice him she did. In fact, Felix soon became an obsession to her and, as the months rolled on, Anika's possessiveness was unbearable. She'd watch love scenes he'd starred in and plague him with questions.

'Were you *really* acting?' she'd asked with narrowed eyes on more than one occasion.

Felix had well and truly grown tired of her. The model took high maintenance to another level. And it wasn't just the actresses Anika was jealous of – she'd even had a pop at Jennifer!

'That woman demands far too much of your time,' she'd once commented.

Felix didn't even gratify it with an answer, just shook his head. However, when Anika had had the audacity to criticise his mother, that had been the real turning point. His relationship with his mother was extra close, having lost his dad at an early age. Staring Anika in that beautiful face that had covered many a billboard, he finally spoke his mind.

'Nobody speaks about my mother like that. We're over, Anika. It's not working.'

Her eyes widened, totally shocked by his words. *Nobody* dumped her. *She* did the dumping.

'I beg your pardon?' she replied in a quiet, icy tone.

It didn't intimidate him. Nor did the explosion which he predicted was about to happen.

'You heard,' he answered flatly. 'I want you out of here, pronto. Your behaviour has been out of line for a long time and I've had enough.'

Thankfully, she hadn't moved into his apartment, so it didn't take long for her to collect her few possessions dotted around the place. Tears stung her eyes as she turned on him one last time.

'You are so going to regret this,' she spat.

He merely held out his hand.

'Key, please,' he said.

Anika was outraged. Throwing it at him, she slammed the door behind her.

Felix had never felt such relief. Now though, her final words were haunting him. Not that he regretted ending the relationship, the exact opposite; but her constant baiting he could do without. He wanted her gone, away from his mind, so he could concentrate fully on directing. It also worried him that she still knew his every move. How did she know about his new house? Who was feeding her the information? It was a concern that had taken root and started to grow. He only hoped blocking Anika from his phone would do the trick, but he somehow doubted it.

Chapter 9

Emma woke early, anxious to prepare the house for Felix and his guest. She had decided that the Rose room would be the most suitable for his visitor. It was next to the bathroom on the landing, so it would be theirs to use. She couldn't help but wonder if the guest was here on a private or business matter. Could this be a new girlfriend perhaps? But then why would she be asked to prepare a separate bedroom?

Emma knew, like the whole world did, of his contentious break-up with that supermodel. However, having got to know the man this past week, she found it hard to believe how the media had portrayed him; she certainly hadn't ever seen any signs of the traits he'd been labelled with. Felix had never shown a violent temper, controlling behaviour or narcistic tendencies at all. From her point of view, Felix was a fairly laid-back, decent kind of guy. It was clear he worshipped his mother from the way he talked about her, which Emma found endearing. She also thought it was sweet the way he regarded his PA Jennifer. As for herself, he was also considerate, asking if her room was comfortable enough and if she had any concerns about anything to tell him. She couldn't have asked for more from an employer. He also paid well, which was a bonus.

She had stocked the bathroom with fresh toiletries and clean towels and was putting flowers in the Rose room when it suddenly occurred to her – what if Felix's guest was male? Would he appreciate flowers in his room? She'd automatically assumed the guest was female. Now why was that? Perhaps because he was single… and handsome to boot, she chuckled. Surely a man such as Felix Paschal wouldn't be short of female company.

Emma had prepared tea and fruitcake for Felix's arrival. She was now learning to master the aga and had baked the cake herself, surprising herself at how domesticated she was becoming. She seemed to have slipped into the role of housekeeper seamlessly. It was such a huge change from her old job at the bank in comparison and she shuddered at the thought of working there now. Although some may dismiss housework as an occupation, Emma was enchanted with the grand house. She loved its interior as much as the outside setting. And as for having a sexy, good looking, famous boss, well, it was tough work, but someone had to do it!

The main pull for Emma, though, was being on set for the drama about to be shot. It absolutely fascinated her to think of how the house was to be used as a location. Felix was right, it was the perfect backdrop. She imagined the place full of lights, camera, action and pictured herself milling amongst the actors, offering cocktails on a silver tray. Or maybe she was letting her imagination run away with her. They'd more than likely be too busy and pushed for time. Judging from the snippets of conversation she'd overheard, Felix was on a tight budget and timescale to wrap up the production.

Music-wise, things were quiet with the band, as was usual for the winter months setting in. There was just one gig scheduled in December, but they were expecting things to pick up in spring. The band mainly performed outside, festivals being their most popular gigs, so tended to be booked in warmer weather. Emma missed playing and singing with her band. Often she'd look at the grand piano in the hall and was so tempted to play it. The acoustics were brilliant, reverberating round the high ceiling.

It was now early afternoon so Felix shouldn't be too long, assuming he'd caught the morning train. Having set the tea tray ready, she made her way into the hall. There it was, that magnificent grand piano, just calling out to her. Oh, go for it, she thought, and quickly sat down on the stool and opened the piano lid. What to play? Ah, what Felix had requested on the house open day? He'd asked for *Champagne Problems* by Taylor Swift. It was a gentle, placid piece with lovely piano music. She started the first few bars, then sang the opening lines, closing her eyes, totally immersed in the song. So much so that she didn't hear Felix and his guest enter the hall. They stood there in silence, listening to her. Only when Emma opened her eyes did she notice her audience. She stopped suddenly in alarm and began to standup.

'Sorry… I was…'

'That was brilliant!' gushed the young woman standing next to Felix.

'It was,' he agreed with a grin.

Emma blushed. 'I've prepared some tea…'

'No rush,' said Felix. 'Emma meet Polly, Polly meet Emma.'

'Hi there.' Polly beamed invitingly.

'Hello,' smiled Emma. Now, giving her full attention, she realised this was Polly Andrews; she'd read about the actress in a magazine after she'd made her name playing Eliza Doolittle on the stage. Blinking in astonishment, then quickly remembering her place, she uttered, 'I'll go and fetch the tea.'

'Great, thanks, Emma. We'll be in the drawing room,' Felix replied.

Emma noticed Polly's suitcase.

'Shall I take your case upstairs?' she asked.

'No need, I'll do that,' Felix answered before Polly could reply. He gave her a quick grin, then showed his guest through the hall into the drawing room.

Emma scurried down into the kitchen, all the time her mind whirling. Polly Andrews! Who would have thought this time last year she would be in such company with two famous actors. She cringed at them catching her playing the piano, hoping Felix didn't think she was taking liberties. He didn't appear to though; if anything, he looked like he was enjoying it.

Emma suspected that Polly was going to be Lady Scarlett, the leading lady in the drama, and when she served them tea in the drawing room, her suspicions were proved right. Felix asked Emma to sit down and join them.

'Polly is here to familiarise herself with the house,' he explained. 'Playing the leading role, we thought it'd be a good idea for her to feel comfortable about the place, before filming starts.'

Polly nodded and smiled in Emma's direction.

'When will the filming begin?' asked Emma.

'Next week,' replied Felix.

'Right.' Emma tried to sound in control, even though her mind was going into overdrive. She wanted clear instructions as to what would be expected of her, but didn't like asking in front of Polly.

'Don't worry, we'll have a chat beforehand,' assured Felix, seeing the expression on her face. News of the imminent filming had clearly affected her. 'In fact, I was going to suggest we all eat together this evening?'

'Sounds great,' agreed Polly with another smile.

'Err... yes,' replied Emma, taken aback. Her? Dining with two famous actors?

'Nothing formal though, just a simple kitchen supper,' said Felix.

'Oh,' Emma was even more surprised, picturing the three of them sat round the kitchen table. Better that than them spaced out over a long dining table having to whizz down the salt.

'OK?' asked Felix with an amused raised eyebrow.

'Yes, fine, kitchen supper it is,' replied Emma, wondering how much more surreal her life was going to get.

Robin and Jack had secured the deal with the help of the bank and bought the warehouse on the quayside in Lancaster. Whilst Robin still had slight reservations it was hard not to be filled with Jack's enthusiasm – it was infectious.

'You won't regret this mate, I promise,' he'd cheered when standing in front of the building.

They had arrived on site to put temporary metal panelling around the warehouse in preparation of the building works ahead. They had envisaged this renovation would take them the best part of two years to complete, so it was going to be a labour of love, but well worth it.

When Robin had outlined the venture to Jasmine, she too had seen its potential.

'Go for it, Robin,' she'd said. 'Opportunities like this don't come up very often, especially in such a great location.'

But then Jasmine would say that, thought Robin, as she herself had done exactly the same, albeit on a smaller scale. The very big difference was that she had bought her derelict cottage sitting on the edge of the bay solo and overseen its renovation.

'I just knew, in my gut, it was for me,' she'd explained to Robin. Then asked, 'Don't you feel the same way about this warehouse?'

'Yes…' replied Robin, 'but we've never borrowed as much from the bank before. That's what's bothering me.'

'But you'll sell the apartments no problem,' disputed Jasmine. 'In fact, I bet they are all reserved before completion, being in such a sought-after location.'

Robin laughed; she was beginning to sound like Jack. When telling her so, she gave a snort.

'Never thought I'd hear those words,' she replied, arching an eyebrow.

Robin was extremely fortunate to have both a good friend and business partner in Jack and a loving girlfriend in Jasmine. However, balancing both relationships could be tricky at times. Whilst he'd committed now to the warehouse renovation, he was very conscious of not neglecting his time with Jasmine.

The London trip he had planned for her thirtieth was booked, all he had to do was run it past her. After a busy day at the warehouse in Lancaster, he intended to spend the evening with Jasmine and had collected a take-away on the way home. Entering her kitchen with a cheery hello, he swooped a quick kiss on her cheek while she took the carrier bag off him.

'You get yourself showered and I'll dish this out,' she told him as she began popping the containers into the warming oven.

Sitting down to relax later, with a glass of wine and having eaten too much, Robin put an arm over her shoulders on the settee.

'Not long before the big Three-O now,' he teased, nuzzling into her neck.

'I know,' she said, leaning into him. She was looking forward to their mini break and having Robin all to herself for a few days.

'So, this is what I've got planned for us so far.' He reached for the laptop on the coffee table and opened up the website for the hotel he'd booked.

'Oh, Robin, it looks fabulous,' Jasmine cried, taking in the Old Coach House Hotel and its leafy surroundings.

'Then I thought we'd go on the London Eye, the evening of your birthday. A pod all to ourselves, with a bottle of champagne, of course,' he told her.

'What a brilliant idea!' she exclaimed. 'We'll be able to see the fireworks all over the London sky.'

'That's what I was thinking,' Robin replied with a grin, loving her reaction. 'I would have liked to arrange 'Jasmine's thirtieth!' lit up in lights, if I could,' he joked with a playful nudge.

'Ah, lovely thought, but not even you could wrangle that,' she laughed, then leaned forward and kissed him full on the mouth. Robin responded instantly and it wasn't long before the kiss progressed. 'Let's go to bed,' whispered Jasmine. Robin didn't need any further encouragement. Standing, he reached down and pulled her up into his arms.

'Let's,' he replied huskily.

Perry had had a busy day too. He'd gone for a tranquil boat ride down the canal and, standing on deck, navigating at the wheel and listening to the gentle chug of the engine, had given him time to reflect. Emma had rung him earlier in the morning and it had bucked him up no end. Just listening to her cheery voice lifted his spirits. They'd even arranged to meet on her day off which was imminent. This had settled Perry, knowing that he'd soon be seeing her.

As he drifted along the water, he took in all the wildlife and nature surrounding him. Kingfishers ducked down in pursuit of food, dragonflies wavered in the rushes, while frogs jumped from one spot to the other. He'd loved this transient way of life, forever on the move from one place to the next. Meeting Valerie, his late wife, had ended it though, shifting his boating from being a lifestyle to more of a hobby. He had no regrets – moving into her stone cottage and being nestled into a ready-made little family was the best thing to have happened to him. Change. It was all part of life's rich tapestry.

His thoughts led him back to Emma. Her life had also changed and she seemed to be enjoying it, to his relief. After hearing her voice full of excitement and vibrancy at what was going on over in Samphire Bay, any trepidations had been quashed. There could be no denying how much Emma was enjoying herself. It was evident just from the tone of her voice. By all accounts Felix was a decent man, despite his reputation in the papers. And as for the TV crew which was about to descend on them, well, she hadn't been able to contain herself. Perry chuckled when Emma had regaled him with how she'd been caught playing the piano in the hall.

Something told him that Emma had made quite an impression on her employer. His daughter's zeal and natural good nature was a joy to be around. Emma lit up the room wherever she was. She had a presence about her which people gravitated towards, hence her ability to draw in the crowds at the band's gigs. Even though he was Emma's dad and therefore prejudiced, he couldn't help but think Felix would be attracted to his daughter. To him, it was inevitable. And, if the inevitable did happen, then what? He knew Emma was a grown woman, with her own choices to make, but his fatherly, instinctive protectiveness reared its head. He also knew how impressed and in awe Emma would be at meeting a production team and cast of famous actors. That said, was she out of her depth? No, he concluded, she wasn't. Emma had enough self-assurance and confidence to hold her own. And rightly so, in his opinion. He'd seen her on stage enough times to know his daughter would take everything in her stride. Emma was no push-over, no matter which company she kept. He chuckled again; just watch this space, he told himself.

Chapter 10

Emma was in the kitchen loading the dishwasher when Felix entered.

'Can we talk?' he asked.

'Yes, should I put the kettle on?'

He nodded. 'Good idea,' he said and sat down at the kitchen table. He'd wanted to see Emma alone so had decided to come down into the kitchen where he knew she would be working. Polly was in the drawing room reading her script in preparation for the filming starting in two days' time.

Once both were at the table with a coffee, Felix began to explain what to expect when the production team arrived.

'All the crew are being put up in a country hotel nearby in Yealand. Polly will be joining them,' he told her. This immediately put Emma at ease. 'If you could provide refreshments mid-day for the cast and team, that would be great.'

'No problem,' Emma replied, thankful that she wasn't required to look after a house full of staying guests. To make lunch for them all wasn't a big ask.

'During filming I'd also ask you to stay clear of certain rooms, but you'll be notified well in advance,' Felix continued.

'Yes, of course.' Emma had already anticipated something like this, knowing interruptions wouldn't be welcome with cameras rolling and, for continuity, they probably wouldn't want her moving items around for dusting.

'There could be one or two evening meetings, depending on how the production's going,' he warned.

'Okay,' replied Emma, taking it all in.

'So,' Felix grinned, sitting back, 'are you ready for the mayhem to begin?' He eyed her carefully. She had poise, he'd give her that. Considering her age, she had a level head on her shoulders. He thought back ten years to when he was twenty-five. At her age, he'd been in a travelling theatre, touring up and down the country, living it up with a crowd of actors most days, performing at night and then getting drunk after the show. A far cry from running a huge house on a deserted peninsula with a film crew about to land. Even Jennifer would have shown a degree of disgruntlement at the notion of having to contend with such a hectic schedule ahead of her. But Emma remained composed, still smiling, those incredible amber eyes of hers twinkling with delight. Her chestnut curls were tied up in a colourful silk scarf. He suddenly got the urge to pull it and loosen her hair free… She frowned at his continued stare.

He coughed and sat up straight. 'Right, is there anything you want to ask?'

'How long will it take to complete the drama?'

He laughed. 'Good question. It all depends, but hopefully by the beginning of summer. There'll be a break for Christmas and a few scenes need to be shot in warm weather. Ironically, it's the opening scenes that will be filmed last,' he explained.

This surprised Emma. 'You mean it's not going to be filmed in order?'

'No,' Felix smiled, this was a common preconception, that all scenes were shot in sequence. 'The drama starts with Lady Scarlett taking a summer vacation at her holiday home, 'Charades'.'

Emma burst into giggles.

'This house, it's going to be called Charades?'

'Yes,' Felix smiled. 'In fact, we've a house sign made. I'll show it you.'

'Oh please!' Emma squealed.

'Come on then, it's in the library.'

Once there, Felix opened the drawer to his desk and pulled out a large sign in matte black, with white lettering in a Mackintosh font. It would run the full length over the front doors.

'Oh, it's fab!' admired Emma. 'Charades feels very apt somehow.' She imagined antiquated parlour games, gaiety and high spirits. 'Did you think of that name?'

'Mhmm, I did actually,' he laughed.

Emma gazed at him musingly. His cheeks formed adorable dimples when he laughed and his pale blue eyes shone. He looked far more relaxed than he did a few days ago. At times he appeared a touch pale and drawn, but his complexion was a healthy tanned today. He mentioned his mother was French, perhaps that's why he had that colouring? Now it was his turn to look puzzled at her assessing him. But Emma didn't hide her inquisitiveness.

'Is Paschal a family name?' she asked unexpectedly.

'Yes, it's my mother's maiden name,' he answered.

'Ah, I see,' nodded Emma.

Their eyes met. It was as though a cloud between them was dissipating, and they were seeing each other clearly for the first time. Emma blinked first, tipping her head towards the house sign.

'Are you going to keep the name?' she joked, in an attempt to lighten the atmosphere and break through the tension that was suddenly fizzing in the air.

'I just might,' he teased back.

—

Poppy had finished with learning her lines and had set about searching for company, nipping down to the kitchen for a coffee with Emma. They had hit it off the other night over supper – it made a refreshing change to be treated as a regular person and the three of them had chatted and laughed easily. Polly had been surprised to learn that Emma had only recently been made house-keeper.

'Really? I thought you'd been here for ages,' she'd commented.

'No, I'm still finding my way around.' Emma gave a wry grin.

'Well, you certainly look at home to me,' replied Polly, meaning it as a compliment. Emma did look at home, in a well-balanced way. She made the place welcoming with her helpful ways and warmth. Not at all like Felix's PA who she'd met a couple of times in London. She'd reminded Polly of her old headmistress.

Felix had thrown his head back in laughter when she'd told him.

'Jennifer keeps me in check,' he'd admitted. He had also admitted to himself he was glad Jennifer was back in London and that he was coming home to a very different lady in Lancashire.

Polly was enjoying her stay in Felix's house but she was ready to join the rest of the cast now. She had found her time here invaluable, rehearsing her lines in the rooms to be filmed and getting a feel for her surroundings. Her favourite was the drawing room, with the huge bow window giving panoramic views of the bay. She well understood Felix's purchase of the place.

As Emma wasn't in the kitchen, Polly went in pursuit up the stairs again and, hearing voices from the library, poked her head inside.

'There you are,' she said when she spotted Felix and Emma together by his desk.

'Hi, Polly, I was just showing Emma the sign of your holiday home,' grinned Felix.

'Ah, yes, Charades,' laughed Polly, who, like Emma, found the name rather twee.

Once again Emma was struck by how Polly made the perfect Lady Scarlett. She had short, black bobbed hair and emerald green eyes, making her look the ideal part already, very retro chic. She could just imagine her in costume, wafting about as lady of this Art Deco house. Then, remembering her place, Emma offered them both tea.

'That'd be lovely, thanks, Emma,' replied Felix, putting away the house sign.

Polly looked from one to the other, sensing she'd interrupted something. Not for the first time had she intuited that the relationship between Felix and his housekeeper possibly ran deeper than just employment. Not in an obvious way, it was far more subtle than that; but there was definitely *something* between the two.

As Emma made her way back down to the kitchen she was having similar thoughts. Feeling a touch flustered, she set up the tea tray with slightly shaky hands. That moment in the library when she and Felix had stared into each other's eyes… Time had stood still for her. She hadn't been looking at the famous actor Felix Paschal, nor her employer either, but a man she was growing more and more drawn to. Not just because of his distinct good looks and strong physique, but the way he treated her, almost like she was a friend rather than the hired help. Never once had she been made to feel like a skivvy, there to only cook, clean and wait on him or his guests. He was kind and considerate. Emma also saw a playful side to him. She remembered hearing him chuckle behind the library door while she was being interviewed and had announced that she'd 'provide the entertainment!'. She also recalled how he'd smiled to himself when he caught her playing his piano. Another employer may have reprimanded her for taking liberties.

Then, daydreaming into space, Emma called to mind the first time she'd met him. The 'Mystery Man' in the dark shades, requesting her play and sing at the house open day. Felix clearly had a genial side to him. Then a feeling of foreboding started to seep into her. Was this a good thing, to be attracted to your employer? But she couldn't help the feelings which had decided to sprout and grow, could she? Common sense told her to just get a grip and keep everything in perspective. Treat her attraction for exactly what it was – a natural reaction to a tall, dark, handsome man, who was a rich and famous actor… who also happened to be her boss. Easy. Wasn't it?

The day had arrived. The TV cast and crew were about to descend on Samphire Bay, albeit only Felix and Emma were the only inhabitants who knew. It was now common knowledge that Felix Paschal had bought the big house on the peninsula (thanks to Trish's valiant efforts), but no news had been forthcoming about when the filming was to start; mainly because Felix had kept Emma in the dark and only prepared her a couple of days beforehand.

Together, they stood in the hall awaiting the mayhem. Emma had prepared a hostess trolley with cups of tea, coffee and biscuits to welcome everyone and Felix intended to say a few words. As it was the opening day of the drama, all involved would be there, the whole production team and full cast.

One of the first jobs would be for the production manager to hand out the shooting schedule. This would become the Bible that ruled everyone's life for the next eight to ten months. It was important to try to film scenes at the right time of year whenever possible, but the availability of individual actors could affect the schedule, making it a complicated business of logistics. Only Polly Andrews would be working throughout the whole filming, the others would come and go according to the scenes they were in. Luckily, for location, it was convenient not having to work round a listed house owned by bodies like the National Trust, so the team didn't have to fit in with their requirements.

Felix was feeling confident. At the last meeting he'd had in London, the production design executive had congratulated Felix on his home and its location. She'd not only been impressed with the house, but the fact it was on a peninsula.

'We'll be able to make decent sound recordings easily, no noisy traffic about. Plus, there's plenty of room in the house for the film crew and it'll be easy to light for the cameras.' Felix had also been encouraged by the comments she'd made about the décor of his home. 'Design-wise, it's very accurate to the Art Deco style. Clearly it's been built and decorated by an enthusiast to the Arts and Crafts movement.'

Felix had nodded in agreement. He'd since learnt that it had been Bunty's mother who had loved that era.

The production manager had shared the same views as Felix regarding filming. As much as possible was to be done on location. It was agreed to use the landscape of the bay as a player in the drama. They anticipated striking sunsets and thunderous storms having the desired dramatic effect.

So, all in all, Felix was well prepared and raring to go, as was Emma. She'd been up early, tending to the refreshments and making sure the place was ready to receive its many visitors.

They both heard the crunch of gravel telling them the vehicles had arrived. Facing each other, they grinned in mutual support.

'Here we go,' said Felix, heart pounding.

'It's going to be fine,' Emma reassured him and strode confidently to the front entrance. With a fixed smile, she opened the doors.

Her jaw dropped at the commotion before her. She hadn't expected so much activity. All the vans and cars were lined up in a convoy outside the house. Filming equipment was being unloaded, cameras, stands, lights and microphones; rails containing colourful costumes were carefully being carried; people with clipboards were busy giving directions. Emma gasped at the scene, for a moment completely bewildered. Then, taking a deep breath, she collected herself and regained composure. Remembering she was the housekeeper and the first point of call, she was determined to set a professional tone.

'Welcome!' she called cheerily. One or two looked up, the rest seemed too preoccupied. Not allowing herself to be intimidated, she shouted louder. 'This way, there are refreshments in the hall!' Then she stood back to allow the entourage inside.

The hall was soon filled to the rafters with all the filming kit and an excited flurry of runners, actors and production team.

'Good morning, everybody,' Felix announced from the first step of the sweeping staircase. A hushed silence fell. 'It's my pleasure to welcome you to my new home and set, for what is going to be an amazing drama.' At this, a round of applause echoed round the marbled hall. Felix beamed. 'I know this is going to be hard work, but, I hope, also an enjoyable experience. We've an excellent team behind this production and first-rate actors.' He spotted Polly from the crowd and signalled her over. Blushing, she came to join him at the stairs. 'May I introduce our Lady Scarlett!' he heralded. More claps reverberated round the hall with cheers and a whoop of delight from one of the young runners.

Tea and coffee followed, then it was straight down to business. As the production manager told them all whilst handing out the shooting schedule, time was of the essence. The cameras and lighting equipment were set up in the drawing room, ready to use in the first scenes. Emma directed the costumes to be stored in one of the bedrooms upstairs. Another bedroom had been designated the makeup studio. She couldn't help but feel energised and thrilled at all the hullabaloo. Although the house was full now, Emma knew this was the busiest it would ever be. After today, only the required actors and filming crew would be present most of the time. As it was autumn, the lack of light meant most of the imminent filming would be indoors. Outdoor filming would require more assistance, but for now there would be minimal numbers.

Once everything had been unloaded and either set up or stored, the runners had vanished and by late afternoon only the actors were left. Emma had made them all lunch and set up a buffet in the dining room. She recognised one or two faces, but hadn't seen most of them before. Polly made a fuss, introducing her to them.

'This is Emma, the real lady of the house,' she teased with a nudge.

'Err... I'm the housekeeper,' Emma quickly refuted with an easy laugh, 'not exactly the lady of the house.'

Polly's eyebrow rose provocatively and she gave a crafty grin.

'Of course not, Emma,' she winked, leaving Emma with her mouth wide open.

Chapter 11

'Right, folks, let's run through it one last time,' spoke Felix to the two actors and cameramen. They were in the drawing room about to shoot the first few scenes. 'Polly, you've just poured yourself a Martini,' he pointed to the mirrored glass drinks cabinet, 'then you walk to the window,' he turned to one of the cameramen, 'make sure you get the bay outside, it's looking dark and gloomy out there today, I want it to reflect the mood,' then he faced Polly again, 'you're pondering, deep in thought.'

'Yep, got it,' replied Polly.

'And, Brian, I want you to be assuring towards Polly, but inside you're alarmed, you've a murderer in the house, yea?'

'Yes.' Brian nodded, a tad irritated by Felix's unnecessary direction. He was an accomplished actor, after all, and didn't need it spelling out quite so patronisingly. He excused Felix's behaviour as it was his first shot at directing.

'OK, let's go… and action!' Felix stood back and watched intently.

Polly was a real pro, she poured the Martini with ease and sauntered over to the bow window. Her green eyes looked over the rim of the raised cocktail glass out to the bay. She let out a sigh of fear and confusion.

'But who would have wanted to kill the cook, Daddy?'

Brian slowly raised from the sofa and moved to stand behind her. Putting a comforting hand on her shoulder, he recited his line.

'Now, now, old bean, you know what the inspector said. Let's leave it to the constabulary.'

She turned to him with searching eyes. 'Jilly, the scullery maid, said she'd overheard raised voices between the cook and Wilson. But surely the butler wouldn't stab the cook in the back, and with her own kitchen knife no less!'

'I think we all need to keep calm,' soothed the father.

'Where was Wilson, when Jilly found the body?'

'Cut!' shouted Felix. They all looked abruptly towards him.

'Polly, I want more… *insistence*, more resolve, yeah?'

Polly nodded. 'Got it.'

'From that line. Action!'

'Where *was* Wilson, when Jilly found the body?' She narrowed her eyes, then twisted back to the window to gaze out in deliberation.

'Now don't go snooping, Scarlett, this is dangerous territory,' warned Brian.

'It's not snooping, Daddy.' She took a sip of Martini and looked her father squarely in the face. 'I have a talent for solving crimes.'

'Promise me you'll not do anything rash? I know how impulsive you can be, Scarlett.'

'Of course not.' She gave a foxy smile. Felix signalled towards the cued cameraman to zoom in for a close-up shot to end the scene.

'And cut!' called Felix, pleased with the take.

Emma couldn't resist listening in behind the drawing room door. She was so intrigued to hear what was going on. On the pretext of collecting the post in the hall, she'd paused as she'd passed by. When she heard Felix shout 'cut' she quickly dashed to the front door to pick up two delivered envelopes. Emma saw one was just a utility bill, but the other was a hand-written envelope addressed to Felix. It looked to be on expensive, thick white paper. Who hand writes letters these days? thought Emma, puzzled. As she walked back, Felix was coming out from the drawing room.

'Felix, this has just arrived for you,' said Emma passing him the letter.

'Oh, right,' he frowned, obviously not expecting something. He then looked up. 'Any chance of coffee? We've wrapped up for the morning.'

'Yeah, sure, I'll bring it up,' replied Emma, pleased to assist.

Within half an hour she'd set up the hostess trolley in the hall and the cameramen, Polly, Brian and Felix were enjoying a well-earned break.

'You not having a coffee, Emma?' asked Felix, beckoning her to join them.

'Oh, err…' Emma hesitated.

'Here, take this,' said Polly, passing her a cup.

'Thanks,' Emma replied with a smile.

She was really warming to the actress. Being a similar age and both artists in their own field, they had quite a bit in common. Ever since that cheeky remark about her being 'the real lady of the house', Emma had shared a bit of banter back. Together they enjoyed gossip and giggles, particularly about the rest of the cast.

'He's got a toyboy,' Polly had whispered about Brian Chapman, the actor playing her father, Lord Pemberton.

'No!' hissed Emma.

This was indeed a scandal, considering the man had been a real lothario in the seventies and was married with four children.

'Yep, honestly. They have a flat together in London. Lives a double life apparently.'

'Blimey,' gushed Emma with wide eyes.

Then Polly had given her a mischievous look. 'You got any hot gossip?'

'Me? No. What would I know?' replied Emma in surprise.

'Sure?' Polly said, raising her eyebrow in the same suggestive way she had previously.

'What are you getting at?' Emma asked, suspecting she already knew.

'Oh, come on, you know what,' retorted Polly with a smirk. 'I've seen the way you look at each other.'

'Sorry?'

'You and Felix. I definitely sense there's something going on between you two,' said Polly, looking at her through slit eyes.

'Well, there isn't.' Emma laughed even though inside she was pleased that Polly had said 'you two' and not just her. Whilst knowing how much *she* was attracted to Felix, it was gratifying to think her feelings could be reciprocated.

'Hmm,' replied Polly, clearly unconvinced, but deciding to drop the subject.

Now, seeing them together though, her suspicions could only be confirmed. They *did* seem very comfortable together. She watched how Felix automatically stood next to Emma, chatting and laughing easily with her. Considering he was her employer, he appeared very tentative towards his housekeeper. He involved her, whether it be for drinks or meals, Emma was always included, and he clearly didn't treat her like a member of staff. Polly liked it, the fact Felix was so down-to-earth and unaffected. Initially, when she'd found out Felix Paschal was directing *Lady Scarlett Investigates* she'd felt a little daunted. Like many others, she'd read the media's portrayal of him. But having now worked with the man, she knew the accounts of him must be lies. Never had she witnessed or experienced any of the shocking anger or rages his ex-girlfriend had accused him of – quite the opposite, in fact. On the occasions she'd forgotten her lines, or missed a particular direction, Felix had shown nothing but patience. He was a dream to work with, always encouraging the team.

She then eyed Emma, who always looked so pretty in a totally unassuming way. Today she wore a cheesecloth, embroidered blouse and denim skirt, and looked amazing. Not the most conventional housekeeper's uniform, she grinned to herself. Emma's curls were free, tumbling down her shoulders, and Polly noticed the way Felix kept looking, as though wanting to touch them. Yes, she concluded, there was most undoubtedly a magnetism between the two.

Felix finally finished filming at the end of a very busy day. Although he was enjoying his new role as a director, he found it immensely tiring. As an actor he had breaks in between scenes, but directing meant no rest at all. He was on hand all the time. At least he didn't have to travel to and from the studios though, he thought, wearily making his way up the stairs. He wanted a well-earned bath before dinner.

Undressing in his bedroom, he remembered the letter which he'd put in his back pocket. He sat on the edge of the bed and looked at the envelope. A sickening sensation hit him in the stomach again at recognising Anika's handwriting. So, she'd resorted to this, handwriting and posting him a letter, which obviously meant she knew his address. Marvellous. Debating whether or not to actually open the bloody thing, he gave in and ripped the white paper open.

So, Felix,

You've had the impudence to block me from your emails, all social media and phone too.

I did warn you that you'd regret your behaviour towards me. Surely the press you've been given is indicative of the power I have over you?

That said, I am a tolerant person and am prepared to put the past behind me. I understand playing second best to a world-famous supermodel like me must be challenging – and for this, I forgive you.

I hear you've started filming now, well done. Perhaps fulfilling your ambition of directing will massage your ego enough to match my status. Let's hope so.

I'll be in touch.

Felix stared incredulously, open mouthed at her words, not quite believing what he'd just read. But it was all there before him in black and white. Anika truly thought she was so superior to him (and everyone else). The girl was delusional. No, Anika was more than that, she was actually *unbalanced*. This was getting scary now. Felix was beginning to feel more than just tired and frustrated with her, he was unnerved. Anika's texts, calls and now letters were not the actions of a sane, rational human being. Neither were her lies to the press for that matter. She had totally discredited him, or at least tried her damndest to.

He re-read the letter and shook his head, still staggered. More than anything, Anika needed help. Some form of counselling to make her understand their relationship was *over*. Her utter refusal to accept he had ended it was frightening. Just what lengths was she prepared to go to? His eyes homed in on her final words, *'I'll be in touch'*. What the hell was going on in that mad mind of hers? He swallowed at the thought of Anika knowing his every move, plus, more threateningly, his address. Somebody was informing her. There had to be a mole in the camp. But who? He genuinely had no idea. Why would anybody he knew want to tell Anika details about him? None of it made sense.

As much as he wanted to just bin and forget the letter, he knew he mustn't. It was evidence. Despite hoping she'd tire of tormenting him, he now acknowledged this wasn't going to happen. Him barring her from his phone had only made her worse. If he believed Anika would simply give up contacting him, then he was as delusional as her. She wouldn't. If anything, she was going to get worse; he knew how Anika operated. With a sinking heart Felix had to admit defeat. It was time to call the police. Anika's actions were tantamount to stalking and, for a fearful moment, his thoughts took an even more sinister turn.

If she knew where he lived and she intended to 'keep in touch', did she plan on showing up at his house? His mind cast back to a previous message of hers, when she'd texted that it was *'time to visit?'*.

If it was just him living here alone, he'd be able to handle it, but he didn't. There was Emma to consider. How would Anika react to another woman, albeit his housekeeper, living under his roof? He imagined Emma opening the door to Anika and a chill ran over him, knowing how jealous his ex-girlfriend got. Poor Emma wouldn't stand a chance looking like she did. Anika was hardly likely to assume she was the housekeeper. At pains to admit how irrational Anika clearly was, and also taking into consideration her foul temper and vindictive streak, he became even more wary. As well as involving the police, he had to warn Emma.

He ran a bath and climbed into its soothing water. Sinking below the surface, he wanted to block out all the hassle. He rued the day he met Anika Genness. Everything about the woman was superficial and false. Rising up, he swept his hair back and rested his arms along the bath sides. He narrowed his eyes in contemplation. Maybe it was time to retaliate and give an interview of his own? After all, he knew enough about her to do some damage, didn't he? Her outbursts of anger were notorious within the modelling world, perhaps he should make it public... Just disclosing her real name would be enough to injure her. Anika hated the fact she'd really been plain old Ann Jones. Then the voice of reason kicked in. Was he really doing himself any favours by stooping to her level? He could hear what his mother's wise words of wisdom would be, *'Do not lower yourself my son'*. And she'd be right. If he started mudslinging, God knows where it would all end. No, he needed to keep calm and inform the authorities.

After bathing, he dressed casually in a white T-shirt and faded jeans and made his way downstairs into the kitchen. Emma was just taking a lasagne out of the oven when he entered.

'I'll have it ready soon,' she said, surprised to see him.

'I was thinking of having dinner in here tonight, with you?'

'Oh, right.' Emma was taken aback. Usually she'd either set up the table in the dining room, or a tray for him in the drawing room, in front of the TV, depending on his mood. Tonight he obviously wanted company.

'Is that OK?' Felix asked with a small frown, suddenly worried he was intruding on her downtime.

Emma smiled. 'Of course.' In fact, she'd like to enjoy his company for a little while; once filming was done for the day and everyone had left, she often found the silence and emptiness of the house quite lonely.

'I'll set the table,' he offered, surprising her further.

'Thanks. Cutlery is in that drawer.' She pointed to the dresser.

'I'll get the wine, more importantly,' he grinned.

'Be careful, the cellar steps are steep,' warned Emma.

Soon they were sat eating cosily at the kitchen table. Outside a storm was brewing and the wind whistled through the windows, but the heat of the aga protected them against the cold of the draughts. With the kitchen lamps on the walls blanketing the room in soft lighting, it was immensely comforting to be hunkered down inside, whilst the elements battled outside. Emma had the radio on in the background, tuned in to an easy listening station.

Felix poured them both generous glasses of wine. It felt good to relax as he sipped his drink taking in Emma. She had a hearty appetite which he liked and reminded him of his mother, who always appreciated her food too. No fussy picking away, just enjoying what was on her plate.

'So, what brings you down here tonight?' asked Emma. It wasn't said with any rudeness, but genuine curiosity.

That was another thing he appreciated about her, thought Felix. With Emma there were no hidden agendas or silly mind games. She just came out with it.

His face turned serious. 'Emma, there's something you need to know,' he started in a sombre tone, making her look up sharply.

'What?' she asked, alarmed.

'Where to start?' he answered resignedly, putting down his knife and fork before sitting back and gulping a mouthful of wine.

'At the beginning is usually best,' said Emma, suddenly feeling sorry for him. He looked so… defeated.

'OK.' He nodded and proceeded to tell her everything. At the end of a detailed account of his and Anika's relationship and her present-day vengeance, Emma sat motionless.

'I'm… stunned,' was all she could say.

'Here.' He reached inside his pocket and passed her Anika's letter.

Emma read it then faced him with wide eyes.

'Felix, this isn't normal.'

He let out a bark of laughter. 'I know that, Emma.' Then, after pausing, added, 'But besides ringing the police, what can I do?'

'Nothing. You'll have to leave it in their hands,' Emma replied gravely. 'Keep the envelope, the police may want to see the post mark,' she advised.

Felix nodded in agreement. How had it got to this?

'I'm sorry, Emma,' he apologised quietly.

'It's not your fault, Felix.' She covered his hand with hers on the table.

The weight of her hand was solid, warm and inviting; the complete opposite to how Anika made him feel. Looking into her amber eyes, his heart melted.

'Thank you for being so understanding. Many in your position would run a mile.'

Hmm, thought Emma, looking into his extremely handsome face, I don't think so.

Chapter 12

Robin and Jasmine stood on the platform, eagerly awaiting the Euston train. It was early morning and the busy commuters milled around them. Shivering, Jasmine pulled up the fur collar on her coat.

'Shouldn't be long now,' said Robin, glancing at the timetable screen. Sure enough, the train pulled slowly into Lancaster station. 'Our coach will be up here.' He led her towards the front of the train.

'First-class?' Jasmine asked in surprise, expecting to travel economy.

'Of course.' Robin grinned. He fully intended to spoil his girlfriend rotten this mini break, wanting her thirtieth birthday to be extra special.

Entering their carriage, it was a blessed relief to be in the warmth. They sat down in their roomy seats with a table between them. Once the train set off, breakfast was soon served, consisting of smoked salmon and cream cheese on rye bread, with a glass of Buck's fizz each.

'This is the life,' cheered Jasmine, clinking glasses with Robin.

'Isn't it just,' replied Robin. 'And there's plenty more where that came from,' he winked.

Jasmine sat back and smiled contently. At the beginning of the year, if someone had told her she'd be celebrating her birthday travelling first-class to London sipping Buck's fizz with such a caring, loving, gorgeous man, she'd have laughed in dismissal. Having lost her husband so tragically, she had found it impossible to see any kind of future at all. Her days then had just merged into a dark, depressing, bottomless pit. The idea of actually acknowledging her birthday would have seemed implausible. But, thanks to her move to Samphire Bay and the motivation that followed, she had met and fallen for the boy next door.

Jasmine looked across and absorbed Robin, not just in sight, but presence also. He had a calming influence about him, leaving her to feel secure and protected. She smiled to herself as he tucked into his breakfast. He deserved this break as much as she did, having worked so hard on the cottage next to her and now his latest huge warehouse project. She was going to savour the time with him this holiday, suspecting the next one would be a long way off.

It only took two hours to arrive in Euston. Wheeling their cases to the taxi rank, Robin was soon loading them into a cab. He gave the address of the Old Coach House Hotel, and they were whisked through the busy London streets, packed with tourists and traffic.

'It's not like home, is it?' Jasmine laughed, gazing out of the cab window.

'Give me the coast and fresh air any day,' said Robin, remembering his days living in north London. He had been a teenager when his parents had decided to ditch the rat-race and up sticks to Lancashire. He had never missed his city life, totally embracing the nature, space and freedom the move to Samphire Bay had given him.

' 'ere we are,' the taxi driver called, in his thick cockney accent.

Jasmine gasped at the Georgian coaching inn, looking so elegant flanked by evergreen plants and trees.

'Oh, Robin, it looks lovely!' she exclaimed.

After checking in, they were shown to their room. True to form, Robin had booked the largest, most romantic of bedrooms, with a huge four poster bed and free-standing copper bathtub in the corner. There was a bottle of champagne chilling in an ice-bucket with two glass flutes ready to be filled. Jasmine's eyes filled, appreciating the effort he'd made.

There was a packed itinerary to follow, starting with a visit to the Tower of London. They both enjoyed being immersed in the history of the place dating back to 1066, built by William I. They marvelled at the Yeoman Warders, solemnly carrying out duties, as they had done so for centuries past.

Next came Westminster Abbey. Jasmine was instantly surprised at its size.

'It looks so much bigger on the TV, doesn't it?' she whispered as they collected tour guide headsets. They tuned in to the voice informing them of coronations, royal weddings, kings, queens, statesmen, soldiers, poets, heroes and villains which were all part of the history to be discovered within its ancient walls.

'It's amazing to think we're walking in the same footsteps as them,' remarked Robin as he took it all in.

By early evening they made their way to the South Bank located along the river Thames, for the last flight of the London Eye. Again, on form, Robin had booked a private 'Cupid' pod which provided a romantic setting with a bottle of champagne. It was dark and the nightfall sights of London's twinkling lights and the gentle rotation of the wheel contributed to a magical and intimate experience. Views of Buckingham Palace, Big Ben and The Shard floated around them against a backdrop of colourful fireworks marking Bonfire Night.

'Happy birthday, Jasmine.' Robin kissed her cheek as her eyes reflected the lights outside.

Turning towards him, she smiled and touched her lips with his. The kiss was long and slow, devouring each other.

'Thank you for everything,' she finally replied.

They held each other, spell-bound with the city skyline before them, truly feeling on top of the world.

Emma stared out of the kitchen window, deep in thought. Felix's words from the other night had made a big impact on her. Not that she regretted taking the job as housekeeper and living in his house, far from it. But she couldn't deny the feeling of foreboding that Anika Genness had left – like a bad smell hanging in the air.

Her imagination had started to run wild. Visions of Glenn Close from *Fatal Attraction* sprung to mind. What if this bunny boiler really did come here and pay a visit? Her blood chilled at the thought. And more sinisterly, what if she happened to be alone in the house? Her eyes homed in on the knife block sat on the worktop and she gulped back the fear. Was she being a tad dramatic? No, not when considering what the police had to say.

Although Anika hadn't actually carried out any physical harm, the defamation of Felix's character had been very real, as were the underlying threats to further sully his reputation and remain a constant menace in his life. After

Felix had shown the police her letter, plus all the other messages she'd sent him, they had taken him seriously. It was evident the woman was unhinged. In their experience of such stalking cases, the perpetrator usually went from mild threat to extreme intimidation, gradually increasing their erratic, disturbing behaviour.

All this of course did little to appease Felix, or Emma for that matter. Having the police call at the house and advise them was unsettling to say the least and only confirmed what Felix had become to realise – Anika was dangerous. He'd also learnt that she had an existing criminal record. She had form for stalking and more, and had been prosecuted under her real name, Ann Jones, some years back. What the police had revealed had sent him cold; false imprisonment. She had actually restrained a former lover under lock and key. Felix had blinked in disbelief. How could she do something like that and carry on as normal? He had assumed Anika had changed her name for reasons of vanity, for a glamorous persona, one to match her super-model standing. Little had he known it was also to shake off and disguise her previous convictions.

Having security cameras installed was advantageous, the police had assured them. They had also told Felix and Emma to ensure all windows and doors were locked during the day as well as at night. Emma had been extra vigilant at seeing the film crew and actors in and out, never leaving the front doors open. She made sure the back doors to the house were securely bolted and had even suggested getting a guard dog. A bloody big Alsatian to ward off any intruder. Felix had said he'd consider it, but didn't particularly relish the idea of a barking dog ruining his filming, but then neither did he want a raving nutcase in his home either.

None of this was helping Felix, especially at a time when he needed a clear head to direct his drama. What made it more infuriating was watching how Anika appeared before the cameras, without a care in the world, like there was nothing wrong. Apparently she'd gone down a storm at the New York fashion show. There she was, striding down the catwalk, beaming into the lens, hands on hips, business as usual for *her*. Whilst he had to quietly second guess her next move, because there definitely would be one, that much he did know. Although the police had prepared him by predicting a stalker's typical conduct, Felix intrinsically knew that Anika was trouble. He had witnessed far too much, for far too long, to know there was no way she'd back off. The kind of person who was capable if imprisoning someone didn't have the capacity to see sense or reason; their head was twisted. *Twisted* — that was the very word which epitomised Anika Genness.

His mind cast back to the tell-tale signs in their relationship; the jealousy, the anger issues, how unreasonable and uncompromising she was, not to mention the physical outbursts. He'd never forgive her for throwing his BAFTA award at him. At the time he'd put it down to her being a diva, a product of the circles she mixed in. But now, looking back, who else did he know like that? He too rubbed shoulders with the rich and famous; he was a well-known actor, for goodness' sake, and he didn't behave in such a way.

The more consideration he gave it, the more cynical he became. How had he not seen it earlier? Why had he tolerated Anika for so long? He recalled the time when he had finally ended their relationship. It was almost laughable that the catalyst had been a comment she'd made about his mother. What if she hadn't said it? If Anika had never insulted his mother, would he still be with her? Of course not, he told himself, that was just the final straw. It was always going to happen, sooner or later. Felix just wished it had been sooner.

Thinking about his mother, he had a sudden need to hear her voice. Perhaps because he was feeling a little vulnerable. He took his mobile and rang her number. She soon picked up.

'Hi, Mum.'

'Ah, Felix, how are you, *mon chéri*?'

Just hearing her voice settled him, giving him an idea.

'I'm OK, but I was thinking… Maybe you could come and visit? See my new home?'

'*Bonne idée*! When would be the best time?'

'Soon,' replied Felix, his voice cracking.

Chapter 13

It was twilight as Perry drove to Samphire Bay. He was having dinner at Bunty's this evening and was thoroughly looking forward to some company. He was still struggling with an empty house, devoid of Emma, made worse by the fact that his daughter had been so noisy that the silence was even more evident. Whether it be stomping up and down the stairs, banging doors or singing loudly, her presence was always known. Even when cooking a meal, pots and pans could be heard being bashed about, with the radio on in the background. Perry softly chuckled, hoping she didn't make the same level of sound over at Felix Paschal's place.

Now though, when she wasn't there, he sorely missed listening to all the stomping and banging, but most of all her lovely voice. That, he could happily listen to all day. Out of sheer despondency, he dug out an old demo tape she'd made years ago. Emma had often laughed when playing it, saying her voice hadn't been as good when she'd been a young teenager. True, her singing had improved after receiving some professional training, but there was no doubt she'd had a natural talent.

As he drove along the coastal road he saw Bunty and Jasmine's cottages softly lit up in the distance. How cosy they looked standing on the edge of the bay, surrounded by such scenery. Even as the days grew longer, Samphire Bay still delivered stunning sunsets, casting burnt oranges and deep pinks across the inky still water. The place seemed magical to him. Not for the first time, Perry reflected on what could have been. Had Bunty's father accepted him all those years ago... Still, it was no good mulling over the past and besides, had he not moved away from Samphire Bay he would never have met his late wife Valerie, or had Emma in his life, and that would have been a tragedy.

He parked outside the cottages and made his way up the garden path, waving at Jasmine over the hedge, who was still working in her studio. He knocked at Bunty's door and stepped inside. The warmth from the wood burner was welcome, as was the smell of the casserole cooking in the oven.

'In here!' trilled Bunty.

Perry went into the lounge to join her. She was on the sofa surrounded by holiday brochures.

'Hello there, what are you busy with?' asked Perry, coming to sit down next to her.

'I've decided, it's time to have a holiday,' Bunty announced, flicking through the glossy pages. 'The cold weather can be so dreary, I'd love to have a break.'

Perry picked up a brochure at random and glanced at its cover. 'Oh yes, anywhere in particular?'

'Hmm, not sure yet.' She frowned. 'There's so much choice.'

Perry nodded, whilst wondering if this holiday might include him. Not wanting to ask outright, he bided his time. His eyes clocked the countries Bunty was considering on the scattered brochures, Portugal, Egypt, Cyprus, blimey, even Dubai. He grimaced. All this was a far cry from the narrowboat holidays he enjoyed. For him, there was nothing better than sailing nonchalantly down a peaceful canal. It was good for the soul and gladdened his heart. He really could not understand why people put themselves through the stress of travelling abroad. The thought of queuing for hours in an airport, to be shackled into a tiny space next to strangers on a plane and frying under unbearable heat in some foreign country where nobody understood you, baffled him. Not when you had the calm and tranquillity of your own boat.

'What do you think?' Bunty showed him a folded page headed, *Turkey – the land of eastern promise.*

Perry's eyes swept over it, then met hers.

'Well?' she urged.

'It's… not what I'd go for,' he answered carefully.

'Oh.' Bunty paused, then asked, 'What would you go for then?'

'None of these countries,' he replied with a grimace, pointing to all the brochures.

Bunty stared at him with a puzzled expression.

'If *I* were to choose a holiday,' he started to explain, 'I'd stay in this country.'

'Oh, I couldn't be bothered driving and—'

'On the boat,' he interrupted.

'Ah, yes, of course,' she smiled, suddenly warming to the idea, but maybe not in winter.

Her reaction pleased him, but he sensed a degree of hesitation. He attempted to sell his idea further.

'Holidaying on the boat is enchanting. It offers a great alternative to the hustle and bustle on land. You can enjoy snug evenings, visit waterside pubs with roaring log fires and wake up to the crisp, clean country air.'

Bunty was considering it, brow furrowed as she tapped a finger against her lips.

'Where would we go?' she asked tentatively.

'Chester? We could go to the craft markets and a concert in the cathedral? Plus, there's the historic tours and city walls.' He refrained from saying he had previously done this with Valerie.

Bunty's face lit up. 'That would be lovely!'

'So, you fancy a holiday aboard *The Merry Perry* then? You'd have a steady hand at the tiller.' He raised a playful eyebrow.

'Yes, yes, yes!' she exclaimed, clapping her hands with glee.

Bunty's eyes twinkled in delight. What a breath of fresh air this man was. She took in his paisley shirt, jaunty neckerchief and long layered grey hair. Her very own sexy buccaneer! She pictured them sailing off into the sunset and was sold.

'Good,' he said firmly, while collecting the brochures up in a pile. 'We won't be needing these then.'

'Cut!' called Felix again. 'Brian, I need more *urgency,* yeah? The scullery maid's gone missing and there's a killer on the loose.' He also muttered something inaudible under his breath in frustration.

Today had been the most taxing so far. It just wasn't happening. Nobody had fully remembered their lines, the timing was out and the ring of the front door bell had been picked up by sound and interrupted filming.

Brian threw him a filthy glare and was very tempted to tell Felix where to stick his urgency. Quite frankly he'd had enough. So what if he couldn't remember every single word? He hadn't got where he was today without a little improvisation.

'And,' added Felix, 'if you can't remember the script, do not make it up,' he stated flatly, earning him another black look. 'Right, from the top, action!'

'Julie's been missing since—' Polly began.

'Cut!' roared Felix. All stopped abruptly. 'The maid is called Jilly!' he wailed, throwing his hands in the air.

'Oh yes, sorry.' Polly winced, nerves starting to get the better of her.

'Again… and action!' called Felix.

As the commotion upstairs took place, Emma was down in the kitchen, getting the mid-morning coffee ready. From what she'd heard coming from the library where they were filming today, the cast and crew would be more than ready for a break. On hearing the doorbell, she'd immediately gone to the hall to answer it but, when she'd opened the front doors, nobody was there. Looking down, she'd spotted a parcel left on the doormat. Emma had picked up the cardboard box and looked around her. Whoever had left it obviously wasn't waiting for a signature. When she examined the box, she noticed it didn't have an address on, let alone any postage stamps. It was simply addressed to 'Felix'. Frowning, Emma took it inside and locked the doors behind her. She put the parcel on the console table in the hall and went to get the refreshments for breaktime.

'OK, it's a wrap,' declared Felix somewhat jadedly. He could do with a brandy, never mind coffee.

Brian, still smarting from his direction earlier, nudged past him into the hall and went straight for the hostess trolly.

'Sorry about before,' apologised Polly. 'I'll try not to let it happen again.'

Felix turned and gave a tight smile. Had he been too hard on them? He hoped not. Then he recalled how he'd treated Jennifer in the past, without realising how much he'd worked her. He ran a hand through his dark hair and coughed.

'Hey, everyone,' he called out to the small crowd now filling the marbled hall. His voice echoed as they all stopped chatting to face him. 'I'm… er… sorry if I've been a touch… picky today—'

'Just a bit,' Brian muttered into his cup.

'But it's only because I want the best for the drama,' he continued, eyeing them all, hoping they'd understand.

Emma, handing out cups, looked up in surprise. This wasn't like Felix. He appeared tired and drawn. Clearly the stress was getting to him, which was no surprise considering that he was contending with rather a lot. Not just the pressure of directing a TV drama for the first time, but all the anxiety his manic ex-girlfriend was causing too. Was it any wonder the guy looked so exhausted? And yet, still so sexy. Emma's gaze homed in on the broad shoulders and muscular arms beneath his fitted black jumper. It highlighted the darkness of his hair against his tanned skin. She knew filming would halt over the coming break and welcomed it. She could do with a rest as much as Felix. She had a gig with the band and was looking forward to that as well. She'd missed being with Gaz, Mitch and Sophie.

Pouring a coffee for Felix, she wandered over to him and passed him a cup.

'Here,' she offered.

'Oh, thanks, Emma,' he sighed and took a drink.

'A parcel came for you, I left it on the console table.' She haltered, then continued, 'It's strange though, it must have been hand delivered, but nobody was outside when I opened the doors.'

Felix's eyes narrowed. Instantly his hackles were up, his whole body on high alert. His first instinct was to take the parcel away and open it in private, but he remained motionless. He still had an afternoon's filming ahead of him and didn't want any further distractions. With another sigh, he momentarily closed his eyes. He hadn't been sleeping of late, his mind forever over-active.

'Are you OK?' Emma whispered, concern etched on her face.

He turned and looked into those mesmerising amber eyes of hers and for a second was lost in them.

'Felix?' she urged.

'Hmm? Sorry… yes, just tired that's all,' he replied and sipped his coffee.

'Good job, you're due a break.' She gave him a small but sincere smile before heading across the room to speak to Polly.

Felix paused and for the first time considered the scheduled break in filming. Would Emma be expecting leave, as the house would be pretty empty then? The thought of spending so much time in this big house without her filled him with dismay. Then another dark thought snaked its way in; maybe he'd never be completely alone, not with a stalker.

He looked at Emma who was chatting animatedly with Polly, looking so carefree and natural. His eyes slid over her slim body in a figure-hugging sweater dress. He couldn't help but admire her curves, then immediately tried to quash the direction of his thoughts. Should he really be having such lustful thoughts about his house-keeper? He wasn't the only one though. He'd noticed one or two covetous looks coming from the cameramen directed Emma's way. Felix had felt a compulsion to warn them off, he was her employer after all. Yes, he was just being protective of her, that was all.

Meanwhile, Polly had clocked Felix's face and it told her everything she already suspected. She'd seen him run his eyes over Emma with desire. He fancied her rotten, it was blatantly obvious. But had he made his move yet, she wondered?

'So, it's at Red Rose Brewery,' said Emma.

'Sorry?' Polly blinked.

'The gig, if you want to come along,' she replied.

'Oh, I'll be at home, with there being a break in filming,' said Polly regretfully.

'Oh well, never mind.' Emma shrugged, then moved the conversation along to Polly's plans until the break was over.

After another hard afternoon filming, Felix finally called it a wrap. He saw the cast and crew off the premises himself and locked the doors. Then he noticed the parcel on the console table and took it into the drawing room to open it up. Preparing himself, he delved inside the card-board box and pulled out a framed photograph. It was of him and Anika on the red carpet at a film premier, looking into each other's eyes. He looked handsome and happy in his dark suit and white shirt, one arm round Anika, lips pursed in a smug half-smile, her silver sequinned gown reflecting the lights of the camera flashes. The picture-perfect couple – not. However perfect this couple appeared, Felix knew different. That very night, Anika had thrown a tantrum because he'd apparently paid too much attention to a female co-star. It had resulted in her smashing a full bottle of champagne and hurling it across the kitchen at him.

Felix inhaled deeply. This picture had been hand delivered. He needed to scan the security camera footage and contact the police. Anger surged through him. What would it take to stop this woman?

Chapter 14

'So, Bunty is going on a narrowboat holiday,' Jasmine explained to Robin as he came back from the bar and placed their drinks on the table.

'Is she?' replied Robin, after taking a gulp of his pint.

'Yes, she said Perry sold the whole idea to her.'

'I thought narrowboats were just for summer holidays,' said Robin.

'Oh no, any season can be a holiday for narrowboaters,' Jasmine exclaimed with passion.

'Really?' Robin frowned, not really getting it.

'Absolutely, Bunty and Perry are going to Chester. It'll be gorgeous, brisque walks in the bright autumn sunshine, all the colourful leaves, hot toddies by an open fire. I think it sounds… dreamy,' Jasmine looked wistfully into the distance.

Robin assessed her and remained silent. Was she thinking of happy times in the past with Tom, her late husband, on their narrowboat? He took another long gulp of his beer. It was at times like this when he really didn't know how to react. He felt a mixture of emotions, ranging from jealousy to sympathy. Was Jasmine with him by default? If Tom were still here… then what? Guilt started to jab at him by having such thoughts. It wasn't poor Jasmine's fault for being in this position, and she'd never given him reason to believe he was second best.

'What are you thinking?' she asked, observing his pensive face.

He shook out of his reverie. 'Oh... nothing.' He averted his eyes, trying to avoid her direct gaze.

'Yes, you were,' she gently accused.

Robin's eyes met hers.

'You were thinking about me, living with Tom on our boat, weren't you?' Jasmine asked him softly.

'Yeah.' He nodded.

'It was another life, Robin,' she said quietly.

'But... do you –' he stopped himself.

'Do I what?'

He heaved a sigh, finding it difficult to ask. 'Do you wish he was here, instead of me?' He swallowed.

Jasmine breathed in deeply, anticipating a question of this kind. She reached out and held his hand. Looking into his eyes, she answered sincerely.

'Before I met you, I wished Tom was with me every day, of course I did. But no amount of wishing could ever bring him back. In time, I learnt that I had to deal with life and what it throws at you. Thank God, it threw you at me. I could never compare; you and Tom are separate entities, different people, at a different time in my life.'

'I see,' Robin answered in a small voice.

'But,' continued Jasmine, making him look up sharply, 'if you're asking me do I love you as much as I did my late-husband, then yes. I love you very much, Robin.' Emotion made her eyes glisten.

This declaration caused a lump to form in Robin's throat.

'And I love you,' he replied in a hoarse voice.

'Wow! You're going on the boat for a... holiday,' exclaimed Emma, totally surprised to hear her dad's news. She refrained from teasing him by saying, 'for a dirty weekend'.

'Is that all right with you, Emma?' asked Perry, somewhat guardedly. He half thought she might take offence, as he'd done the same with her mum.

'Of course it is,' came the instant reply, 'I'm pleased for you.'

Perry smiled wryly to himself, his trip would probably be the last thing on Emma's mind, still, he needed to know his daughter didn't bother about him being away.

This was true, her mind being somewhat occupied with other pressing matters, like having a stalker on the scene. She had decided not to tell her dad about the Anika Genness business, not wanting him to worry, which he inevitably would. Why ruin his holiday with Bunty?

'I'll be here for your gig though,' Perry told her.

'Good.'

'Will... anybody else be going?' he tentatively enquired.

Emma frowned. 'Such as?'

'Felix?'

She laughed. 'I don't think so. I'm not sure Red Rose Brewery would be Felix Paschal's scene.'

'Hmm, I wouldn't bank on that,' Perry remarked sagely. His gut instinct, from a man's point of view, was that his daughter couldn't fail but make an impact on Felix. Or was he just biased because he was her dad?

Emma rolled her eyes. As if.

Bunty was considering what clothes to take on her narrowboat holiday. Hating the cold, she was thinking thermals, thick stockings, chunky jumpers, woolly hats, gloves, fury boots and padded coats. Not quite what she'd had in mind when thinking of a mini break, but still, Bunty expected fun. Simply being with Perry made life enjoyable. Often, she would wonder how she'd coped for so long without him. His very presence lit up her being. But Bunty, being Bunty, craved more.

She wanted to live with Perry. They had so much lost time to make up for, why not? Unless that is, Perry still needed his own space? Well, only one way to find out, thought Bunty; she'd ask him. Yes, she was going to take matters into her own hands. The bitter resentment caused by her father years ago had never left, thereby making her all the more determined to control her own destiny now. Bunty was finally going to right the past. In fact, she would go the whole hog. She was going to propose to Perry.

Chapter 15

It was Sunday and there was no filming today, which meant Felix could relax in bed and have a much-earned lie-in. Except he was finding it incredibly hard to relax. After contacting the police with an update about the hand-delivered framed photograph, together they had accessed the security camera footage, which had revealed a tall, slim figure in black, wearing a hoodie and a face mask, ringing the doorbell and leaving the parcel.

Felix knew it was Anika. The way she had confidently swaggered off, without a care in the world, told him so. Anyone would have thought she was parading down the catwalk, not trespassing on his property. The brazenness of the woman was absolutely staggering.

'Are you not able to intervene?' Felix had asked.

'So far she hasn't actually showed any physical signs of hostile behaviour. Yes, she's left a package, but nothing endangering and that's not illegal,' the police had told him.

'But she's definitely in the vicinity,' he replied in despair.

'Stay extra vigilant,' warned the police officer.

All this he could well and truly do without, especially as his mother was due to visit very soon. He wanted it to feel special for her arrival, eager to show off his new home, not have to worry about the likes of his mad ex-girlfriend.

Although he could well imagine how she'd deal with Anika if they ever came face to face again. He couldn't help but smirk to himself.

Then, there was Emma to consider. She appeared to be handling this whole stalker fiasco remarkably well, but he knew it must have unnerved her. How could it not? She was already being extra vigilant, checking and double checking all the entrances and windows were locked. Nobody got through the front of the house without her bolting the doors firmly behind them and the back doors were constantly locked.

So, where was Anika? Nearby, that was for sure, or at least had been at some point. Felix had a compulsion to get in his car and drive all over Samphire Bay, scour the place and hunt the stupid woman down.

He hated to admit that Anika had won, in that she'd ruined what should be a special time for him. He'd bought a beautiful Art Deco house, in a stunning location and was fulfilling his ambition of directing. Yet, it had all been overshadowed by *her*.

His thoughts were interrupted by a gentle knock on his bedroom door.

'Felix, are you awake?' Emma called quietly.

'Yeah, come in.' He sat up in bed.

Emma poked her head round the door. 'Sorry to interrupt, but I was wondering if I could maybe practise… for the gig? Err… do you mind if I use the piano?' All the time she spoke, she was taking in his wide, muscular shoulders and the smattering of dark hair on his naked torso.

'Not at all! Be my guest,' he grinned.

'Great… well, thanks.' She closed the door. What a sight for sore eyes! she thought, flushing slightly. Hell, he was in good shape.

Still struggling to get the picture of a semi-naked Felix out of her mind, Emma sat down at the piano and steadied herself. Right, down to business… But what a body… Emma! Her inner voice reprimanded. She cast a glance over the sheets of music and the playlist on the music stand.

The band were kicking off with well-known favourites from previous gigs, the first song being *Fields of Gold*. She sang the opening lines, her voice reverberating round the high marbled walls and ceiling, the acoustics were fabulous.

Felix sighed as he lent back against the pillows and closed his eyes. She had the voice of an angel. He pulled back the sheets and decided to get dressed and join her.

Emma tried to concentrate when she noticed him saunter down the stairs, looking very alluring in faded jeans and an olive-green cable jumper. She faltered slightly when he stood at the side of the piano, just as he had done the very first time they'd met at Bunty's open house day.

He watched closely, admiring the way her graceful hands danced over the ivory keys. Then his eyes slowly wandered up her toned arms, her rising chest as she sang, then up her slender neck to her *very* pretty face, finally resting on that wild, chestnut mane that tumbled onto her shoulders. He felt his heart rate kick up, again. This was becoming a habit, he cautioned himself, and a part of him felt uncomfortable. Another part of him, though, the male, red-hot blooded side of him, didn't. After all, it wasn't as if he hadn't clocked her looking at him, like before. Emma was only twenty-five, yet one of the most grounded people he knew. He was ten years older than her. Was that too much?

She finished singing with the closing lines and he clapped.

'Brilliant.' Felix smiled, then added, 'Who chooses the playlist?'

'We decide between us, it's pretty much a group decision.'

Felix nodded. 'What's your favourite song?' He was gazing at her, curious to know.

Emma's face lit up. 'I love ending on *Hey Jude*, all the crowd join in with the chorus.'

'Yeah, I can imagine,' he grinned. Suddenly the image of the audience singing along with cheer gripped him. He wanted to be included. He wanted to be a part of *her* world, just like she was experiencing his. He paused before asking. 'Where did you say the gig was?'

'Red Rose Brewery,' Emma replied, eyes narrowing. He wasn't thinking of coming along was he? Surely not. She continued explaining where it was in Lancaster. All the time Felix was listening with interest.

'After you've finished practising, do you fancy showing me round?'

'What, Lancaster?' she asked in surprise.

'Well, it is my local city now, isn't it? And who better to show me the sights?' he grinned with a raised eyebrow. His lips twitched at seeing her reaction, she looked a tad taken aback.

'Err… yeah, if you want.'

'Hmm, I do want,' he replied almost laughing now.

'Do you want to go now? This can wait.' Emma started to close the piano lid.

'No. I tell you what, I'll make us a bite to eat, while you stay here and carry on. We'll go after we've eaten,' Felix told her assertively.

Emma blinked. 'Are you sure?'

Felix laughed. 'Yes, I am capable, you know.'

'But that's my job,' replied Emma.

'Well, not today.' He shook his head. He looked at the playlist. 'Maybe we could do a duet?' he teased.

Emma burst into giggles, imagining the very scene. 'Stick to the day job, Felix,' she spluttered.

'Yeah, perhaps.' He smiled and made his way to the kitchen.

He took a while in preparing them bacon sandwiches, wanting Emma to have enough time to practise. He hummed merrily along to the set she was singing, currently Norah Jones' *What Am I To You?* Good question, he thought – and one he was increasingly asking himself. Was he strictly Emma's employer, or had he become something more? She was certainly becoming more than just his housekeeper to him, that was for sure. It was no good denying it. Felix got so caught up in his thoughts he almost burnt the bacon. Get a grip, man, he thought sternly. Having poured the tea into mugs and put a few biscuits on a plate, he went up with it all on a tray.

Emma was just finishing when Felix placed the tray down on the console table in the hall and applauded.

'Bravo!' he called.

'Why, thank you.' She got up to curtsy, then joined him.

'Come on, let's eat this in the drawing room,' said Felix, taking the tray.

After finishing their tea and sandwiches, they wrapped up to face the cold air outside. Felix wore a beanie hat and thick scarf, covering most of his face. Emma wondered if it was because of the cold, or as disguise. He drove them into Lancaster under Emma's direction, chatting all the way as she guided him into the nearest car park.

'Are you worried someone might recognise you?' she asked, tipping her head towards his scarf.

'It's more habit than anything.' He shrugged. 'In London it happened a lot, but perhaps here not so.'

'Yeah,' agreed Emma, 'I mean, who would expect the likes of me to be out and about with a famous actor?'

He turned to face her, pausing before answering.

'Why not?' He frowned.

Emma stalled. 'Well… you know…'

'No, I don't.'

'Right, forget it. Come on, let's go.' She made to unfasten her seatbelt, but he stopped her, his expression staid.

'Emma, please don't think that way. You're a beautiful, talented lady and great company. Why on earth shouldn't we be out and about together?' He cocked his head on one side.

Emma blinked, taken aback by his declaration. She was speechless.

'Right, where to first?' he asked, rubbing his hands together.

'Well, I could really do with a new outfit for the gig,' said Emma, not really sure Felix would enjoy being traipsed around the shops.

'OK.' He nodded. 'Then what?'

'I could show you the castle? Or, what about the theatre?' She suddenly realised he could be interested in that.

'Sounds great,' he smiled in reply.

It was surreal showing Felix round the vintage and second-hand shops she normally went to. They did get one or two looks, but nobody actually stopped them. He seemed to be enjoying himself, helping her pick clothes and giving his honest opinion until, finally, Emma settled on a tie-dyed dress in golds, oranges and browns, really matching her colouring.

'It looks amazing,' stated Felix when she came out of the dressing room.

'Sure?' Emma chewed her lip with uncertainty. For a second, she was reminded of when she dressed for the interview with his PA and almost giggled to herself. Who would have thought she'd be here now, with Felix, shopping in a charity shop?

'Yes, definitely, it suits you,' he replied assertively.

'Good, that's sorted, now I'll show you the sights.'

After enjoying a tour round the castle and calling at the theatre, they were in need of a well-earned sit down. Felix had loved looking round Lancaster's small theatre. Although a rather modest building from outside, inside was surprisingly much grander and seeing the up and coming advertised performances reminded him of his early acting days. He had always looked back on his time in the theatre fondly.

'Come on, lunch is on me,' said Felix.

They snuck into the nearest pub, trundling to a cosy nook at the back.

'I'll go to the bar,' said Emma, thinking he'd be wary about getting served.

'No, I'll go,' Felix told her firmly. 'What are you drinking?'

'Oh, a white wine would be lovely, thanks,' she replied. She watched him go, observing the reaction of the barman, whose face did seem to flicker with recognition, but didn't act upon it. He probably thinks he's his body double, thought Emma, grinning to herself.

Felix returned with her glass of wine and an orange juice, along with the menu.

'Right, what to eat,' he said, eyes scanning the list. Emma already knew what she wanted. She'd gigged a few times here with the band and was familiar with the menu.

'I'll have the steak and ale pie, please.'

'Hmm, I think I'll join you,' replied Felix, after a few moments. He got up to order the food. This time when Felix was at the bar, the young lad serving spoke to him.

'Has anyone ever told you, you're a dead ringer for Felix Paschal?' he questioned politely.

Felix just smiled. 'Yeah, I get that a lot,' then ordered their food.

Emma giggled to herself, amused by the way he'd handled the interaction.

After lunch they slowly made their way back to the carpark. On doing so they passed an antique shop window, a stunning Art Deco Tiffany lamp was on display, which caught Emma's eye.

'Oh, look!' she gasped, pointing to it.

Felix stopped to see and knew immediately what she was thinking. 'Should I buy it?'

'It would definitely look the part. It's what our house deserves. I mean, *your* house,' she quickly corrected.

Felix looked into those spellbinding amber eyes twinkling with joy and his heart skipped a beat. He liked the reference of 'our' house, it made him feel... connected to her. And at that point he knew. He knew Emma was the one.

'Come on then, let's bring it home,' he replied, never feeling so happy.

—

The next morning Felix woke up in great spirits. Spending time yesterday with Emma had done him the world of good. Also, having a less busy working schedule helped. There were just two days left, time-tabled for the end of the week, which meant he had another free day. He got up early, showered, dressed and made his way into the kitchen, expecting to join Emma.

On entering though, the kitchen was empty. Feeling a touch surprised (and disappointed) he frowned, wondering where she was. He noticed the cellar door was ajar and went down the stone steps into the darkness. He called out her name, but there was no reply, so he decided to see if she was upstairs in the drawing room or library. But she was nowhere to be found. Perhaps she was in her bedroom? Beginning to feel anxious now, he tapped on her door. When there was no answer, he opened it and poked his head round. No, she wasn't there either. His stomach contracted in fear. Where was Emma? His chest started to pound, hammering against his rib cage. All sorts of hideous scenarios flashed through his mind. He raced back down the stairs, shouting her name. Then, looking out of the hall side window, he saw her in the garden. She was stood by the flower beds, cutting roses, and his eyes closed in relief. Thank God for that.

Felix tapped on the glass to gain her attention. She turned round and waved at him. Just seeing her smiling face instantly calmed him. He waved back, then quickly hauled his jacket on and went outside to join her.

'I saw these and thought they'd look lovely inside. May as well enjoy the last of them,' Emma told him as he approached her.

'So I see,' he replied, 'here, let me.' He gathered all the prickly branches together, after putting his gloves on inside his jacket pocket.

'I wondered where you were,' Felix said as they entered the hall. He couldn't help but sound a touch accusing.

Emma lifted her head up in surprise. 'I was only outside,' she replied, a tad confused at the tone of his voice.

Felix gave a sigh as he placed the rose branches down on the floor.

'Please don't do that again.' He looked straight at her with a serious expression.

'What?' Emma laughed, genuinely puzzled by his behaviour.

Felix paused, not wanting to frighten her, but still keen to get his point across. Then the penny dropped and Emma's eyes widened.

'Oh my God, you thought Anika had done something to me, didn't you?' she gasped, covering her mouth in shock.

Felix reached out and pulled Emma to him. Wrapping his arms protectively round her, he breathed her in.

'I just... panicked, that's all,' he tried to soothe, still holding her tightly.

Emma felt warm and tingly inside, loving the warmth and security of Felix's body. Maybe he had overreacted a little, but she was touched by his concern and also quite flattered by it.

'Hey, Felix.' She pulled back and stared into his troubled eyes.

He shook his head. 'Sorry, I feel so... responsible I guess.' He gave a weak smile and swallowed.

'Listen, you mustn't let her get to you,' Emma appeased.

Felix was once again struck by her mature, sensible attitude, despite the ten-year age gap between them. Feeling a little foolish now, he smiled back at her.

'You're right, sorry.' He looked down at the pile of roses. 'I'll put these in the kitchen.'

Then, they both jumped at hearing the doorbell.

'Are you expecting anyone?' asked Emma quietly.

'No. I'll get it,' replied Felix, then turned, 'you stay here, Emma,' he ordered. His chest was pounding again, as he opened the front doors, preparing himself for the worst, an irate Anika. His eyes widened at the sight before him. 'Mum?'

'A little earlier than planned, I know, but thought I would surprise you, *mon chéri*!'

That evening, after supper with Felix and his mother, Emma went to bed in a contented but exhausted state. Despite sinking into a warm bubble bath and restfully taking stock, her mind was in overdrive. It had been such an eventful day with so much to consider. Mainly, the way Felix had behaved when he couldn't find her that morning.

He had looked genuinely distraught and the way he'd grabbed her to him in a tight hug... She'd been taken aback. A tiny part of her questioned if that was the normal actions of an employer. Emma giggled at the thought of her old bank manager, Mr Butterworth, reacting in such a way!

Then, there was how he had spoken in the car, after she'd joked about him being seen with her shopping in Lancaster. Felix had looked so sincere when gently reprimanding her, and she blushed at the memory of him calling her beautiful and talented. Again, was this to be expected of her boss?

It all left Emma a tad confused, but happy nonetheless. Truth be told, she *liked* it. The more time she spent with Felix, the more attracted to him she was becoming. Her thoughts flashed back to how he'd dealt with the barman in Lancaster, easily brushing away any attention he'd received. Some would have gloated in it, but not Felix.

Supper had been a very pleasant affair and she had thoroughly enjoyed Felix and his mother's company. They were humorous together, banter bouncing back and forth, making Emma squeal with laughter. She had expected to feel intimidated by his mother – between her sophisticated French accent, dry sense of humour and chic outfit, Emma felt positively dowdy next to the woman. But she'd been surprised by the warmth and geniality that Madeleine – as she was instructed to call her – had offered instead, inviting Emma to join in her teasing of her son with a wink.

Once or twice she'd caught his mother's watchful eyes rest upon her in an almost questioning way. She did know why she was here, didn't she? It crossed Emma's mind that perhaps Madeleine may think her a friend of Felix's, such was the manner in which he treated her; topping up her glass with more wine and actually assisting with cooking the meal. Emma had rustled up a spaghetti carbonara with garlic bread and Felix had been on hand to help, setting the table and serving it up. It touched Emma that he had done so, as opposed to having her run to his beck and call. Yet, she conceded, wasn't that what he paid his housekeeper to do?

Her mind then rewound to him buying her lunch, letting her choose the Tiffiny lamp… was this the done thing between an employer and employee? She pictured them again, in the dimly lit, cosy kitchen, hunkered down beside the wood burner. All three of them sat together, chatting easily as they ate. Madeleine had complimented her cooking, as had Felix. In no way was Emma made to feel inferior, or even as staff, for that matter. Hence, the quizzical looks from his mother.

They'd shared stories from Felix's childhood, like the way he had always been a performer, staging plays he'd made up from the age of seven, which Emma had found endearing. Only when Felix went down into the cellar to get another bottle of wine did Madeleine make a slight enquiry.

'Are you from Samphire Bay, Emma?'

'Nearby, in Lancaster,' she answered, expecting more questions to follow. They didn't. Madeleine seemed content with the limited knowledge she had. Or perhaps Felix *had* informed his mother all about her?

Emma just wasn't sure. In fact, there was quite a lot she was beginning to feel uneasy about, like the state of her ever-increasing attraction towards her boss for one. The line between a professional and personal relationship was gradually blurring. Emma felt drawn further and further into a situation out of her control; but as the same time didn't want it to stop.

Meanwhile, Felix was having a nightcap with his mother in the drawing room.

'So, what do you think of the house?' he grinned, sitting opposite her.

'*Magnifique*,' she smiled, nodding her coiffured brunette head, she held her glass up, '*Santé*!' she cheered him. Then, settling back comfortably on the sofa she assessed her son broodingly.

'What?' he half-laughed, knowing something was brewing.

'Emma?' she simply said.

'...Is my housekeeper,' he replied in an innocent tone.

'I see.' She smirked openly at him.

'She *is*,' he protested a touch defensively.

'Maybe for now, *mon chéri*,' she gently teased.

Felix knew better than to deny it. It appeared his mother's intuition wasn't far off the mark.

Chapter 16

Jasmine was busy working in her garden studio admiring the view of the bay. Although it was too cold to enjoy a morning swim, she still absorbed the beauty of the clear, still water surrounded by smooth, white dunes. She smiled at a young family who were walking along the shoreline. Two small children ran ahead whilst the parents lagged behind. Mum and Dad were obviously letting them run off pent-up energy, she laughed to herself.

Jasmine turned back to the laptop to finish off the book cover she was working on. She had a tight deadline to meet and had to get it finished today. However, her eyes kept glancing up at the family on the beach, distracting her. The parents had now caught up with their offspring and were lifting them in the air. She watched them giggle in delight and a sudden yearning swamped her. Like radar, she homed in on their cute little bobby-hats and mittened, tiny hands and a *need* filled her body.

It was an unfamiliar sensation and one which had struck unexpectedly, but it was very real. I'm broody, thought Jasmine, a touch shocked. Since her late husband's death, Jasmine's body had only recently recovered. The cataclysmic trauma it had endured meant that her monthly cycle hadn't functioned as it should. She had sought medical advice, thinking there was a serious problem, but had been reassured it was just her body's natural response and that, in time, everything would operate as it should. And, thankfully, it had.

Meeting Robin had helped enormously, plus her move to Samphire Bay. Often she would reflect on the days with Tom in their narrowboat, but instead of crying she now smiled at the memory. Maybe this broody feeling was the next stage? Was she ready to move on to another chapter of her life? And what would Robin think about all this? Jasmine realised it was too early in their relationship to consider a baby. She wasn't being rational.

Her gaze followed the family on the beach as they wandered back. The children were clearly tired now as they sunk into their parents' arms, heads resting on shoulders. She sighed and tried to focus on work.

Her concentration was interrupted by the buzz of her mobile. It was Robin.

'It's officially the weekend,' he declared cheerfully, 'and it's time to stop working.' He and Jack had called it a day and were in good spirits. Both of them richly deserved a break, having laboured constantly on the warehouse renovation.

'Not for me,' replied Jasmine regretfully.

'Oh, come on, Jasmine!'

'I've a deadline to meet,' she moaned.

'In an hour then? I'll bring you lunch,' coaxed Robin.

She smiled. 'Okay then, thanks.'

'See you soon.'

For the first time ever, Jasmine resented her work. She begrudged having to apply herself when really all she wanted was to just close her laptop and enjoy the weekend like everyone else.

Robin, in an attempt to cheer Jasmine up, decided to make a real effort with lunch. He called at the local shop and bought sandwiches, a selection of cheeses with biscuits and a bottle of prosecco. Within an hour he was bringing it all to Jasmine.

'Time to stop work and relax,' he announced and began laying out the food on her desk.

'Yes,' she agreed, laughing, 'it is.' Finally she'd finished the book cover and sent it off to the editor. Job done. Now it was time to relax. 'I'll open this.' She grabbed the bottle of prosecco with relish.

Bunty, having decided to pop the question to Perry, was in a bit of a quandary. How to do it? She knew where to propose – aboard *The Merry Perry*, his most beloved place – but should she ask after a romantic candle-lit dinner, or when they were happily sailing along the canal? And how, by getting down on one knee? She snorted at the thought, doubting she'd manage to get back up again.

It was his birthday coming up. She'd bought him a lovely card, not too gushy, but very tasteful, with the words '*To someone special*' on the front, along with his favourite aftershave and an Aran jumper. Then an idea came to her. Why not write, *Will you marry me?* inside his card? Yes, she grinned to herself, that would surprise him.

It was hard to contain herself, knowing what she had planned. Perry had sensed a change in her.

'Why are you acting so… odd?' he'd asked.

'What do you mean?' she casually replied.

'All edgy?' He frowned.

'Must be excited for the holiday,' she breezed.

In truth, she really was looking forward to their mini break. It would be a holiday to remember and cherish. She recalled previous holidays with her father, which basically consisted of her tending to his every need, as usual. There was very little in it for her, apart from a change of scenery. One particular holiday resonated, the French Riviera, where he'd taken her to get over Perry leaving Samphire Bay. It hadn't worked.

Taking a deep breath, she poured a large gin and tonic. Instead of looking out to sea, as she usually did to calm herself, she turned to a picture painted by her father on the wall. It depicted her as a toddler, playing in the sand. She put her glass down, walked towards it and removed it from the wall. She didn't want to see herself through her father's eyes any more. Instead, Bunty replaced it with a framed photograph of Perry, at the tiller of his boat, smiling broadly into the camera, eyes crinkled with joy. She couldn't change the past, but she could damn well choose her future.

Chapter 17

It was the final day of filming before the cast and crew finished for the autumn break. A cheery atmosphere filled the air, with everyone looking forward to a rest. As there would be no more filming in the hall, Emma decided to display the flowers she'd picked in there, avoiding any changes to the set. The bright blooms cheered the place up. She also put the Tiffany lamp Felix had bought in Lancaster on the console table. As expected, it looked perfect.

'How lovely,' said Polly as she entered, admiring the many vases dotted about. Then her eyes caught the Tiffany lamp. 'Is that new?'

'Yes,' replied Emma.

'Who put it there?' Polly knew she hadn't seen it before.

'Me and Felix, well, I spotted it in an antique shop and he bought it,' came her reply, knowing full well what the response would be.

'Of course,' Polly winked, then for devilment added, 'very cosy.'

Emma just shook her head in good spirit, not bothering to rise to the bait. Madeleine however had overheard the exchange and couldn't resist chipping in.

'*Oui*, they make a good team.'

Emma turned abruptly, taken by surprise at her comment. They were interrupted by Felix's loud voice.

'OK everybody, let's get on and wrap this up by lunch time. Emma, very kindly, is putting on a good spread, so let's get cracking.' He smiled at Emma in gratitude, and she returned with one back.

'Like I said, very cosy,' whispered Polly mischievously in her ear.

The place was hectic and Emma had a job in overseeing the front entrance as well as providing refreshments. Thankfully Madeleine was on hand to help, much to Emma's relief. She'd proved most helpful assisting in the kitchen.

'What are you doing over the break?' she'd asked Emma, whilst arranging sandwiches onto plates. She automatically assumed Emma would be having some time off too.

Emma shrugged. 'I'm not sure if it's a break for me too… but anyway my dad's going away for a few days on his narrowboat with his lady friend, so—'

'Then you must have a break here! And a rest from all the household chores,' Madeleine instantly replied.

'Oh, but—'

'*Non,*' Madeleine raised an elegant hand to silence her, 'you *must* stay here, Emma,' then continued, 'and I shall cook.' She gave a firm nod as if to end the subject.

Emma knew better than to argue with Madeleine, but she was actually glad. She'd half envisaged herself at the cottage, alone.

Emma stood back to assess the kitchen table. It was brimming with sandwiches, savoury tarts, salads, pastas and cakes.

'There, now to get it all up to the dining room,' she said.

'I'll help,' replied Madeleine.

'No, it's fine, honestly I can manage.'

'You must allow me to assist, Emma,' she told her in a stern voice.

'Thank you,' Emma grinned, thinking what a formidable woman Madeleine was. Only slight in build, yet full of energy. Her appearance was always impeccable, from first thing in the morning to retiring to bed in the evening. Her slim, petite figure looked good in the tailored trouser suits and smart dresses she wore. Emma compared this to her mum's wardrobe and how she'd mainly been comfortable in jeans and sweatshirts, clothing she could throw on without a second thought. A pang of emotion jolted through her, which Madeleine noticed.

'Are you alright, Emma?' Her perfectly make-upped face creased with worry.

Emma liked the way she pronounced her name, with emphasis on the first syllable, *Em*-ma. Her own mum used to shorten it to simply 'Em'. This memory made her even more sentimental and to her horror she could feel her eyes fill.

'Emma?' Madeleine asked with urgency.

'I'm fine, really,' she quickly pulled herself together, 'I… was just reminiscing.'

'About what?' Madeleine asked directly, eyes locking with hers, straightforward but inviting.

'My mum,' came the quiet reply.

'Ah, I see.' Madeleine came and put an arm round her shoulders. 'Yes, Felix explained that she passed away some years ago. It must have been hard for you, *non*?'

Emma was touched by her concern. 'To be honest, me and Dad usually cope OK. I think it's because things are different now, with me living here.'

'But you like living here, do you not?' Madeleine gently enquired.

'Oh, yes, very much,' Emma hastily replied.

'Good, because I know Felix likes you living here.' She stared straight into Emma's face, then hesitated before saying, 'Tell me—'

'Need a hand?' Felix suddenly appeared, making them turn round sharply. He rubbed his hands together. 'This looks terrific.' He looked at them both. 'Thanks, much appreciated.'

'Yes, Emma is worth... how you say, her weight in gold, *non*?' Madeleine smiled affectionately at her.

They all carried the buffet to the dining room, where the actors, camera men, runners, costume and make-up assistants eagerly awaited them. Felix wanted a celebratory gathering and had supplied several bottles of wine. Once everyone's plate was full and the drinks flowed, Polly suggested some music.

'Emma, why don't you sing for us?' she asked.

'Good idea,' smiled Felix, who was standing nearby. 'I've heard her latest set and it's amazing.'

'Hmm...' Emma wavered.

'Oh, go on!' cheered Polly, full of bonhomie.

'Alright then,' she grinned and went into the hall to the piano. She was soon followed as her voice began to fill the place. Felix fixed his eyes on her. She sang with a natural confidence, no awkward inhibitions, just an innate talent shining through. Her sweet voice was breath-taking, making all who heard it stop in their tracks. His gaze once again travelled down her swan-like neck to the swell of her breasts that rose and fell with her singing.

Polly, who'd had quite a few glasses of wine by now, clocked how Felix's gaze once more locked onto Emma. Sidling over to him, she murmured, 'So when are you going to make a move then, Felix?'

Without turning he gave a slow smile. 'I have no idea what you're talking about,' he replied.

'Oh, I think you do,' Polly chuckled softly.

Madeleine had also witnessed her son's look of yearning and gave a calculated smile to herself. A sense of liberation passed over her. After the nightmare which had been Anika Genness, it was such a blessed relief that Felix had met Emma. She had warmed to the girl immediately and a mother's intuition was never wrong. Madeleine had never liked Anika, but had remained silent in her opinion, until Felix had come clean about his relationship with her. She'd been both appalled and angry at what her son had had to endure. Emma, it was blatantly clear, was the polar opposite to Anika. She was down-to-earth, uncomplicated. The fact Emma was Felix's housekeeper Madeleine found rather amusing. Where better to meet someone than on your own doorstep? Much preferable then at some fancy film premier, full of pretentious or fame-hungry actresses. No, Emma was just what Felix needed. It never occurred to Madeleine that Emma might not see Felix in a romantic light. Which girl in their right mind wouldn't?

After a few more songs, the party lunch was winding down. The cast and crew were mindful of the tidal road and wanted to get back to their hotel to pack and go home.

As Emma locked the front doors, she bent down to collect the post. A few envelopes were addressed to Felix, apart from one, which was addressed to her. Surprised, she carried them into the hall and put the envelopes on the piano stool and opened the one with her name on it. Unfolding the white A4 paper she inhaled sharply. There, in bold black writing read the words:

Stay away from him, bitch. Or else.

The nasty warning couldn't have come at a worse time. Emma was shaken to say the least and she had to perform that evening. The gig at Red Rose Brewery loomed and instead of feeling upbeat and energised like she usually did, Emma was extremely nervy and unable to focus.

After showing the message to Felix, he had gone ballistic and rung the police immediately. Madeleine was horrified and anger seethed inside her. How *dare* Anika Genness continue to ruin her son's life and threaten Emma?

'I… I don't know if I can sing tonight,' Emma stammered. They were all sat in the drawing room.

'Of course you must. Do not allow this woman to distress you, Emma,' Madeleine said firmly.

Easier said than done, thought Emma, knowing Anika's past behaviour. Like it or not, the fact was that Felix's deranged ex was nearby. She was clocking their every move. Her warning of 'keep away from him' meant that she had obviously seen her and Felix out together. She must be watching the place, their comings and goings.

Fear tingled down Emma's spine. Flashbacks of her and Felix going shopping in Lancaster came to mind. Anika must have witnessed it. Was she spying on them now? Her eyes dashed to the big bow window, but darkness was falling and she couldn't see very much.

Felix, following Emma's stare, got up to draw the curtains. He, too, had been thinking along the same lines.

'This is all my fault,' he said in a flat tone, sitting back down to face them. He hated seeing Emma like this, so pale and drawn, and tonight of all nights, when it was the gig she'd been building up to.

'It is *not* your fault, Felix,' interrupted Madeleine crossly, losing patience, the whole situation beyond absurd. 'What exactly are the police doing about this mad woman?' she demanded.

Felix gave a hard sigh and ran his hand through his dark hair. 'They've taken it very seriously. This time Anika has made actual threats, physical threats, and it's classed as harassment under the Public Order Act. Technically she could be sent to prison for this,' he stated.

'Your security cameras, have they not picked anything up?' asked Madeleine.

'Not since Anika delivered that framed picture in a hoody and dark clothing,' replied Felix.

'Nothing else?' asked Emma.

'No, we've checked,' he answered, looking regretful. He so wanted to put things right, for Emma as much as himself. Adamant she wasn't to miss the gig, he said, 'Listen, I'll escort you tonight and make sure you get home safely.'

'But… you could be recognised, and—'

'*Non.* I will drive the pair of you to Lancaster and book a taxi for your return,' cut in Madeleine.

'But, Mum—' Felix tried to reason, really not liking the idea of his mother in this big house alone.

'No buts!' Madeleine's hand came up in objection. 'I insist. You two,' she pointed at Felix then Emma, 'are to go out *together* to enjoy yourselves,' she finished resolutely.

Emma watched her and not for the first time admired the lady's spirit. She was right. Why should Anika Genness ruin things? The band's gig was a big deal to her and the rest of its members. If she let them down at such short notice, they'd never forgive her. Well, perhaps they would if they knew an obsessive lunatic was after her; but this was their *Gig*, the final one of the year. There was no way she could gib out. No, the show must go on, she concluded.

'You're absolutely right, Madeleine, it's business as usual,' Emma stated, shoulders back.

Felix looked at her, approving her attitude. My God, she was beautiful when she was angry.

'That's my girl,' smiled Madeleine, then turned to Felix, 'and you, my boy, are to go out tonight and… how do you say, let your hair down.' She nodded with conviction.

Bunty was at Perry's cottage. They too were going to see Emma's band at Red Rose Brewery that evening. Perry couldn't wait to see his daughter perform; he'd so missed hearing her sing. Bunty smiled at his attire. A red silk waistcoat over a collarless shirt, complete with a neckerchief. He certainly had it. For a man of his years, Perry still cut quite a dash.

'I know.' He winked, noticing her admiring glance.

'Know what?' said Bunty.

'How good I look,' he replied, then broke into laughter.

'And don't you know it,' replied Bunty, raising an eyebrow.

'But nowhere as good as you,' he said, then put an arm round her waist and kissed her cheek. True, Bunty did look great in her long denim dress and navy jacket. Together they made a very stylish older couple.

The sound of a horn outside interrupted them.

'Come on, the taxi's here,' Perry ushered Bunty to the door. He fully intended to enjoy tonight's gig and had no intention of driving or letting Bunty either. They, in his own words, were going to 'get plastered'.

Alcohol was the last thing on Jasmine's mind. A nauseous sensation kept drifting in and out of her stomach. Whilst she and Robin had made plans to go to the gig, her body really didn't feel up to it. She felt tired, worn out. Although Jasmine had been working hard to meet various deadlines, this was alien to her. She was used to tight timetables and couldn't fathom why the recent schedule had affected her so badly. But it had. Jasmine was washed out and had now started with a migraine.

'Sorry, Robin, I don't think I'll make tonight,' she said, reaching for the paracetamol tablets in the kitchen cupboard. She ran a glass of cold water and downed them. Robin looked at her pale white face and frowned.

'You look awful, Jas,' he said in concern.

'Thanks.' She gave a faint smile.

Robin got up and peered closely at her. 'I think you should ring the doctor in the morning,' he told her.

'No, I'm just tired, that's all,' she dismissed.

'Well, come on then, I'm tucking you into bed. You need sleep,' Robin replied assertively.

Jasmine didn't refuse. She didn't have the energy. The thought of a nice, warm, comfy bed was too tempting. It wasn't long before Robin was pulling up her bedcovers, after installing a hot-water bottle.

'Now sleep.' He bent down to kiss her on the lips. Jasmine closed her eyes and within minutes fell into a deep slumber. Robin hovered by the doorway, not wanting to leave her. He was worried. He suspected something was off kilter with Jasmine the other day when, even though she'd been pleased he'd brought them a lovely lunch and prosecco to her studio, she'd hardly touched it. He noticed her wince at the first sip of drink, which was far from her usual reaction. He remembered how Jasmine had thrown it back in London, enjoying every minute of the fizz he'd provided at their hotel, on The London Eye, then at dinner. He also recalled their unrestrained lovemaking… so wanton he'd not always been as careful as he should. A startling thought unexpectedly hit him hard.

His eyes fixed on Jasmine, softly breathing, her chest gently rising and falling. Then his eyes slid further down to her abdomen and he gulped.

Chapter 18

Emma gazed into the bathroom mirror, hardly recognising herself. Not really one for lots of makeup, tonight's face looked a tad dramatic in comparison to her normal natural look. Mascara and bronze eyeshadow emphasised her amber eyes, while the cherry-red lipstick and touch of blusher added extra depth and dimension she didn't even know her face possessed. Her chestnut curls were tied up in a silver scarf, which matched the silver biker jacket she'd worn for her interview with Jennifer. That seemed almost a lifetime ago, thought Emma as she'd slipped the cold leather on against her bare arms. The tie-dyed dress she wore underneath didn't give much warmth either, but the adrenaline surging through her veins would soon heat her body.

Felix and Madeleine were waiting in the hall as she came down the stairs.

'Ooh la la!' called Madeleine in delight. 'You look just the part,' she exclaimed.

Felix swallowed. Words failed him. Emma looked tentatively in his direction, waiting for some kind of reaction.

'Amazing, you'll knock 'em dead,' he said as jovially as he could muster, when inside he was crashing. The last thing he wanted to do was watch every man at the gig lust after her – just like he was.

'Well, let's go, my dears,' Madeleine shooed them to the front doors, 'the taxi will be ready to collect you at midnight,' she instructed.

Emma smiled at her. 'Thank you, Madeleine.' They both knew she wasn't just thanking her for the lift and arranging transport, but for her support too. It meant a lot to Emma, especially as her dad didn't know about all the business with Anika. Once he came back after his holiday she'd fill him in, but didn't want to worry him beforehand.

'Not at all, you must enjoy every minute,' she replied, ushering them all out of the doors.

Felix, for once, wasn't hiding himself. He wore jeans and a black quilted jacket but no mask, shades or hat to cover his face. Emma glanced sideways at him as they both got in the back of his Range Rover.

'What if someone recognises you?' she said.

'They'll be too busy looking at you,' he smirked. To be honest, he was past caring. He lived in Samphire Bay now and wanted to be accepted as a local, which also meant the surrounding area getting used to seeing his face. Once it was common knowledge, he'd be yesterday's news. After all, what was the alternative? To stay prisoner in his own home? And what was the worst that could happen? He was already being stalked.

He and Emma agreed he'd enter the brewery discreetly, rather than make an entrance together.

'I feel nervous.' Emma shivered as Madeleine set off to Lancaster.

'It's only natural to feel nervous. Once you're out there, you'll be brilliant,' he assured her.

'Is that what it was like for you, when acting?' asked Emma looking at his dark profile. How handsome he was.

She knew despite his remark he'd be getting attention tonight.

'When I was in the theatre, yes,' he answered.

'But not in front of the camera?'

'Not really. It became the norm.'

They were soon entering the heart of Lancaster and Emma directed Madeleine to the back of the brewery.

'It looks like a good venue,' Felix remarked, taking in the huge, red-bricked Victorian building. There was a pebbled courtyard, enclosed with black railings in the centre, leading to large wooden double-doors where the main back entrance was.

'It is,' agreed Emma.

They parked up and after a final 'Good luck!' from Madeleine, set off to the rear entrance and up to the mezzanine balcony overlooking the brewery downstairs. Already the place was filling as Mitch and Gaz were setting up.

'Hey, Emma!' called Sophie from the far end of the room.

Emma turned and mouthed 'Wish me luck' to Felix following at a distance behind her then darted off.

Felix watched quietly from the bar. He saw the four band members group hug and smiled to himself, whilst a small part of him envied their closeness. Ordering a double Jack Daniels and coke, his eyes scanned the crowd, now building momentum. He felt a tap on his shoulder and turned abruptly.

'You've dropped something mate,' said a man standing beside him.

'Oh, thanks.' Felix bent down and picked up his wallet, then shoved it into his back pocket.

Within quarter of an hour the place was heaving and the band was almost ready to start. Felix noticed an older man weave his way to the front and give Emma a big hug. That must be her dad, he thought fondly.

Disappointingly for Felix the opening song was sung by Sophie, who, in his opinion wasn't a patch on Emma. Whilst Sophie sang Felix queued to get another drink. Once being served, he turned back to see Emma now take the microphone. He took a long sip and savoured the taste of whiskey as much as the sight of Emma.

A new song started, one Felix hadn't heard her sing before. He leant against the bar, absorbing her. She was an absolute natural with the crowd, who sang along. Emma played to her audience, dancing and waving, occasionally pointing the odd person out and beaming at them. She ducked down to shake one teenage boy's hand, who cheekily pulled her scarf out so all her glossy curls came tumbling down, to the cheer of the crowd. Felix groaned inwardly, finding it unbearably sexy. There was no doubt, Emma had charisma and far more presence than the previous singer, Sophie.

The whole band sang *Moves Like Jagger*, with both girls singing the female lyrics and the two boys the male. This was met with a roaring applause. Felix ordered another drink and really started to relax. Then came the ultimate song, well, for him anyway. Emma sang *What Am I To You* and the whole place was on fire, whooping and clapping to her seductive movements. Felix stared rigid, his body tingling from head to toe.

'Has anyone told you, you're the spitting image of Felix Pascal?' said a female voice in his ear.

Annoyed at the interruption, he spoke without taking his eyes off Emma.

'Never heard of him,' he replied flatly.

The woman knew when she was snubbed and walked away.

After several more songs, the band finally finished with *Hey Jude*, sung by both Sophie and Emma together. As anticipated, everyone swayed and sang to the chorus, including Felix.

All in all, the gig had been a resounding success. After the band bowed to a thundering applause, the crowd gradually started to disperse. Emma didn't feel comfortable introducing Felix to the other band members, who assumed she'd been dropped off by her dad. They still didn't know who she worked for. Instead, after the usual celebrations and saying goodbye to her dad and Bunty, she secretly stole away to meet Felix at the back of the brewery as arranged, where a taxi was waiting for them.

Emma was on a high from the triumphant performance and hastily got into the back of the car, where Felix sat with a huge smile. He too was feeling suitably ebullient, not surprising given the many drinks he'd had.

'Brilliant, Emma, you were absolutely brilliant,' he congratulated, opening his arms out to her. She sunk into his embrace, inhaling the smell of his tangy aftershave.

'Thanks,' she sighed in joy, as the taxi set off home.

In their contented state, Felix didn't completely let go of Emma, but kept his arm round her shoulders all the way home, much to Emma's pleasure. She adored his reassuring touch and wallowed in it. Once the taxi had arrived, Felix got out and opened the door for her. As the car drove off, they climbed up the stone steps together.

Emma felt Felix lean into her a little and took the keys from him, suspecting she'd be far more adept at unlocking the front doors. After several giggles and 'shushes' not to wake Madeleine, they stumbled into the hall arm in arm. Unable to conceal his desire, Felix reached out and stroked her hair.

'I love this wild mane of yours.' His eyes met hers and for a moment time stood still. He slowly moved his mouth towards hers. Emma met him halfway, pulled towards him as if by an invisible string, and their lips touched. The kiss was passionate, all the pent-up emotion from both of them spilling out. It became urgent, and they grabbed at each other, bodies pressed together and hands roaming. Finally, Felix pulled back and with a ragged breath spoke gruffly.

'Stay with me tonight?' He wanted her and couldn't stand the thought of them separating at the top of the landing into separate bedrooms. Emma slowly nodded her head in agreement. She too was tired of pretending. She wanted him too.

–

Felix and Emma walked up the staircase holding hands as quietly as possible. The last thing either of them wanted was for Madeleine to be disturbed and catch them in the act. Silently creeping into Felix's bedroom, Emma's eyes homed in on the big double bed. Felix didn't waste any time in undressing and was soon in there.

Emma was transfixed by his muscular physique. He drew back the covers and beckoned her to join him. She began to undress, but then halted. Had she locked the front doors? She couldn't remember and the nagging practicality meant she was unable to relax.

'What is it?' Felix frowned, praying she hadn't changed her mind.

'I'm not sure I locked up,' she hissed.

He paused, at pains to dismiss her worry, but couldn't, not in the current climate.

'I better go and check,' she said and hurried off.

Felix sighed and closed his eyes. A wave of fatigue hit him hard. All the alcohol had caught up with him and within seconds he drifted off.

Meanwhile, Emma was rapidly turning the front door handles and making sure they were bolted. Good, she had locked up. She was just about to go back up the stairs when she heard a loud crash coming from the kitchen. *What the hell was that*? She made her way there to investigate.

Emma flicked on the kitchen light and saw a bottle of wine smashed on the slate floor, its glass shards in a red pool. She stood, startled. How had that happened? Then she gasped at seeing the sash window half open.

'I warned you to stay away from him,' said a low, menacing voice from behind her.

Emma jumped in fright. With her heart thumping, she turned to face Anika, standing by the door. She was dressed all in black, her blonde hair hanging limply, covering half her face.

'What are you doing here?' Emma yelped, petrified by the way this woman was glaring at her.

'What are *you* doing here more like,' replied Anika in that same deadly tone.

Emma swallowed, trying to stay calm whilst terrified inside. A layer of sweat broke out over her skin. She slowly started to walk backwards, heading towards the cellar door which was open, but Anika edged forwards to her.

'I... I work here. I'm the housekeeper...' she tried to appease.

Anika let out a harsh laugh.

'So, he's sleeping with the bloody staff, is he?' she spat.

Then, to Emma's horror, Anika bent down to pick up the neck of the broken wine bottle from the floor and advanced threateningly in her direction.

'Stop, please—' begged Emma.

'Shut up, you slut!' shouted Anika, then raised the sharp glass in the air. Emma screamed as she watched it high in the air, right above her head. Then, as it was about to come down, suddenly Anika fell forward with force and was pushed through the cellar door, down the steps. 'Aargh!' she shrieked.

Emma's eyes widened and suddenly Madeleine was there, standing where Anika had just been standing.

'Quickly, Emma,' she urged, pointing to the cellar door. Without delay, Emma bolted it. They could hear Anika groaning in pain as she crawled back up the steps.

'Let me out!' she roared, hammering on the door.

'I'm calling the police,' said Madeleine, 'you go and wake Felix.'

Emma ran at breakneck speed up to Felix's bedroom. Shaking him awake, she was hyper by now.

'Anika's broken into the house,' she gabbled.

'Wh—what?' Felix rubbed his eyes.

'Anika. She's here,' hissed Emma.

That was enough to rouse him. Anika, here? In his house? He quickly dressed and followed Emma back downstairs into the kitchen. By now Anika too was hysterical, ramming on the cellar door.

'Let me out, you bitch!' she yelled.

Madeleine was remarkably calm.

'The police are on their way,' she said in a cool voice.

Felix took in the scene — the open window, the smashed bottle of wine and a very shaken Emma.

'She... was about to stab me,' she whimpered in a strangled voice, then burst into tears. Felix pulled her into his arms.

'Shush, it's all right.' He rocked her whilst looking over her shoulder at his mum with alarm.

'I came in the nick of time,' said Madeleine, crossing her dressing gown around her. 'I heard something smash and made my way downstairs. When I came into the kitchen, Anika was holding a piece of glass over Emma's head.'

'Oh, my God.' Felix closed his eyes in utter horror and clutched Emma tighter. 'She's going down for this,' he choked in a thick voice.

The police arrived and arrested a very subdued Anika. Having fallen down the steps, plus ranting, raving and hammering on the cellar door for over half an hour, she had worn herself out. Two burly police officers bundled her into a van, where she was taken to the station. It looked like Anika was going to be spending time behind bars, adding attempted murder to her previous convictions.

Way too alert to sleep, Emma, Felix and Madeleine sat in the drawing room drinking coffee. Felix had laced Emma's with whiskey to help with the shock of her encounter with Anika.

'I'm so, so sorry, Emma,' Felix apologised once more.

'But it's not your fault,' replied a very pale-faced, traumatised Emma.

'Emma is right. Anika is one crazy woman, who needs locking up,' stated Madeleine.

'You're not wrong there,' replied Felix.

'It is over now,' continued Madeleine. 'It was a pleasure to push her down the cellar steps.' Indeed the satisfaction it gave her was immense. Her son was no longer to be haunted by this woman any longer, or Emma for that matter. They could all rest easy.

'I'll need to get the kitchen window fixed,' said Felix, once the police established how Anika had broken it to gain entry.

'Don't worry about that for now,' replied Madeleine. 'We have had quite enough excitement for one night.'

They all slowly made their way upstairs, each heading to their own bedroom. As Felix's head hit the pillow, he had a lot to contemplate. What a night. Just when he'd finally made his move on Emma Anika had decided to break in and… it didn't bare thinking about. Even so, the fact Anika was finally in police custody gave him some gratification. That and knowing the absurd stalking had at last ended.

Emma too was processing the eventful evening. Eventually, as the early hours came, her mind surrendered to sleep.

Madeleine, however, didn't have any trouble sleeping at all. She was soon out like a light, in the satisfying knowledge she had sorted out that hideous ex-girlfriend of her son's. As usual, mum to the rescue. Not a lot had changed.

Chapter 19

Perry and Bunty were sailing serenely down the Chester canal. A slight frost had dusted the trees and banks.

'It's a magical wonderland,' sighed Bunty, hugging a hot chocolate for warmth. Her eyes couldn't take enough in, having so much to see by the canal side. There was a lovely community spirit about it, with fellow narrow-boaters waving up and greeting them.

'It certainly is,' agreed Perry as he steered the boat with one hand and sipped his drink with the other. He was glad Bunty had not only agreed to come away on *The Merry Perry*, but that she'd fully thrown herself into the experience. To look at her, you would assume she'd been boating all her life. She'd soon picked up the terminology of the narrowboat and instinctively worked it. Bunty had quickly mastered the tiny kitchenette and woodburning stove, not to mention adjusting to the cramped bathroom and cassette toilet. Perry admitted it wasn't *all* twee glamorous living on a narrowboat. There were many practicalities to adapt to, like replenishing water, keeping an eye on fuel and being mindful of electricity use. Not to mention emptying the toilet! But Bunty was taking it all in her stride.

However, he still couldn't help but detect something was bothering Bunty. She had an air of... well, he couldn't quite put his finger on it. She was just acting a little odd. When he'd questioned her about it again, she'd dismissed it as excitement for their holiday, but he wasn't convinced. He glanced sideways at her now, all bright eyed and rosy cheeked. There was no doubt she was in her element, enjoying herself, he was pleased to see. Bunty must have felt his stare as she turned to smile at him.

'Everything all right?' she asked.

'Everything fine with me,' he grinned, then narrowed his eyes, 'and you?'

'Ah, perfect,' she breathed in deeply.

Truth be told, all *would* be fine, once he'd accepted her proposal. What seemed like a good idea at the time was playing on her mind now. But, she'd gone through with it. His birthday card was written, with the words, 'Perry, will you marry me?' inside it. Now all she had to do was give it him.

Robin had stayed over at Jasmine's all week, not wanting to leave her whilst she was unwell. The nausea hadn't left her; it still kept coming and going in waves. But the fatigue was lessening and she had actually risen before Robin that morning.

Robin woke and rolled over in bed to find Jasmine not there. He got up and went downstairs into the kitchen to join her. She was sat at the kitchen table drinking tea, staring into space.

'Hi, you OK?' he asked.

She looked up and smiled at him. 'Yeah, just couldn't sleep.'

He came to sit down opposite her, sensing something was afoot. Not surprising really, as something was defin- itely troubling him. Ever since Jasmine had first taken to her bed exhausted, then had begun to feel bouts of sickness, his mind had spun into overdrive. But he had kept quiet, not daring to address the matter. Instead, he'd been waiting for her to approach him. He sat, preparing himself.

'Robin,' she gulped, 'I think I may be pregnant.'

There was a moment of stillness as both digested the news. Jasmine looked searchingly into his eyes. His hand reached out for hers.

'Well… I'd be very happy, if you were,' he answered tentatively. 'What about you?'

She broke into a slow smile. 'I… think I would too,' she replied in a small voice.

Robin came round the table to hug her. They embraced, taking it all in. Robin pulled back and held her face.

'We better make sure. I'll get a testing kit today.'

Jasmine nodded.

Then, looking sheepishly at her, he added, 'I'm sorry for not being careful enough—' but she shook her head to silence him.

'No, I wasn't prepared, Robin. To be honest, my body clock's been all over the place. It's only just returning back to normal,' she explained.

'Even so, I should have made sure, when we were in London—'

'Do you think that's when it happened? In London?' she cut in.

They exchanged a knowing smile, remembering the passion they'd shared.

'Without a doubt,' Robin said with a wry grin. Jasmine gave a tinkle of laughter.

'Right, I'm going to attend to your every need, starting with breakfast. What do you fancy to eat?' he asked.

'Nothing at the moment.'

'Feeling sick again?' Robin's face etched with concern.

'A little,' she replied, then continued thoughtfully, 'you know, it's strange, the other day I was watching a family on the beach and for the first time ever felt broody.'

'Hmm, maybe it was your body's way of priming you?' suggested Robin.

Jasmine gave another laugh, 'What, you mean gear myself up?'

'Well, yeah,' he reasoned.

'Yes,' Jasmine's head tilted in contemplation, 'maybe. Nature's a wonderful thing, isn't it?'

Robin stared at her in admiration, taking it all in her stride, just like she had every other life changing event she'd faced. What a woman. And now, hopefully, she was carrying his baby.

Later that afternoon, after Robin had gone into Lancaster to buy a pregnancy test, they both sat in the bathroom with bated breath for the result.

It was positive. Jasmine was officially pregnant. They held each other with utter joy.

Although unplanned, their child was very much wanted. Of course this meant big changes were about to come, like living together, for one. They both agreed that Robin's smaller apartment would need to go on the market and he would move into Jasmine's. Then, they discussed when to tell their parents, which they both knew would ultimately lead to the burning question of marriage. Not wanting to feel pressured in any way, they decided to only go public after three months, giving them time and space. A lot was about to happen and they had to go at their own pace. It was equally an exciting, thrilling time as it was overwhelming.

'I'm going to mass this evening,' announced Emma as she served Felix and Madeleine breakfast. Felix looked up in surprise, whilst Madeleine wiped her mouth with a serviette. Truth be told, Emma was feeling extremely vulnerable. Attending church made her feel close to her mum. She and Perry had often gone together to light a candle for Valerie. It was comforting and… peaceful. Yes, Emma definitely needed a sense of peace after the horrific episode with Anika. They all did.

'Yes, I would like to go too,' Madeleine replied.

'We could all go,' said Felix.

'Great, the church may be full though,' warned Emma, thinking again that he might not want to be recognised. It was Sunday and she suspected a lot of Samphire Bay's residents liked to attend. It didn't seem to bother Felix though, who just shrugged.

'It would be nice to go and be among normal people,' remarked Madeleine, who was of course referring to the recent events.

Since Anika's arrest, the police had been in contact and given them the details surrounding her break in, which she'd disclosed under questioning. Anika had hired a holiday cottage very near to the tidal road, which had given her an excellent view of the traffic coming and going to Felix's house. Basically, she'd been monitoring his every move. When she'd seen all three of them leave for the gig in Lancaster, Anika knew the house was empty and had broken in before Madeleine had returned by smashing the top pane of glass in the kitchen sash window, putting her hand inside to unscrew the lock, then easing the frame up to climb inside. There inside the kitchen, she had waited. After a short while she heard someone come back and assumed it was Madeleine on her own, as she couldn't hear voices. Then, realising she was probably in for a long wait before Felix came back, she crept down into the cellar to get a bottle of wine. Only Anika had the audacity to sit drinking wine in a house she'd just broken into.

The alcohol and adrenaline pumping through her veins, together with all the anger, hate and jealousy she'd been storing up for weeks, had kept her mind occupied until, finally, she heard voices, at which point she'd quietly walked up the kitchen stairs to see Felix and Emma kissing passionately in the hall. Fuming, she returned to the kitchen to plan her next move.

Needing to get Emma in the kitchen, Anika did what she usually did in a temper and threw the wine bottle on the floor, smashing the glass loud through the silence of the house, then hid by the door to await her entrance. The plan had worked. Emma had entered the kitchen, but what she hadn't planned for was Madeleine following minutes later. And she most certainly had not anticipated being pushed down the cellar steps. It had proved to be a fatal mistake not bolting the cellar door after she'd been down there for a bottle of wine. Had she done so, she wouldn't have been pushed through it.

All this was related to a staggered Felix, Emma and Madeleine, who had sat open mouthed in shock at hearing the events from the police officer.

'What's going to happen next?' Felix asked, sat on the edge of the settee.

'Well, the charges are racking up now, stalking, threatening behaviour, breaking and entering and possibly attempted murder,' answered the police officer.

'Possibly? She was going to stab me with that glass,' said Emma, incensed.

'Anika denies that,' he replied.

'I saw her raise it over Emma's head,' cut in Madeleine.

'For now, rest assured Anika is behind bars and likely to stay there for the foreseeable future.'

'Good,' said Felix with force. It had crossed his mind what the media would make of all this, should the news get out. He personally wasn't going to tell a soul. All he wanted to do was draw a line under the whole thing. He sought solace in the fact Anika was incarcerated, knowing what this would do to her. That, and the fact he could live safely with Emma in peace. It also meant he'd be able to look ahead to the future with no worries or fears. His head was in a good place and, after the break, he'd be able to carry on directing without any distraction.

He glanced at Emma who was still looking a tad miffed at what the police officer had told her. He couldn't blame her really, under the circumstances. His mum didn't appear entirely gratified with the situation either. Maybe he was too tolerant? Since when had he become so? Since meeting Anika. He now realised how appeasing he'd learnt to be, constantly calming situations and avoiding arguments, instead of facing the fact head on. Anika was a raving nutcase who he wished had never set eyes on him.

So, yes, attending church that evening would be a blessed relief, mixing with 'normal' people as his mum put it.

In a rather reflective mood, all three of them set off later that evening. They passed the cottage that Anika had been staying in and Madeleine had turned to give Emma a supportive look. Felix saw the exchange and gripped the steering wheel. He would always feel guilty for what Emma had gone through, no matter what she or his mum said. It was *he* who had brought Anika to Samphire Bay.

They arrived at the church and walked in with all the others. Felix wore a beanie hat but no scarf and Emma could see one or two people eyeing him. Madeleine looked elegant as ever in a cream woollen coat and matching cream beret. Emma pulled the hood of her quilted coat down, freeing her curls. Felix's eyes homed in on them cascading onto her shoulders. He'd so wanted to speak to Emma privately since their kiss and very near night together but had never got the chance. A part of him would be glad when it was just him and Emma in the house. Emma turned and their eyes met. There was so much he needed to say to her. Instead, he gave a heartfelt smile and she returned it.

Emma too yearned to get Felix alone and would be glad when Madeleine returned home to France. So much had happened in the last few days and she was still taking it all in. It helped enormously that Anika was now safely off the scene. At least she was no longer on high alert the whole time. She was also touched that Jennifer had contacted her and offered a few words of comfort and encouragement. As Felix's PA, she more than most had had her fill of Anika and was horrified to learn of her breaking in and threatening Emma, but absolutely delighted at the outcome. Unlike Felix, Jennifer wasn't going to be discreet. If an opportunity presented itself, she'd drop the woman right in it, no problem, and let the whole world know exactly what Anika Genness was.

'She's an absolute nightmare,' Jennifer had told Emma. 'You and Felix deserve a medal for what you've had to endure.'

Then there was the other issue – Felix. Emma was beginning to think maybe he'd simply been drunk and not really in control of his actions. Did he regret kissing her? Inviting her to spend the night together? Whilst Emma had been on a natural high from the gig, she *had* been completely sober. And she hadn't regretted a thing. She had shuddered at the thought of Anika opening Felix's bedroom door and catching them in bed together. My God, how would that have panned out?

Madeleine led them to the narrow pews and they shuffled along, sitting down silently, with Emma in the middle. Suddenly she felt Felix's hand reach out to hold hers. She took it. Bending down he whispered in her ear, 'I'm so sorry, Emma.'

She looked up into his pale blue eyes. 'Let's put it behind us.'

He gripped her hand tightly and nodded. Yes, it was time to draw a line under Anika Genness.

After the service Emma went to the side of the altar to light a candle, while Felix and Madeleine made their way out. Watching the bright flame, Emma closed her eyes in prayer.

Oh, Mum, I so wish you were here. With her dad being away on his narrowboat, she felt even more insecure without either of them. Then a comforting glow settled within her. She wasn't alone an inner voice told her, she had Felix.

Chapter 20

Bunty woke to the gentle chug of the narrowboat engine. She found it soothing. Back home upon waking her first sight was the view of the bay through the large bedroom window. Often she'd leave the blind open, not wanting to shut out the stunning, panoramic scene before her. Out of habit, she turned to the miniature window beside her now, pushed back the small curtain and sighed contently. Outside was that winter wonderland. The frost covering the canal side shone like glitter under a bright morning sun. All was quiet, apart from the throb of the engines as boats glided along the waterways.

'Good morning, Bunty.' Perry entered the cabin with a plate of bacon sandwiches and a mug of tea.

'Oh, lovely, thanks, Perry,' she replied, sitting up in bed and taking the plate. He placed the mug on the cabinet next to her. 'And happy birthday. It's me who should be doing this for you.'

He leaned over and kissed her full on the lips.

Bunty's heart skipped, as it often did when he kissed her, but more so today, because today was *the* day. It wouldn't be long before she gave him his card and gifts. Once more a feeling of trepidation hit her.

'You all right, sweetheart?' Perry frowned, seeing a flicker of emotion pass over her face. Bunty quickly shook herself.

'Yes, of course,' she replied with a tight smile.

'Good, because after breakfast I've planned a full-packed day,' he chuckled, rubbing his hands.

Yes, thought Bunty – and that's not all. Her birthday card lay propped up on the dining table, along with the wrapped presents. She swallowed with anticipation. Exactly how was he going to react?

'You sure you're OK?' Perry asked again.

'Yes, fine.' She forced another smile.

'No regrets spending a holiday on the boat?' he persisted warily.

'Not at all!' she replied with gusto.

'Good,' he paused, then added, 'and you enjoyed the concert last night?'

'Oh yes, it was amazing.' Bunty reflected on the singing in the cathedral, the soft light of the sun casting shadows on ancient stone walls and the sweet choral voices echoing throughout the church was purely magical.

Perry beamed a smile at her. 'I'm glad you enjoyed it.'

'Yes, and I'm sure we'll both enjoy your birthday too,' answered Bunty. By then they would (hopefully) be engaged, she thought happily.

'Come on then, eat up,' he chivvied her along. 'It's a day to enjoy.'

'It certainly is,' she grinned craftily.

It wasn't long after breakfast when Perry looked eagerly towards the dining table laden with his birthday presents and card.

'May I?' he asked, eyes twinkling.

'Of course!' laughed Bunty. 'Card first,' she insisted.

He slid it out of the envelope and smiled at the scene of a sailing boat on a pure blue ocean. Then he opened it. Bunty held her breath. Perry's eyes scanned over the writing inside, 'Perry, will you marry me?' There was a pause.

'Say something, Perry,' Bunty said in a quiet voice. He looked into her eyes.

'Bunty, open this.' He took a small, wrapped box from inside his waistcoat pocket and handed it to her. Bunty's heart was hammering as she fumbled to unwrap it. It was a ring box. She lifted the lid and gasped, suddenly spun back in time. It was the same ring, from all those years ago.

A memory kick-started, playing like an old film in her mind… a picnic on a little fishing boat, sipping champagne, sitting together on the deck, gently bobbing up and down, listening to the waves as they lapped against the boat sides. Perry had suddenly presented a ring, a stunning Aquamarine diamond which glittered in the last of the sun's rays. Bunty gasped at its beauty.

'Marry me, Bunty,' Perry had insisted, praying the ring he'd produced would persuade her into accepting…

Staring at it now, lit this time by the sun streaming through the boat's windows, her eyes filled with tears. 'It's my ring,' she whimpered.

'It is. Now are you going to do us both a favour and put the thing on this time?' he cajoled.

'Yes,' she half laughed whilst a tear ran down her cheek. Perry took out the ring and placed it firmly onto her finger.

'Now then,' he smiled. 'It's finally where it belongs.'

Bunty's arms flew around his neck. Holding him tight, she never wanted to let go.

–

'Bon appetit!' cheered Madeleine, raising her glass of wine.

'Bon appetit!' chorused Felix and Emma in unison.

'This looks fabulous,' Emma gushed, mouth watering at the mountain of food Madeleine had prepared for them.

'Mum always cooks a great roast dinner,' said Felix.

Madeleine nodded with a smile, glad to be of help. She was sticking to her promise to Emma, instead of letting her do all the cooking. Laughable, really, when she was in fact the housekeeper. But her mother's intuition had clocked Emma as the lady of this house in every aspect. She knew her son and it was blatantly obvious where his feelings lay. That was mainly the reason why she'd now decided to return to France, to give the two of them space. Madeleine was no fool; she would rather get out of the way and let nature take its course. Soon the filming crew would be back, so time was precious. As a farewell meal she had pulled out all the stops and made a real effort in the kitchen.

After a splendid dinner with all the trimmings followed with cheesecake, then cheese and crackers, they all retired into the drawing room for coffee. Instead of watching TV, Madeleine insisted on playing charades.

'Really?' laughed Emma, surprised at her request.

'Absolutely, it's fun!' she exclaimed.

Felix went first and had them all in stitches, as he tried (after several glasses of wine) to act out Grease, by imitating John Travolta combing back his quiff and pulling up his jacket collar. Eventually Madeleine got it, but only because he'd done the same before.

'He does it every time,' she groaned, rolling her eyes.

'I've got one!' Emma blurted out, getting into the spirit. Then she too, somewhat tipsily, tried to act like Polly by going over to the bow window, looking out to sea and then, turning dramatically with a gasp, she placed the back of her hand on her forehead.

Felix smiled lazily, instantly getting it. She was mimicking Lady Scarlett but he kept silent, enjoying her performance. He glanced at his mum and suspected she was doing the same.

Emma looked from one to the other in exasperation, then tried again, this time she went to the glass drinks cabinet and pretended to pour herself a drink. She raised her cocktail glass with a theatrical stage wink. Still, nothing from either of them. Oh, for goodness' sake, she thought. Then she broke the rules and spoke.

'By Jove, I've solved the case,' she chirped in the best Lady Scarlett accent ever.

Felix burst into hysterics, while Madeleine leant over in giggles.

'You knew!' Emma exclaimed as indignantly as she could, whilst trying not to laugh too. Her phone bleeped in her pocket, diverting her attention. It was a text from her dad.

Big news, Emma, was the caption under the photograph of Bunty's hand wearing her engagement ring.

'OMG!' trilled Emma. 'Dad and Bunty are getting hitched!'

Chapter 21

The news of Bunty and Perry's engagement had been received with delight and Emma couldn't contain herself, bursting with questions when she called her dad to get all the details.

'Have you set a date yet?'

'Give us a chance, Emma,' laughed Perry.

'What about the venue?' she persisted.

'Let's just calm down. We've plenty of time to arrange it.'

Bunty had overheard the conversation, thrilled by Emma's reaction to the news. She got on well with Perry's daughter but had to admit she'd been nervous about how Emma might react to their engagement; she didn't want her to feel like she was trying to replace her late mother by any stretch.

Jasmine, too, had been elated to learn about the engagement. When she told Robin, he had looked somewhat pensive.

'Do you think we ought to… you know…' he asked a touch awkwardly.

'What, get engaged?' replied Jasmine.

'Well… yeah, seen as how we're having a baby.'

Jasmine laughed. 'Well, I've had more romantic proposals,' she joked.

'You know what I mean,' Robin rushed to reply.

'I do,' she reassured, 'but no. Let's wait till the time is right, yeah?' She smiled, knowing full well what Robin meant. They had discussed the matter of marriage previously and had already agreed to put it on hold. A part of her appreciated the kind of old-fashioned decency Robin had about him, finding it endearing.

Meanwhile, Madeleine was glad to be leaving on a high. Seeing Emma so excited was a joy and, giving her a hug goodbye, she whispered, 'All the best. Until next time.'

'Safe trip, Madeleine,' said Emma, feeling a little sad to see her go. She'd warmed to this petite, elegant lady with a sharp eye and strong spirit.

As Felix drove his mum to the airport, he glanced sideways at her.

'So, overall, what do you think?' He was of course referring to his new home and Samphire Bay.

'I think you've made a good choice,' Madeleine replied, staring out of the windscreen, lips curving.

They both knew she wasn't talking about the house.

Emma made good use of her time alone in the house. As she'd been made to feel more of a guest lately, she had a lot of housework to catch up on. Cleaning a house this size certainly kept her fit. Hoovering the sweeping staircase alone involved much bending and stretching, not to mention the biceps that were forming from all the scrubbing and wiping down. Emma enjoyed it though, finding it gave her headspace, plenty of time to think. And she did have much to think about.

Truth be told, Emma hadn't really been able to completely process all the events of late. The house had been occupied with Madeleine, preventing her from talking properly to Felix and asking questions that needed answers. Like, what were his intentions, for one? *Did* he have any intentions? Was the kiss and his suggestion of them spending the night together just a drunken moment? Her gut instinct told her it wasn't, not judging by his behaviour since; he was still attentive and considerate towards her. Her mind flashed back to him reaching for her hand in church. Not only that, but how he had treated her, as though she was one of the family.

Emma knew Madeleine liked her – had she not, it would have been obvious – and it warmed her to have his mother's approval, seeing how important the two were to each other. But was Madeleine's esteem for her son's choice in housekeeper, or potential girlfriend? And if they were about to embark on a romantic relationship, how would that change things? *Would* it change things? Sure, the dynamics would alter, but Emma liked her job. She loved the house with all its character and charm, every nook and cranny, and hated the thought of anyone else tending to it. Then there was the reaction of... well, everyone. Not just Felix's rich and famous friends, or her friends for that matter, but his colleagues, the film crew. Then she laughed out loud, remembering how Polly had teased them. She doubted Polly was the only one to suspect something.

She abruptly paused and sat midway on the stairs. Turning the hoover off, she sank her head into her hands and sighed. Was she getting a bit carried away, being just a touch fanciful? A horrible sense of trepidation seeped into her conscience. Did he expect her to... accommodate him? Hideous scenarios filled her, reminiscent of days gone by, when the Lord of the manor thought it his right to take advantage of the young housemaids… She stopped herself. Of course Felix was nothing like that! But did people like her really end up with handsome, famous stars?

His voice rang in her ears, *'Emma, please don't think that way. You're a beautiful, talented lady and great company. Why on earth shouldn't we be 'out and about' together?'* Those were his very words, that day they'd gone shopping in Lancaster. It said it all, didn't it? Still, she needed to confront Felix and gain clarity, not to mention peace of mind.

'Au revoir, mon chéri.' Madeleine stretched out her arms and embraced her son.

'Bye, mum,' Felix hugged her hard. 'Ring me when you get back,' he told her.

'Of course,' she nodded and began to wheel her suitcase towards the check-in desk. She turned midway for one last wave. 'And look after Emma!' she called.

'I will!' he called back, not at all surprised by his mum's words.

The journey home gave Felix lots of time to contemplate. For him, it was a no brainer. Emma was everything he wanted. A perfect bundle of joy. The complete package. She had it all – good looks, a sense of humour, she was caring, talented and above all, had a level head. No silly awestruck ways about her. Once again, their age difference concerned him slightly. He was ten years older than her. Was it too much? Did it even matter?

He knew Emma wouldn't be fazed by the circles he mixed in. Look how she'd handled the cast and crew. And Anika. His blood ran cold. Yes, Emma had indeed endured a lot and taken it all in her stride. Felix considered what her father would make of it all. Perhaps he ought to meet him, explain in person the turn of events. It was his daughter after all.

His mood lifted when he reached the tidal road. It was a real comfort to know his house was the only one on the peninsula. Felix wanted to make the most of the remaining break. Once filming started again, it would mean various meetings would also be scheduled and he'd have to go back to the city. The thought filled him with dread, such was his affinity to Samphire Bay. He knew better than to suggest further meetings be held at his house. Initially it had been ideal for all to see the location, but the team were hardly likely to travel again when they were all based in London. So, he'd have to get used to the hustle and bustle again. Still, it was only temporary. At least now he had an escape, a haven to return to – and Emma.

A sudden chill ran over him. What if Emma decided to go? She'd made no secret of her ambitions. Supposing she wanted to give it a shot with her band and go off touring? The very notion of returning to an empty house, with no Emma inside was unthinkable. He didn't want this to happen; he *couldn't* let this happen. But at the same time, he knew how selfish he was being. Emma had real talent, of course she should be able to pursue it.

With a jolt, inspiration struck. Why had he not thought of it before? He gave a slow smile and leant back into his seat, an enormous sense of satisfaction blanketing over him.

Emma was hoovering her bedroom when Felix arrived home. He automatically climbed the stairs two at a time to see her. Following the sound of the vacuum, he paused before entering her bedroom.

'Felix?' called Emma.

He pushed the door open and smiled. 'Hi,' he said, feeling a touch uncomfortable being in her private space.

'Hi. Madeleine get off okay?' she asked, turning off the hoover.

'Yes, her flight was on time.'

'Good.'

There was a slight hiatus before they both spoke at the same time.

'Felix, we—'

'I was—'

'No, you first,' said Emma.

'I'd like to meet your father,' Felix replied, taking her by surprise.

'Oh, right…'

'It seems appropriate, doesn't it?'

Emma looked searchingly into his face. Felix gazed into those mesmerising amber eyes and melted.

'Appropriate?'

'Well, after everything that's happened,' he continued.

'Yes… I suppose…'

'Good. How about tomorrow? I thought maybe a meal here? Is that OK?'

'Er… yes. Bunty too?' asked Emma.

'Lovley, why not?' smiled Felix.

Chapter 22

'So, dinner at the big house,' said Perry somewhat musingly.

'That'll be nice, won't it?' replied Bunty. She, more than anyone, knew Perry's feelings on her former family home. She'd never forget how intimidated he'd been made to feel inside it. And she knew Perry wouldn't either. 'It's where Emma lives now and I think it's rather sweet that Felix wants us there, don't you?'

'Yes… and no,' answered Perry.

'What do you mean?' asked Bunty, puzzled at his reaction to the invite.

'I don't know. It just feels a bit…'

'What?'

Perry shrugged. 'I can't put my finger on it. But yes, I definitely want to meet the man.'

Bunty laughed. 'Do you feel threatened by him?' She was well aware of how protective he was as Emma's father.

'No. Not threatened, but what parent wouldn't be concerned about their child living in a stranger's house, alone, in a pretty isolated spot?'

Bunty nodded, understanding Perry's apprehension. 'Emma seems happy enough, doesn't she?'

'Yes, she does,' he conceded.

'Well then, let's go with an open mind.'

Meanwhile, Emma was busy preparing for the supper. Whilst she'd first been surprised at Felix's suggestion of inviting her dad, she was also pleased. She did want them to meet. It was important to her, and clearly to Felix too, which then opened up even more questions for Emma. *Why* did he want to meet her dad? Out of politeness, as her employer? Or because he wanted to make a good impression, as a potential boyfriend for his daughter?

Despite Emma's intention of having a much-needed conversation with Felix, it had been difficult. Time had been taken up discussing the arrangements for that evening, along with the shopping and preparation for the meal. Felix had ordered the groceries and was unpacking the delivery whilst Emma had replenished the drinks cabinet and was now in the kitchen chopping vegetables. It was to be a three-course meal. They'd chosen carrot and coriander soup, followed by a roast beef dinner and raspberry pavlova, all washed down with copious amounts of champagne, or beer, as was Perry's preferred drink. Emma had made sure there was plenty of gin in the drinks cabinet, knowing that was Bunty's tipple.

It should have felt strange, working alongside Felix as his housekeeper, but it didn't somehow. Probably because he'd never treated her as an underling. However, all this only added to Emma's quandary. She desperately needed some form of clarity. Here they were, acting like a couple, getting ready to receive family, all on Felix's instigation. She stole a look at him as he unpacked the shopping. Whilst he'd wanted to be helpful, she couldn't help grinning at the fact that he hadn't a clue where everything went.

'Just put the champagne in the fridge for now. I'll put the rest away,' she told him.

He turned. 'What should I do to help then?'

'Set the table?'

'Ah, yes.' Then he paused.

'Cutlery's in the top drawer.' She tipped her head towards the dresser. It seemed surreal telling the owner of the house where his stuff was.

'Of course it is,' he smirked. It wasn't lost on him either.

Jasmine and Robin had also arranged to go to her parents' for dinner. Jasmine, despite feeling a tad tired, looked well. The morning sickness had at last abated and she was positively glowing. Instead of a pale face, her complexion was rosy, her eyes sparkled and her hair shone.

'Wow,' remarked Robin as she came down the stairs.

Jasmine smiled, glad he appreciated her appearance. She'd made an effort, wanting to feel special after having felt so nauseous and wiped out previously. She wore a flattering black dress, which fit loosely, accompanied by black, suede boots. A deep red pashmina finished the outfit off nicely and her freshly washed hair hung silkily on her shoulders.

'Come on, let's go. We don't want to be late,' she said.

'No, we don't,' replied Robin, keen to set a good impression with Jasmine's parents. He had met them, but not as their daughter's boyfriend. Before he'd simply been Robin-from-next door, the friendly neighbour who had gone out of his way to help Jasmine. It troubled him a little the way they were keeping the baby a secret, for now. He only hoped their parents understood and didn't take offence when they did learn about Jasmine's pregnancy.

As Jasmine had fully expected, and true to form, her mum was utterly gushing around Robin.

'Welcome, welcome, Robin!' she'd prattled, giving him a bear hug. 'Do sit down, Robin'.

After a very nice, but very filling meal, they all sat in the comfy chairs for drinks. Once fussing round Robin and sorting his drink out, they rested on her daughter. 'Not drinking Jasmine?' she noted, as Jasmine pushed her glass away.

'Oh no, thought I'd give it a rest,' she'd replied as casually as possible. Then swiftly added, 'And I'm driving home, aren't I?' she smiled at Robin for support.

'Yes, very kindly, so I can have a drink,' he quickly answered, then cringed. How did that sound?

'Hmm, I see,' replied Jasmine's mum with narrowed eyes, not before stealing a swift glance at her daughter's front.

She knows, thought Jasmine. Nothing got past her mum.

It felt extremely strange for Bunty to be climbing up the stone steps at the front entrance of her former home. Perry rang the doorbell and it was soon answered by an excited Emma.

'Hi, come in,' she welcomed, standing aside for them to enter.

Immediately Bunty's head whipped round the grand marbled hall. A sharp pang hit her, suddenly realising how much she did in fact miss her childhood home.

'Congratulations!' said Emma, once they'd shed their coats. Taking Bunty's hand to look at her ring she gasped. 'Oh, it's so beautiful,' she cooed.

Bunty gave her an endearing smile. 'It is indeed,' she agreed and looked at Perry, who was enjoying the exchange between the two ladies in his life.

'Come on through, Felix is in the drawing room.' Emma ushered them into the room.

Bunty clocked her beloved glass drinks cabinet where Felix stood and another sentimental jolt of emotion hit her.

'Dad,' Emma said, bringing the two men closer, 'meet Felix.'

Perry held out his hand.

'Pleased to meet you,' said Felix, with a firm shake.

'And you too, Felix,' Perry replied.

The two men watched each other carefully for a brief moment, as though sizing each other up.

'And this is Bunty,' cut in Emma.

'Ah, yes,' Felix said affectionately. He obviously felt a connection with the older lady already, having shared the same home. He shook her hand too. 'And congratulations on your engagement.' He gave her a winning smile.

'Thank you.' She nodded politely, then asked, 'All settled in then?'

'Absolutely, I love the place.' He gestured around the room, taking in the huge bow window, high dusty pink walls, ornate coving, the elaborate mirrors and various gold framed pictures. 'It must have been a wrench to leave,' he added.

There was a slight pause before Bunty spoke.

'Yes, but the time was right to move on,' she quietly replied. The usually larger-than-life woman suddenly seemed smaller, frailer, as she took in the room.

Perry looked towards her, his brow pulled in concern, then rested his gaze on Felix.

'Right, what's everyone drinking?' asked Emma, breaking any potential awkwardness.

'I'll have a beer,' said Perry.

Felix reached for the bottle cooling in the cabinet, popped off the top and passed it Perry with a pint glass. Perry nodded his thanks.

'A gin and tonic for me please,' replied Bunty. Again, she was struck by how strange it was watching someone else make a drink from that cabinet.

Emma observed her face, guessing what she was thinking. She dearly hoped tonight was going to be a success, but did she detect a slight atmosphere? Throwing back her glass of champagne, she was relieved when her dad spoke next.

'So, how do you find Samphire Bay compared to the bright lights of London?' he asked Felix.

'Bloody marvellous,' he answered directly, making them all laugh. 'Seriously, this place is a sheer haven.'

Perry clearly hadn't expected that reply, judging by his expression.

'Honestly?' he asked, bemused.

'Honestly. Believe me, I'm in no hurry to go back to London,' confirmed Felix.

Perry seemed pleased with Felix's answer. Emma looked from one to the other, feeling a touch more relaxed. She caught Bunty staring at her and smiled. Bunty gave her a wink back, as if reading her mind.

After several more drinks the ambience lifted to a more jovial tone. Once they were all sat in the dining room eating and talking easily, as agreed with Emma, Felix chose to tell Perry about the events surrounding Anika Genness. Both Perry and Bunty listened in shock. When Felix had finished talking, a deadly silence followed. Emma's eyes moved sheepishly around the table.

'Why didn't you tell me, Emma?' Perry faced her, his lips grimly pressed tight.

'I didn't want to worry you, Dad,' she tried to explain.

'Good God,' he whimpered and closed his eyes. Bunty put a reassuring hand over his.

'Rest assured, Anika is behind bars and likely to remain so for some time,' Felix cut in, eager to console Perry.

'I should hope so,' said Bunty indignantly.

Once the difficult conversation was over and a few more bottles of champagne were drunk, the taxi Bunty had booked arrived. They didn't want to outstay or cramp Felix and Emma's hospitality. As they said their goodbyes in the hall, Perry couldn't resist having a quiet word with Felix.

'Can I ask, what are your intentions towards my daughter, Felix?' he asked bluntly, feeling the right to do so. He was at pains to know his daughter was in safe hands. It was also blatantly clear their relationship ran deeper than just employer and employee.

Felix looked him in the eye, unfazed. 'Entirely honourable, you have my word, Perry.'

'Good,' replied Perry, before adding, 'because if you break her heart, I'll break your legs.'

Felix blinked, thrown by his words, whilst admiring the old boy's spirit.

'Come on, Perry, taxi's waiting!' called Bunty.

After kisses and further handshakes, Perry and Bunty sped off down the coastal path into the dark night.

'Well, that went well, didn't it?' Emma's eyes searched Felix's face. He smiled, leant down and kissed her lips.

Chapter 23

His lips were soft and warm on hers. Emma closed her eyes as desire washed over her, then with a determined effort, pulled back to face him.

'Felix, I think it's time we talked,' she stated.

'It is,' he nodded in agreement. He took her hand and led her back into the drawing room.

It was a perfect setting, with its dim lights giving a cosy glow and the open fire gently crackling. Felix sat them both down on the chesterfield sofa.

'Emma, you must know how I feel about you,' he started, staring into her eyes, watching as the firelight reflected in them.

'That's just it, Felix, I don't,' she replied, a note of desperation entering her voice.

He gave a frown, clearly confused by her reaction.

She continued, explaining herself. 'I'm here as your housekeeper—'

'Have I ever made you feel inferior?' he interrupted.

'No, but that's why I need some clarity. You've *never* made me feel like I'm the hired help.'

'Well then,' he said, as though she shouldn't have any difficulty with the situation.

'But I *am* the hired help, Felix.' She looked squarely at him. 'I'm here as your housekeeper.'

He stilled. Thoughts of her running away, jacking in her job to fulfil her ambition with the band flashed through his mind again. He took a deep breath and decided to face it head on.

'Do you still want to be here?' he asked.

'Yes, of course,' she replied with a touch of impatience, 'but under what terms? As the hired help, or as—'

'My partner,' he cut in firmly.

She stalled, not quite knowing what to say. Felix took advantage and swiftly continued.

'I want you here, with me, in a relationship.' There, could he be any clearer? He watched her eyes widen momentarily. 'Say something, Emma.'

'But...' she stammered, a million thoughts dashing through her head.

'But what?' he asked, bewildered.

'You're a famous actor and I...' All her previous reservations came flooding back.

'You're a beautiful, talented woman.' He kissed her lips once more, then leant back to survey her. 'As I've told you before.'

'What... will everyone think?' Emma asked hesitantly.

'That I'm a lucky bastard?' he half laughed.

Emma couldn't help but grin. He really was the most charming, handsome... Oh God, was this really happening? He moved forward again and this time she flung her arms round his neck and met him head on. After a long and passionate kiss, they eyed each other and burst into happy giggles.

'I've been waiting to do that for days,' Felix said, pulling her onto his chest and wrapping his arms tightly round her.

'Me too,' sighed Emma dreamily. But Emma, being Emma, still needed to know exactly how it was all going to pan out. 'Fe-lix,' she said quietly.

'Hmm?'

She tilted her head to look up at him.

'You still want me to be your housekeeper, don't you?' Emma simply couldn't bear the thought of someone taking her place.

'No,' came the reply, and her face fell. He was secretly pleased she didn't have any notion of leaving him for the band. 'But you could always be my girlfriend, looking after the house we live in, if you like?' he added with a grin.

'I do like,' she beamed back.

Then, because he felt compelled to, broached the subject of her music.

'Will that be enough for you? What about the band?'

Emma shrugged. 'I could still do gigs with them.'

'And is *that* enough?' The idea he'd had driving home from the airport reoccurred.

'Well… yeah, why?' she asked. She appreciated his concern – after all, how many twenty-five-year-olds would be happy to act as housekeeper on a remote peninsula? – but she had honestly fallen in love with looking after this house and helping out with the film crew. And if she found she ever needed more, she would reassess then.

'Just checking, that's all,' he replied, whilst his mind was working overtime. He'd keep his plan to himself for now, no point in building her hopes up.

That night, as they walked up the stairs hand-in-hand, Emma didn't turn right to her bedroom. Instead, she allowed herself to join Felix in his.

The next morning Felix woke first with an over-whelming feeling of contentment. He looked down at Emma still softly sleeping and admired her curls spread across the pillow. Then she slowly opened her eyes and gave a tender smile.

'Hello, you. Sleep well?' he asked with a sexy smirk.

'Eventually,' she replied with a chuckle. Was it possible to feel any happier? Stretching, she gave a yawn and gazed up at him. How attractive he looked with dark stubble. She wasn't used to seeing him up close first thing in the morning.

'What should we do today?' she asked.

'Make the most of it,' he replied, ever mindful of the hectic schedule ahead of him. Filming was due to start tomorrow.

'Let's go for a walk, along the bay,' suggested Emma.

'Let's,' he smiled and leant down to kiss her.

Within an hour they'd showered and breakfasted, then set off to face the elements. The sun was out and a sharp chill stung their cheeks. Their breath could be seen in the air as they spoke.

'What time will filming start tomorrow?' Emma asked.

'First thing, business as usual,' replied Felix, a little subdued.

'What is it?' she replied, instantly picking up on his mood. 'Aren't you pleased to be back directing?'

He gave a sigh. 'Yes, it's not the directing that bothers me,' he answered.

'Then what?'

'I fear there's a mole in the camp.'

198

Emma halted and looked anxiously at Felix. He hated seeing her like this, truly wishing he could put the whole stalking business behind them.

'Somebody who knew my every move must have been informing Anika. It's got to be someone close by, who I work with.'

'But it's no secret that you're directing a drama, or live here,' said Emma frowning.

'Yes, but Anika knew *immediately* when I'd bought the house. She also knew exactly where it was, and what's more, she knew I'd got the director's job before it was common knowledge, and when the filming was due to start.'

'But who?'

'I don't know,' he shook his head.

'Someone on the inside, obviously.' She paused. 'You don't think it's Polly, do you?' She hoped not, having formed a real attachment to her.

'No. She doesn't know Anika.'

'Jennifer?' she suggested, not really thinking it would be his PA.

Felix laughed. 'Definitely not. Jennifer hates Anika.'

'Well, yes, that's true,' conceded Emma, then added, 'but now that the stalking's stopped, does it really matter?'

Felix looked out across the bay, its frozen water smooth and clear as glass.

'Yes, it does matter, Emma. I don't like working with people I can't trust.'

Perry's opinion of Felix had improved. Not that he'd particularly thought badly of him, but since he'd assured him that his intentions towards Emma were honourable, Perry could relax. He knew in his bones that Emma was in safe hands over there on the peninsula. In fact, the way Felix had behaved towards them all gave him confidence. He was a decent bloke, and a rich one at that. Emma could end up being extremely well looked after, thought Perry. Not that money mattered to him. He knew first-hand how a father could ruin his daughter's happiness, especially by obstructing their love life. Felix could be a pauper for all he cared, as long as it was Emma's choice. They appeared very suitably matched, as Bunty pointed out on their way home.

'Emma looks very comfortable with Felix. There's clearly chemistry between them. I think they make a good couple,' she'd commented. She'd also burst out laughing when Perry had told her about Felix's 'honourable inten-tions'. 'Sounds like a scene from one of his dramas,' she'd retorted.

'I think they make a good couple too,' agreed Perry.

'So you feel better about the situation?' she asked.

'I do,' he smiled. 'I just wish Emma had told me sooner about her ordeal, but at least the mad woman's behind bars and she's safe now. It's reassuring to see how much Felix is protective of my daughter too. Now it's time to concentrate on *us*, our wedding.'

'Yes, I've given it some thought,' replied Bunty.

'Good. So what's happening?' he chuckled, knowing she'd have everything worked out. For him, he'd just have a simple registry office do, with minimum fuss, but doubted Bunty would settle for that. And, actually, why should she? He'd been married before, but Bunty hadn't.

'Something a bit different. Not a conventional one,' warned Bunty, trying to gauge his reaction.

'Go on.' He gave a wry grin.

'Well, I thought,' she paused, 'of a hog roast on the beach.'

Perry's heart leaped, loving the idea. 'When?' he asked.

'Spring, when the weather hopefully picks up.'

'Hmm, a bit risky though. What if it's pouring down?'

'We'd have to have it undercover in the garden. A small marquee, but the beach would be so much better, wouldn't it?'

She could picture it now – clear blue skies, a sunlit, sparkling bay, family and friends laughing on the golden sand, merry music filling the air, the delicious waft of hog roast, her in a white floaty number, Perry in a white linen suit, both barefoot on the beach…

'It certainly would, sweetheart.' He adored watching her face light up. Nobody deserved this more than Bunty and he'd do anything to make their wedding day as special as she wanted.

'So, I think we ought to set the date, in April.'

'Sooner the better.' He blew her a kiss.

'Oh, Perrywinkle,' she teased with affection.

Robin was labouring hard with Jack. Ever since buying the warehouse by Lancaster quay, they'd never stopped. The sheer size of the place meant that both men would have to work tirelessly to complete the six renovated apartments. Jack, who had been the driving force behind the project, estimated they'd be completed within two years. Robin, ever conscious of how his life was about to change that summer, felt compelled to tell Jack about Jasmine's pregnancy. It only seemed right that his business partner and best friend was given notice, and Robin needed to explain to Jack that he'd need to have some time off when the baby was born. They might decide to bring in extra help, even on a temporary basis, to cover paternity leave.

After discussing the matter with Jasmine she'd agreed to tell Jack, on the condition he wasn't to tell a soul.

'If it got out before our families knew, it'd be terrible,' she cautioned.

'Don't worry. I'll make him swear to secrecy,' replied Robin, knowing his mate could be trusted.

'Hmm, look how the news of Felix Paschal got out,' countered Jasmine, not totally convinced.

'No, that was different. This is personal to me, to us, and Jack wouldn't betray that,' he assured.

So, with that in mind, Robin was trying to find the right time to tell Jack. They were working on the roof, up on the scaffolding. One of the main, crucial jobs was to get the building watertight. It was late morning and they were due a tea break. Robin stopped to take in the city skyline. The vista was impressive up there high on the scaffold; the castle and its turrets, the priory spire, the dome roof of the Williamson Park monument, Georgian sandstone architecture and ancient cobbled roads – a true historic city.

'Fancy a brew?' he called to Jack.

'Good idea.'

They downed tools and sat on the wooden planks, legs dangling. After pouring coffee from their flasks, Robin glanced sideways and Jack, sensing he had something to tell him, turned to Robin.

'What's up?'

'Come summer, we may need to get someone new in.'

'Why?' asked Jack, startled.

'Because… I'll be a dad by then.' Robin couldn't keep from smiling; he just couldn't help himself. The words made him tingle inside.

'Oh, mate!' Jack held out his hand.

'Thanks,' said Robin, shaking it, 'but it's hush-hush for now. We've not told anyone, not even our parents yet, early days, you know.'

'I won't breathe a word,' Jack told him with certainty. 'When is Jasmine due?'

'Early July.'

'Wow.' Jack smiled and nudged Robin's elbow. 'Well done, mate.'

'So, I'll have to have some time off,' said Robin, eager to warn Jack.

'Of course you will.'

'Not too long, but I want to be there for Jasmine and—'

'Listen, it's fine, honestly,' cut in Jack, putting Robin totally at ease.

'Thanks,' he nodded.

Jack genuinely was pleased for Robin, of course he was, but still a small part of him also envied his friend, because that's what he wanted too, deep down. He may come across as Jack-the-lad, having a reputation as a bit of a lady's man, but… well, things change. After seeing how happy Robin was with Jasmine, he realised that he essentially wanted the same – a loving, stable relationship.

'You all right?' asked Robin, eyeing him carefully.

'Yep, fine,' replied Jack with a forced smile.

'Sure you're OK with me taking time off?'

'Absolutely. It'll be a precious time in your life, Rob,' he almost choked.

Chapter 24

As predicted, the resumed filming began with a blast of energy surging through the house. Emma couldn't keep up with all the activity. As most of the filming so far had taken place inside, Felix now planned to shoot several of the outside scenes. This was proving to be far more hectic than ever. At least they didn't have the security issue hanging over them, conceded Emma. She could relax a little over routinely checking every door and window was locked. Instead, she was manically overseeing refreshments for the cast, crew and now the extras who were on set. As the number of actors increased, so did the makeup and costume assistants.

The place was heaving. Every now and again Felix would catch Emma's eye and they'd share a secret smile. This of course wasn't lost on Polly, who had clocked one or two of the furtive exchanges. Who did they think they were kidding? she chuckled to herself. They did look good together though, Polly concluded. Emma was very bright-eyed and bushy-tailed and as for Felix, he was positively glowing. His mood had lifted somewhat too, she'd noticed. No longer did he snap with impatience over forgotten lines, much to Brian's relief, who still chose to improvise when his memory lapsed. Instead of exasperation, Felix showed consideration when the older actor slipped up. Everyone had expected the director to roll his eyes (as Felix was renowned for doing), but instead he cocked his head to one side and remarked, 'Hmm, I like what you did there, Brian. It works better.'

Although busy, it was a pleasant atmosphere, tinged with excitement to be back together filming after the break.

'How did the gig go?' asked Polly during the coffee break. She and Emma were stood outside on the back lawn. A scene had just been shot with Lady Scarlett supposedly coming back from a horse ride and she wore tight jodhpurs and a black riding jacket.

'Great, thanks,' smiled Emma.

'Did Felix go?' Polly grinned with a raised eyebrow.

Emma paused before answering. She was suddenly aware of how many questions Polly asked. Was it just girly chit-chat, as they'd previously shared with giggles, or was it something more sinister? After all, what business was it of Polly's?

'I'd better get on,' replied Emma and hurried to the refreshment trolly, busying herself stacking empty cups. Polly looked on with a puzzled frown.

Felix too was far more guarded with those around him. That's what suspicion did to you. He may not have the worry of a mad woman stalking him now, but she almost certainly had an accomplice. But *who*? His eyes sceptically ran over the cast and crew. He'd observed Emma's swift exit from Polly, but was convinced it wasn't her. His narrowed gaze fell on Brian, but again, he didn't know Anika and neither did the camera men he reasoned. What about the assistants? It was possible one of the makeup women knew Anika. But then he winced at how appallingly she had treated them and doubted their cooperation. He sighed into this coffee cup.

'You OK?' A hushed voice came from his side. He gave a wry grin.

'You don't need to whisper, Emma,' he said, turning to face her. 'We are allowed to talk in public you know.'

Emma laughed at how she must appear.

'Sorry, I just feel like I'm being watched,' she said, still a tad quiet.

'I know,' he agreed, 'but remember, no harm can be done now Anika's behind bars. It's more…' he struggled to find the words.

'A betrayal?' supplied Emma.

'Exactly,' he nodded. 'I hate that someone close to me openly supplied Anika with every last detail of my business, without any consideration or loyalty.'

'Especially when they must have known how contentiously your relationship had ended,' agreed Emma, feeling his anger.

'I've a meeting in London next Friday,' said Felix, changing the subject. He'd had enough of thinking about 'the mole'.

'Right. What about the filming?'

'We'll finish on Thursday,' he replied, then added, 'fancy coming with me?'

'To London?' Emma sounded surprised.

'Well, not to the meeting,' he joked. Having said that, Emma's attendance at the next meeting may make sense. He intended to put forward his plan then.

'Why not?' She beamed and leaned forward to kiss him, but hastily stopped herself midway. Felix looked into her amber eyes.

'Later,' he said with a sexy smile, making her insides melt.

Bunty was with Jasmine in her garden studio, looking at wedding dresses online. It was hard trying to envisage herself, as an older bride, in any of them.

'Why are all the models young, slim chits of girls?' she complained.

'I know,' agreed Jasmine, who was also subconsciously looking for herself.

'I mean, come on,' Bunty tipped her head towards the laptop screen, 'really?'

Jasmine broke into laughter at the sight of a young bride literally bursting out of a white satin corset style dress, tied with ribbon down the spine. The model looked to be in pain, wearing not only vice, clamped-like bridal wear, but a tight smile too.

'We need to filter our search,' said Jasmine, then tapped 'mature bride wedding dresses' into the bar. Immediately a plethora of images appeared before them. Bunty's eyes widened.

'That's it.' She pointed her finger.

'Are you sure? There's plenty more to look at,' replied Jasmine.

'No, I'm sure. That's the one.'

Jasmine clicked on the picture of a cream dress with delicate layers of tulle that gathered into ruffles. It was scattered with silver sequins.

'"With textured ruffles to create beautiful movement, this truly unique wedding dress will look sophisticated for years to come",' she quoted. 'I must admit, it does have an ageless quality about it.' Jasmine was closely examining the image.

'Exactly. It reminds me of my mother's dress,' replied Bunty.

'Oh, the one Emma wore at the house opening?' Jasmine remembered Emma sat at the grand piano in the hall, wearing a Charleston flapper dress.

'Yes.' Bunty gave a wistful smile at the memory.

'Well, that was easy,' remarked Jasmine, saving the page.

'Should we look for you now?' asked Bunty with a cheeky wink. As always, her gut feeling was bang on the money.

'Me?' Jasmine faked surprise but wasn't fooling anyone.

'Yes, you. Don't tell me you weren't considering it.' Bunty's eyes twinkled with mischief.

Jasmine gave in with laughter.

'OK I admit it. I may have been tentatively looking, but perhaps we ought to just concentrate on you for now.'

'Why?' Bunty asked directly, staring at her.

'Because... it's *your* special time, not mine,' replied Jasmine.

'No other particular reason?' pressed Bunty.

Honestly, thought Jasmine, the woman was way too intuitive for her own good. What was she supposed to say? 'No point in looking at wedding dresses for me just yet, Bunty, because I'll be the size of a house come summer'? She eyed the older lady dubiously. Had she guessed too? Jasmine was sure her mum had sussed out she was pregnant. Maybe Bunty had done the same?

'No other reason,' said Jasmine with an innocent smile.

'I see,' Bunty murmured dryly, sounding anything but convinced.

Chapter 25

Felix sat in the meeting room, waiting for the others to arrive. Making use of the drinks machine, he'd poured a strong coffee and positioned himself at the far end of the table, facing the door. He wanted to get a good view of everyone entering, assess each member of the meeting fully. It had become a personal mission of his, to uncover the informer. Was he being a tad dramatic? No, on reflection he didn't think he was. Surely everyone was entitled to their privacy? And, as Emma had pointed out, even more so if an ex-girlfriend with an axe to grind was pumping someone for information. Everybody knew how badly his and Anika's relationship had ended. Hell, the *whole world* knew!

In Felix's mind, there was no excuse to be so indiscreet. Whoever had informed Anika knew full well he wouldn't want her to be privy to all his personal details. They obviously valued Anika over him. But who? That was the question he kept asking over and over.

Whilst he was in London, Felix had arranged to see Jennifer. Although they spoke often and exchanged emails, he missed her presence. Jennifer had always managed to keep him on the straight and narrow, not just career wise, but personally too. She kept him calm, stable. When all the bad press Anika had thrown at him was circulating, it was she who had given him good counsel. It was Jennifer who had saved him from breaking down, fearing his career would be over.

'Who'll want me, with this reputation?' he'd said in defeat.

'Your reputation is that of a damned good actor. This,' she stabbed at the newspaper article, 'is just a cheap pack of lies, as those stupid enough to read it will know.'

And, thank God, Jennifer had been proved right. She'd also advised him not to retaliate.

'Never explain. Never complain,' had been her direction, echoing the royalty party-line. That too had worked. Felix's tight-lipped stance had created an air of intrigue and also esteem. Seeming to be above Anika's malicious vendetta had earned him respect, especially in the film industry. The phrase, 'all publicity is good publicity,' had been proved true in Felix's case.

Although Felix had no intention of speaking to the press about Anika's arrest, he knew better than to assume it wouldn't leak. Of course it would. A story like that was hot, sensational stuff and hardly likely to go unnoticed; the world and its wife would know exactly what he'd had to endure. He was about to become the injured party, and this time the good publicity would be most welcome.

All things considered, Felix was in a good position. The drama was on track, going well. He loved directing and... he loved Emma. It hit him like a bolt of lightning. Truth be told, he'd pretty much fallen for her when first hearing her sing. He pictured her sat at the grand piano in his huge, marbled hall singing, when he'd been struck not only by her sweet voice, but her beauty also. After seeing her again at the interview, he'd been drawn by her sparkling personality and sense of humour. Getting to know her further, he'd understood how both caring and grounded she was. She was the one and he'd do all in his power to keep her.

His thoughts were interrupted by Andy, the location manager.

'Hi, Felix,' he said, entering the room and helping himself to the drinks machine.

'Hi, Andy,' Felix replied, eyeing him carefully.

Andy turned and gave a cheery smile. 'Had a good holiday?' he asked, sitting down next to him.

'Yes, thanks.' Felix looked for any possible signs of guilt, but saw none. Andy was just his usual friendly self. Then in came mouselike Flo, the associate producer, followed by Mel, the casting director. As always, Flo appeared twitchy and agitated, but nothing new there. Whereas Mel was his usual confident self, though he did give Felix a rather uneasy glance before greeting him, which raised his suspicions.

Both the production and design managers were attending, but more crucially to Felix, the music director too. Laurence Willis had connections to the London Philharmonic Orchestra, and Felix needed to speak to the man.

As the meeting got underway, Felix reported that they were bang on schedule and hoped to get all the outside filming done within three weeks. This was met with nods of approval. Springtime would see the drama conclude, with the exception of the opening scenes which needed to be filmed early summer.

'Or maybe late spring, if the weather's decent,' Felix advised.

'Good to know it's all on track,' remarked the production manager, then turned to Laurence. 'We've now to concentrate on the music, particularly the theme track.'

Felix waited with bated breath for the music director to speak.

'Yes, I've been working on this,' he replied with gusto, 'and I really feel it requires lyrics to accompany the jaunty tune.'

Result, thought Felix. This was exactly what he'd been hoping for.

'I see,' said the production manager.

Felix coughed and cleared his throat. 'Do you have a singer in mind?' he asked.

Laurence looked surprised by the question. 'No, not really. Why? Do you have any suggestions?'

'Actually yes, I do,' replied Felix assertively.

'Who?' asked Mel.

'Emma Scholar,' answered Felix, still looking at Laurence.

'I don't think I've heard of her…' Laurence frowned.

'No, you won't have, but I'd like you to meet her,' said Felix.

'Emma? Isn't that your housekeeper?' Mel snorted with laughter.

Felix turned and gave him a deadly glare.

'No, Emma's my girlfriend,' he stated, all the time observing the effect the information had on him. Mel did indeed look astonished by the news. Was this more juicy gossip to report back? He'd hated the way Mel had belittled Emma and had jumped in rather defensively. He faced Laurence again. 'Emma is an extremely talented singer and I'd love to introduce you to her.'

'I'd be delighted.' Laurence smiled politely. Ever the gentleman, he too hadn't cared for Mel's attitude.

'Okay, we'll leave that with you both and you can give us an update next meeting,' said the producer.

And so the meeting continued, lasting another hour. As it drew to a conclusion Felix felt a real sense of achievement. He couldn't wait to tell Emma the news. As they all filed out of the room, he once more eyed Mel, who, he noticed, refused any eye contact with him. Could this be the mole?

Jennifer sat back in her armchair and considered what Felix had just relayed. He'd called at her home in Richmond and they were in the living room drinking tea. It had been strange to see her pouring from a teapot in front of the fire, instead of tapping a keyboard behind a desk. After digesting Felix's words, she slowly nodded her head.

'Yes, I think it could be Mel, judging from what you say,' she concluded.

'But why?' asked Felix. 'Why would he let Anika know by business?'

'Maybe he was doing it inadvertently? Being pumped for information without realising it?' Then she leant forward. 'Do you remember at the first casting meeting, he'd suggested Selina McKenna for the role of Lady Scarlett?'

'Yes, he did, Selina McKenna, Anika's close friend,' replied Felix with a sense of realisation.

'So why did he suggest her?' asked Jennifer.

'Coincidence? She is a good actress.'

Jennifer gave a harsh laugh.

'Or maybe he was being schmoozed by her, being buttered up to gain a part.'

Felix had been in show business long enough to know this did happen with casting directors. Some actors would stop at nothing to land leading roles.

'But she didn't get the role,' said Felix.

'No, but Mel did put her name forward, which makes me think they'd had some form of dialogue. She'll have flattered him, bought him dinner, supplied him with wine and praised him to death,' stated Jennifer with vigour, latching onto her theory.

'And in return, he'd have her as a contender for Lady Scarlett's role… and chirped like a canary.'

'Exactly!' agreed Jennifer. 'The silly old ham was being reeled in. Selina may have got a plum role as well as gaining information for her friend.'

'But all this is speculation,' said Felix.

'Well, confront him then,' retorted Jennifer with an arched eyebrow.

Emma was in her element wandering round Felix's penthouse suite. She'd never known such luxury.

'If you need anything, just ring the concierge,' said Felix before leaving for his meeting that morning.

How the other half live, thought Emma from the rooftop terrace, gazing down at Hyde Park. She observed the joggers, the dog-walkers, the young mums pushing prams and the tourists strolling along the pathways. It amazed her how lush the grounds looked, considering it was late autumn and in the heart of London. Then she turned to the swimming pool on the terrace, covered now for the cold months, but imagined how inviting it would be come summer.

Inside was just as impressive, with thick cream carpet throughout, a large black leather sofa and recliner, inset electric fireplace and a large, state of the art kitchen. Huge picture windows ran along the south-facing side, flooding the apartment with natural light, offering panoramic city sky-line views.

Emma had also been impressed with the welcome they had received. Although clearly a new face, she'd been treated with the same utmost courtesy as Felix from the staff on reception. They'd arrived the night before and Emma had gaped in awe at the city sparkling below them in the darkness. She'd felt safe, high up on the top of the apartment block, well out of the way. She understood why Felix had chosen to live here. It was private, but in a different way to his property on the peninsula in Samphire Bay. Emma knew which home she preferred and was already missing the beloved Art Deco house.

In her excitement, she decided to ring her dad. Perry picked up straight away.

'You wanna see this place, dad,' gushed Emma.

Perry chuckled. He knew she and Felix were in London and was glad for the call.

'Not too shabby then?' he laughed.

'It's amazing!' she trilled.

There was a slight pause. Perry hoped his daughter wasn't about to take a real shine to London. The last thing he wanted was Emma spending more time there than at Samphire Bay. As if reading his mind, Emma continued.

'But I miss my beautiful Art Deco house.'

'Oh, it's *your* house now, is it?' teased Perry with a grin.

'Well, no, but *I'm* the one cleaning it,' she replied tartly, making Perry chuckle again.

Then, a thought occurred to Emma.

'Dad, you will be living at Bunty's, won't you, when you get married?' she asked.

'Yes,' said Perry, guessing what was coming next.

'But what about Fisher's Cottage?'

Perry had already decided on this. Technically, it belonged to him, but it had been Emma's home before he had married Val. So, in his mind, it was Emma's house.

'That depends on what you want to do with it,' he answered. 'As far as I'm concerned, Fisher's Cottage is your home.'

'But—'

'No buts, Emma,' cut in Perry firmly, 'it's your house. You may decide to sell or rent it out. Give it some thought,' he wisely finished.

'Oh, right,' Emma chewed her lip in thought, not expecting this scenario.

'So, what have you got planned today?' asked Perry.

'I'm waiting for Felix to come back from his meeting, then we're going out for dinner tonight.'

'Very nice,' smiled Perry, enjoying her enthusiasm. If his girl was happy – then so was he.

Later that evening Felix and Emma were led to their table at a top restaurant tucked discreetly away down a side street in Knightsbridge. Felix had waited to tell Emma all the details about the meeting, despite her asking how it had gone.

'We'll talk about it later,' he'd said, wanting to set the scene nicely over a candle-lit dinner. Once they'd chosen from the menu Felix ordered a bottle of the best champagne, feeling the occasion warranted it. After it was poured, Felix raised his glass. 'I'd like to propose a toast,' he announced.

'Oh yes?' Emma smiled, wondering where this was leading.

'To your singing career,' he cheered.

Emma frowned, not expecting that. 'Err… right,' she said. Then added, 'What career exactly?' Surely, he hardly thought performing the odd gig with the band constituted a singing career?

'The one, I hope, you're about to embark on,' he declared with a wide smile. He then proceeded to tell Emma all about the meeting and how he'd planned to introduce her to the music director.

Emma sat, jaw dropped and eyes wide.

'You mean… I could be the one singing the theme song to *Lady Scarlett Investigates*?' she spluttered.

'Yep.' Felix nodded, working hard to contain his grin.

'OMG,' she gasped. A terrifying thought struck. 'But what if he doesn't like my voice?'

'Of course he'll like it,' snorted Felix. 'You have the voice of an angel.' He gave a sexy grin and quietly uttered, 'And the body of a goddess.'

Emma giggled and raised a provocative eyebrow.

'And yours isn't that bad either,' she replied clinking his glass.

The following day Felix had arranged for Emma to meet Laurence at the recording studio. Laurence started by playing the theme tune on a keyboard. It was, like he'd said in the meeting, a jaunty, upbeat melody, reflective of the drama. The music was very reminiscent of the roaring twenties, but, as Laurence had also previously stated, cried out for lyrics. When he'd passed the song sheet to Emma, her eyes had lit up.

'Oh, it's so apt!' she cried, reading the lines with glee. This seemed to please Laurence.

'I'm glad you think so. Now, shall we have a practise?'

Emma gave a deep breath. This was it. The moment she'd been waiting for her whole life.

'Let's,' she replied as confidently as possible.

Felix put a reassuring hand on her shoulder.

'Try to relax,' he whispered soothingly.

She gave a wobbly smile. 'I'll try.'

'You've got this,' he winked.

Emma was given headphones and directed into a glass booth. Grasping the song sheet tightly, she waited for Laurence to give the nod. He played the opening bars and signalled Emma's introduction. Shoulders back, she sang her heart out.

'Lady Scarlett, super sleuth,
With her emerald eyes and raven hair,
She'll figure it out,
Without a doubt,
Such a quick mind and elegant flair!
Lady Scarlett is on the trail,
Hunting for clues and fingerprints,
She's on the case,
Looking for a trace,
The culprit will get caught in an jinks!'

She finished and stared directly at Laurence, who thankfully was beaming. Giving her the thumbs up, he spoke through the headphones.

'That was great, Emma.'

Oh, the relief!

'Let's try again, taking a slightly longer pause between the two verses, yeah?'

'OK,' she nodded. Felix gave her another encouraging wink. Off she went again – and again, until finally Laurence clapped his hands in approval.

'I think we've got it!' he proclaimed.

Emma could have cried for joy. Her life's ambition was fulfilled. Her voice had been recorded. *She* was about to sing to the nation.

Chapter 26

Bunty peered into Jasmine's studio window but was surprised not to see her working there. Usually she'd find Jasmine sat at her desk staring into a screen, but it was empty today. Deciding to try the house, Bunty walked up the garden path and tapped on the back door. There was still no answer. About to walk away, the door suddenly opened.

'Oh hi, I didn't think you were in,' said Bunty on seeing a very pale faced Jasmine. She looked closer and scrutinised her. 'Jasmine, are you all right? You look terrible.' She was concerned at her friend's appearance. Dark shadows smudged under Jasmine's yes.

'I've had better greetings,' replied Jasmine dryly, 'but no, actually, I feel like death warmed up this morning. Come in.' She stood back to let Bunty inside.

'Here, I'll put the kettle on. You sit down,' Bunty directed, pulling a chair out for Jasmine at the kitchen table.

Jasmine was happy to sit down. She'd had practically no sleep that night. She had also vomited that morning, which filled her with dismay, having thought the morning sickness had passed for good. Robin had also been concerned about her, but that was nothing new. Jasmine had batted his worry away, saying she'd soon mend. But she wasn't mending. If anything, the nausea was building momentum.

Bunty placed two mugs of coffee on the table and sat down opposite her. Jasmine lifted her cup, took a sip, then winced. Moments later she was stood at the kitchen sink retching.

'Darling!' Bunty rushed over and put an arm round her back.

'S…sorry,' gasped Jasmine and then spilled the entire contents of her stomach into the basin. Finally she stopped and poured the cold tap on full force. Cupping her hands, she splashed water over her perspiring face.

'Jasmine, come and sit down.' Bunty carefully guided her back to the table and gently sat her down. After a few seconds she softly tipped Jasmine's chin up to face her. 'I can keep a secret you know.' Her voice was warm and tender. Jasmine let out a small sigh and briefly closed her eyes.

'You know, don't you?'

'That you're pregnant? Yes, darling, it's pretty obvious.' Then added, 'To an old dear like me it is anyway,' she grinned, making Jasmine smile.

'I knew it. I knew you'd guessed. So has my mum, I'm sure.'

'Probably,' agreed Bunty, nodding. Then asked, 'But why the secrecy? Why not tell your parents? I'm positive Robin's mum and dad will be delighted.'

'Oh, I know they will and mine too, it's just early days… and… we thought…'

'I understand.' Bunty shook her head perceptively. 'When will you let them know?'

'After my scan,' replied Jasmine.

'When's that?'

'Next week,' said Jasmine. She'd be glad when the scan was completed, then they could be more open and not have to tiptoe around the truth.

'Not long then.' Bunty patted her hand encouragingly. 'Congratulations, darling, I'm thrilled for you both.'

Jasmine looked into the older lady's face and was touched. Joy shone from her sparkling eyes, wrinkled at the edges from a lifetime of smiles and laughter.

'I take it Robin will be moving in, once the baby's born?'

'He's practically moved in already,' replied Jasmine with a wry smile. 'But yes, Robin intends to sell his flat and we'll all be together here.' She couldn't help but feel warm and tingly at the thought; her very own family, here, in this house.

'Well, he won't be the only one,' said Bunty. 'Perry will be moving in with me. So we'll both have new next-door neighbours,' she laughed.

Jasmine had anticipated this and couldn't be happier. It was good to know the couple would be living close by.

'We won't be short of babysitters then?' she joked.

'Certainly not,' Bunty replied with a beam.

Then, changing the subject, Jasmine asked how the wedding plans were going.

'We've booked the church,' Bunty told her. 'It'll be a spring wedding, early April, so we will be sending out the invites shortly.'

Jasmine looked a tad surprised to hear this.

'Oh, right.' She'd assumed it would be a summer wedding. She quickly calculated how many months pregnant she'd be – six and most definitely showing.

'I won't ask you to be a bridesmaid,' teased Bunty, guessing what was going through her friend's mind. They both fell into giggles.

'Can you imagine, me parading up the aisle behind you with a swollen belly?'

'I'm sure you'd look splendid,' laughed Bunty, then paused in thought, 'though I think Emma should be one.'

'Of course,' agreed Jasmine, which prompted her to ask after Emma.

'Oh, she's happy as Larry,' replied Bunty and told Jasmine about Emma's London trip to Felix's penthouse.

'Who'd have thought the mysterious buyer was none other than Felix Paschal.' Jasmine shook her head in wonder. 'What does Perry think about him?' She'd learnt from Bunty that the relationship between Felix and Emma was more than just a platonic professional one. The question made Bunty smirk faintly.

'I think he had reservations to begin with, but that was Perry being his usual protective self. Once he'd met Felix and gave him the 'you-better-look-after-my-daughter' speech, he seems fine.'

Jasmine grinned. 'Most fathers would be thrilled their daughter's bagged a rich movie star.'

'Not Perry. He just wants Emma to be happy with Mr Right, regardless of his wealth.'

They sat in silence, ruminating on those wise words. It wasn't lost on either of them how they resonated with the past. Bunty was of course referring to her father's interference with her and Perry's relationship in the early days. It was so sad, to think of the wasted years. All the more reason to celebrate their forthcoming wedding, thought Jasmine and said so to Bunty.

'Yes, absolutely,' agreed Bunty resolutely. Looking pensively into Jasmine's eyes she continued, 'And you, my darling, this is *your* special time too. Yours and Robin's, nobody more so deserving.'

If ever there was a moment which screamed hug, it was now. The two reached up in unison over the table and embraced. Two women, young and old, firm friends.

The filming was taking place in the kitchen, which was highly inconvenient for Emma.

'But how can I prepare the refreshments?' she'd asked Felix when he'd told her they were due to set up there.

'We'll just have to make do with cold drinks for today,' he'd replied airily. For Felix, it was imperative they shot the scenes down in the kitchen as soon as possible, whilst there was good light.

It was late January and a bright day, so he was keen to make the most of it. Even with the daylight shining through the two sash windows, the cameramen had also stood standing lights in the corners of the kitchen.

Frustrated but not thwarted, Emma had improvised refreshments by making up a few flasks of boiling water just before they'd set up and put teabags and instant coffee in bowls for people to make their own hot drink. There were also jugs of milk, juice and water.

However, it was unlikely a tea break was about to happen any time soon; Felix was getting tetchy. Whilst the main cast were all on form, one or two of the cameo roles had struggled. So much so, Felix had been left wondering just how they'd managed to get a part in the first place. At first, seeing the young actor playing the butcher's boy fall off his bicycle while shooting outside this morning had been comical. Even he had seen the funny side of it, dusting himself off with rosy cheeks.

'Sorry about that,' he'd laughed. 'I'll soon get the hang of it.'

Except, after five takes, he clearly hadn't. They'd hired the vintage bicycle from the props department and Felix was concerned about the state it was going to return in. Already he'd bent the handlebars and damaged the back wheel.

'From the top, again,' directed Felix, waving his hands for the young actor to set off riding down the garden path once more. Finally, he was filming a convincing butcher's boy about to make his delivery. After managing to ride pretty competently, halt and dismount, he then took the wicker basket off his bike and knocked on the back door.

'And cut!' Felix had shouted with utter relief.

Now, inside the kitchen, a young girl was playing the role of Jilly, the parlour maid. She answered the door with such nervous energy, it flung back hard, banging against the wall.

'Again please, with a little less gusto,' said Felix flatly.

The second take went well, with all the cast reciting their lines word perfect. It was only when Felix was about to cry cut, did the cameraman notice the espresso machine in view. When he pointed this out, Felix closed his eyes and pinched the bridge of his nose in despair.

'Who left that there?' he thundered, pointing to it.

The last thing he needed was a modern appliance sitting on the worktop of a 1920s kitchen. An awkward silence hung in the air, when a small voice answered. Emma had been nearby when she'd heard Felix and, creeping gingerly down the stairs, she steadied herself for the onslaught.

'It was me, sorry. I forgot to move it when everything was being set up inside.'

Felix spun round. '*Em*-ma,' he groaned.

'Sorry.' Her amber eyes were filled with sincerity and his shoulders relaxed at the sight.

'It's OK.' He shook his head, regretting his loss of temper.

Upstairs, in the hall, the rest of the cast exchanged sly smiles, having heard the exchange. It was blatantly obvious Emma brought out the best in Felix. Polly was awaiting her cue to enter the kitchen. Once Emma scurried back up, Felix called 'action!' and she made her way down the stairs to make her entrance.

'Morning, Lady Scarlett,' curtsied the maid.

'Morning, Jilly,' she replied, then turned to the basket on the table. 'Is that a fresh delivery?'

'Yes, m'lady, it was the last order cook made,' said a tearful Jilly.

Lady Scarlett's eyes narrowed in thought.

'Hmm, when did cook make the order?' she questioned.

'Oh, err… I'm not rightly sure, m'lady.'

'Think, Jilly, it's important,' urged Lady Scarlett, leaning on the kitchen table.

'Could this be a clue, m'lady?' asked the awestruck maid.

'It certainly could be,' came the reply, as the camera closed in on Polly's face.

'And cut!' exclaimed Felix.

At last they all gave a sigh of relief and made their way up into the hall to get a drink.

'Naughty you,' chided Polly gently to Emma, whilst making herself a cup of tea.

'I know!' hissed Emma. 'I can't believe I forgot to put the coffee machine out of sight.'

'Glad it wasn't one of the crew,' replied Polly, 'Felix would have gone ballistic.'

Emma gave a roguish look, but didn't comment. She wasn't really sure how to play Polly any more. Whilst now knowing who 'the mole' was likely to be from Felix, she still felt a little dubious revealing too much about her relationship with him. It was personal, after all. Instead, Emma changed tack and moved the conversation onto her singing the theme song for the drama.

'That's amazing!' trilled Polly, truly pleased and impressed. 'I know it's going to sound fabulous with your voice.'

'I hope so,' replied Emma modestly.

'Oh come on! It can't fail but be a hit,' Polly said sincerely.

Felix joined them, smiling at overhearing the tail end of the conversation. He was super proud of Emma and wanted the world to know how talented his girlfriend was.

'Emma was just telling me about her singing the theme song,' said Polly, facing him in delight.

'I know,' he nodded, 'and she absolutely nailed it.' The admiration in his voice was evident. He put an arm round Emma and gave her a quick squeeze. Again, this caused one or two side glances among those nearby witnessing the act of intimacy. Polly decided to come straight out with it. She was growing tired of all this namby-pamby, pussyfooting around.

'So, are you two an item, or what?'

Emma looked a touch taken aback and remained speechless. Felix, however, took full control of the situation effortlessly.

'Yes. We are,' he stated with force, a little too loudly for Emma's liking. She'd been at pains to keep their relationship on the quiet so far, but asked herself, why? Felix certainly wasn't staying hush-hush about it. The opposite in fact. She looked up into his eyes and grinned happily. Then, on impulse, reached up to kiss his lips. There, that showed them. Nobody could be in any doubt now.

Chapter 27

Jasmine and Robin walked down the maternity ward corridor with mixed emotions. Glimpsing the baby photos on the corridor walls, they made their way into a small scanning room. It was a pivotal moment for the new parents, full of bright anticipation, mingled with the inevitable tinge of worry. Would everything be fine? Would the ultrasound scan reveal a healthy baby, all as it should be?

The nurse gave a wide smile and directed Jasmine to lay on the bed, whilst Robin sat at the side. After the nurse smeared Jasmine's bare abdomen with gel, she ran the scanner smoothly over it. Robin and Jasmine held hands tightly, waiting with relish to see the first sight of their baby. Immediately a small head appeared on the grey blurry screen.

'And here we are,' said the nurse, staring at the image. 'Baby's head and spine.' She pointed to the minute row of bones. The nurse then used the scanner to take measurements and recorded them.

'Is everything OK?' asked Robin, eyes like saucers as they fixed on the screen. Jasmine too was transfixed on the tiny life growing inside her. There was a slight pause, which alerted both of them. They sharply turned to face the nurse, who seemed to be hesitating.

'Y-es, I just need to…' She ran the scanner further downwards on Jasmine's abdomen and gave a tinkle of laughter. 'Ah-ha, that explains it,' she concluded. Realising both parents were looking at her intently, she pointed back to the image on the screen. 'Look.'

Jasmine and Robin inhaled dramatically. There, on the screen, before their very own eyes, was *another* baby.

'Oh, my God, it's twins!' yelped Jasmine.

'It certainly is,' replied the nurse warmly.

Jasmine tore her eyes away from the screen to look at Robin, who had turned a whiter shade of pale by now. He couldn't speak. Instead, he was mesmerised by the two tiny mirages before him. Except they weren't mirages, they were real, very real, moving with life. His children – plural, they were having *babies*, not *a* baby. Jasmine couldn't help but giggle at him.

'Robin?'

Eventually his eyes slid to rest on hers and he gulped.

'Didn't see that coming.' He blinked and looked back at the screen. He tightened his grip, making Jasmine wince.

'Oi.'

'Sorry.' He quickly released her hand. 'Jasmine, we're having twins,' he said, as if she didn't have a clue.

'Yes, I know,' she laughed.

'Let me just take the measurements of baby two,' said the nurse.

Baby two, thought Jasmine, already wanting to name them, which prompted her to ask the next question.

'Can you tell what sex they are?'

'Do we want to know?' Robin cut in quickly.

The nurse looked from one to the other before replying.

'You can't always tell from the first scan, especially when the baby is so small. Being twins, your babies are especially small, which is why I looked further. I suspected there was more than one baby.'

'I see,' said Jasmine, turning back to admire in wonder at her tiny babies. She understood why Robin might not want to know the sex of them, but, ever practical, Jasmine thought otherwise. The pragmatic side of her kicked in. Knowing the gender of their babies, whether girls or boys, would prove extremely useful in preparing for them. Then another thought swiftly followed. They could be having both, a girl and a boy. Nothing had primed her for this, or Robin for that matter. She stole another glance at him. He'd at least got a bit of colour back now, the shock having sunk in. A loving warmth swamped her. Robin would make a wonderful dad – *is* going to make a wonderful dad. She suddenly became tearful.

'Hey, you all right?' Robin stroked her arm in comfort.

'Yes,' she choked.

'All done here. I think you both deserve a good cup of tea,' said the nurse, wiping the gel off Jasmine.

'We do,' nodded Robin, helping Jasmine to get up off the bed.

They drove home in a companiable silence, each lost in their own thoughts. There was such a lot to consider. Both their worlds had turned upside down, but already Jasmine and Robin were full of love for the new lives they'd created. Robin was thinking of work and how having two newborn babies was going to affect it. Would having an extra baby mean more time off? Then there was the expense. Did it really matter in the grand scale of things anyway? He felt as though his brain was being torn between pure joy and celebration and trying to figure out all the boring practicalities.

Jasmine was thinking of names. She had plenty to choose from with both sexes to consider and two babies to name. Then her mind turned to more rational matters, thankful her home was three-bedroomed. In a way she was pleased to be having two babies together. Although she shared a loving relationship with her brother, she'd often envied the closeness of twins; that special bond between two embryos, growing jointly from day one. She pictured her babies, each a foetus now with its own arms, hands, fingers, feet and toes. All the time they were growing, being formed together, side by side, or top to tail in her case. They were lying across each other, which was why 'baby two' hadn't been spotted straight away. The wonders of nature, thought Jasmine in awe. How magical. Once more she looked sideways at Robin driving. He was staring out, gripping the steering wheel so rigidly the whites of his knuckles showed. She cleared her throat.

'How do you feel about all this?'

He gave a slow smile.

'Now that I'm over the initial shock, I feel...' He paused in contemplation.

'What?' asked Jasmine, closely assessing his face.

'Bloody brilliant,' he beamed.

That had pretty much been the reaction from everyone.

'Oh, my God, twins!' exclaimed Jasmine's mum.

Robin laughed. 'That's exactly what Jasmine said.'

'Like mother, like daughter,' replied Jasmine's dad.

'Do you know what they are? Girls or boys?' asked her mum.

'Or both?' chipped in dad.

Jasmine shook her head at all the questions and the excitement oozing from her parents.

'No, we don't know,' Robin told them in a composed tone, hoping it would take effect.

'Come on, let's all have a sit down and a cup of tea,' said Jasmine's dad, wisely detecting the need for calmness.

'And that's exactly what the nurse said.' Jasmine chuckled.

Later in the early evening, after they'd visited Robin's parents with the good news, Jasmine called next door. Out of all their friends, Jasmine wanted Bunty to be the first to know about the twins.

'Oh darling, that's wonderful news!' she cried. 'No wonder you've been suffering, with double the amount going on in there.' She pointed towards Jasmine's stomach.

'Hmm, one thing's for sure, I'm going to be huge come your wedding.'

Bunty threw her head back and chortled.

'You'll look positively glowing, darling.'

'Not sure I'll be dancing barefoot in the sand, under the stars for too long though,' replied Jasmine.

Felix was on the train to London. He didn't have a meeting, but did intend to see Jennifer at some point and, more importantly, act on her advice. He was making a special trip to confront Mel Nichols. Felix needed to know if it was him who had leaked information and he wanted to see for himself the man's reaction when challenged. More than anything, Felix wanted closure. Once he ascertained that Mel was undoubtedly the culprit, he knew never to work with the likes of him again, if he wanted to keep his private life private.

Not that he envisaged any further scandal in his personal life. Quite the opposite, in fact. Living with Emma was the complete antithesis to life with Anika. Emma was supportive and happy in her own skin, she didn't see Felix as competition like Anika had, always comparing herself to him and his success. If Felix was getting plenty of media attention, Anika sulked, which was ironic, considering the amount she'd created for him. Another startling contrast was Emma's total trust in him. She never showed any signs of insecurity or jealousy. He remembered how Anika used to watch his films and plague him for days about his women co-stars. The love scenes particularly brought out the worst in her. No, with Emma, he unquestionably had found his soul mate.

Felix's mother had been thrilled to hear of his relationship with Emma, having already predicted it. She, like Jennifer, had told him to 'oust the rat' when learning about Mel's betrayal too.

So, here he was, about to disembark the train at Euston station. After jostling through the crowds to the taxi rank, he was soon climbing into the back of one and gave directions to the studios. He knew Mel was about to start auditions for another drama so would be there. Arriving, Felix walked up the steps into the brick building. Mel's office was on the ground floor and he strode with determination to the door marked 'Melvin Nichols – Casting Director' and knocked loudly.

'Enter!' called a voice.

Felix inhaled deeply and marched in. Mel was sat behind a large desk and looked surprised to see him.

'Felix, what brings you here?'

'I'm going to ask you something, Mel, and I want the honest truth,' said Felix, eyes blazing.

Mel shifted uncomfortably in his chair.

'Did you, or did you not, give information about me to Selina McKenna?'

Mel's face grew crimson and he reached for the security buzzer on his desk. Felix's hand quickly slammed over his to stop him.

'Don't even think about it,' he warned in a low, threatening voice. He stared at Mel for an answer.

'Well… I… I… might have mentioned one or two things…' stammered Mel, getting hotter and hotter under the collar.

'You told her where I lived, knowing full well she'd tell Anika,' said Felix, still in the same menacing tone.

'She… could have asked.'

'Yes, and you bloody told her!' shouted Felix, making Mel jump. 'You told Selina McKenna *everything* she wanted to know, didn't you?'

'I'm not sure,' replied Mel lamely.

'Oh, I'm sure,' spat Felix. 'I'm absolutely sure you were wined, dined and flattered by a young actress who was paying you plenty of attention. And you,' he pointed at him in disgust, 'are a pathetic, sad, old man, who lapped it all up. Didn't you realise you were being used?'

Mel's mouth opened in protest, then shut. Felix continued the rant.

'I mean, come on, Mel, why else would Selina McKenna be showing you any interest?'

'For a role?' answered Mel icily.

There was a slight pause.

'Yes, and she nearly got one, didn't she?' replied Felix with slit eyes. 'Is that how you operate, Mel? Dish the parts out to those who show the most willing?'

The suggestion wasn't lost on Mel. Whilst Selina had indeed sweet-talked and cajoled him, and however much he enjoyed being the centre of her attention (silly, vain man that he was) he hadn't actually given her a part. However, the rumours surrounding him casting several other leading men's roles did lead to much speculation.

The simple truth was, Mel Nichols abused his position as casting director. Another truth was he liked men, young men, many who were desperate to become stars. And Mel had the power to make them stars. End of. It wasn't nice and it wasn't professional, but so far he'd got away with it, until now. Was Felix Paschal about to blow his career into smithereens?

A charged silence hung in the air. Both men stared each other out. Mel blinked first.

'I apologise, Felix. I ought to have known better.'

'You will be sorry, Mel,' Felix answered and turned on his heel, slamming the door behind him.

Jennifer sat, eyes wide with interest as Felix recounted the whole incident.

'The complete and utter snake,' she said when he'd finished. Then, after a moment's consideration, added, 'And to think, if I hadn't lied about Selina McKenna being ill, she could have got the role of Lady Scarlett.'

'I know, thank God you thought on your feet,' replied Felix.

Jennifer frowned. 'I'm surprised he didn't know she wasn't really ill.'

'I'm not. She'll have dropped him when he'd served his purpose and never seen him again.'

'I expect so,' Jennifer agreed, then shuddered.

'What is it, Jennifer?' Felix asked concerned.

'Just what you said about Mel, using his power like that, with vulnerable, young actors.'

'I know.' Felix grimaced in repulsion.

'Do something about it, Felix.' She stared at him, eyes pleading.

'You mean report him?'

'Yes.'

'But it's all hearsay, whispers and rumours. There's no evidence,' Felix stated.

'What about the young actors he's manipulated? Do you think they'd speak?' Jennifer leaned forward.

'Sadly, no, I don't think they would,' Felix said with regret. 'Mel Nichols will still have a big influence over their careers.'

'He's not the only casting director in the business,' replied Jennifer.

'No, but he's a big bug at the studio, they definitely wouldn't want to ruffle his feathers.'

'But it's so *wrong*!' she retorted.

'It is.' Felix could only agree.

'And look at the trouble he caused you, disclosing your address, allowing Anika to come and—'

'I know,' Felix cut in, really not wanting to contemplate what could have happened to Emma. The injustice of it all filled him with rage. Still, he took comfort in the fact Anika had been arrested; and Emma, well, just thinking about her calmed him. 'I better make tracks, Jennifer,' he said, glancing at his watch. The sooner he was in Samphire Bay the better.

All the way home Felix kept going over what had happened. Jennifer was right, it was so unethical the way Mel Nichols operated. Surely there must be something he could do?

Chapter 28

Perry sighed deeply and looked round Fishers Cottage. A place full of memories, mostly happy, but some sad too. His mind cast way back to the earliest memory, when Val had first brought him inside and Emma had been excited to show him her room. Even then as a little girl, she'd loved music and had covered her bedroom walls with posters of various pop groups and singers. She'd played him her Maroon 5 CD with pride and joy. Now Emma would need to clear her bedroom if she wanted to sell or rent the cottage out.

He had to collect all his belongings in order to move into Bunty's house. Eventually, depending on what Emma chose to do with Fishers Cottage, the whole place would need emptying. Perry seriously doubted Emma would ever live here again, not when considering her present circumstances. He'd never seen his daughter so happy, and she clearly wasn't leaving Felix or his magnificent house any time soon. Long term, however, he still wanted his daughter to have choices and would be advising Emma to invest her money wisely. Fishers Cottage would fetch a tidy sum, with its quaint stone exterior and characterful interior, and it was also in a very good location, just by the picturesque canal and a walkable distance to the city centre.

Whilst the cottage had been a haven for his small family, he couldn't deny that it still held painful reminders of losing Val. Within its four walls he'd nursed his wife until her final departure in the early morning hours, peacefully drifting away, out of his and Emma's lives. He'd never forget that gut wrenching heartbreak or the look of utter despair in Emma's eyes. The experience had made him even more protective of her. But – he took another deep breath – they were both in a happy place now.

He set about emptying the rest of his wardrobe. A lot of his clothes were already at Bunty's, but he needed all of them there now, along with his full record collection, his books, photo albums and precious keepsakes. Like the framed wedding photograph of him and Val, with little Emma in the middle. He obviously wasn't thinking of putting it up in Bunty's house, but there's no way he could ever part with it.

Once he'd finished and all his possessions were neatly bagged and boxed up, he sat on the edge of his bed and flicked through the photo albums. Cherished moments waved up at him, from family holidays aboard *The Merry Perry* to Emma's first gig as a teenager.

All in all, Perry had mixed feelings about leaving Fishers Cottage. Whilst he was looking forward to a new life with Bunty, he hated to think of this cottage, which had been such a treasured home, being left cold, damp and empty. It needed new life breathing into it, a place of refuge for another family. He decided to try and catch Emma. Hopefully she'd have time for a quick chat, and he brought out his phone to ring her.

'Hi, Dad,' she answered.

'Hi, love. I'm at Fishers Cottage, picking up a few things.' He swallowed, suddenly overcome with emotion.

'Dad, are you all right?' Emma asked with concern, sensing the tension.

'Yes… yes, just thinking about, you know, the future.'

Emma froze. Don't say he was having second thoughts about marrying Bunty? Surely not. She coughed nervously.

'The future?' she asked.

'Yes, about what's going to happen with the place,' Perry replied.

Emma inwardly sighed with relief.

'Oh, right. Yes, I've given it some thought like you said.'

'And?' Perry waited with bated breath.

'If it's OK with you, I'm thinking of selling it,' she said.

'Probably best,' he agreed, suddenly feeling like a great weight had been lifted from his shoulders. The last thing he wanted was for him and Emma to have the responsibility of renting the house out, which would have involved them still having a tie to it and all the hassle that being a landlord entailed. He didn't like the thought of having to see someone else live in Fishers Cottage when they still had connections to it. Much better to wipe the slate clean and say a final goodbye to the place. Fresh starts all around.

'Good, I'm glad you think so,' replied Emma, who had had reservations about telling him of her decision. The last thing *she* wanted was to cause any offence or upset.

'Well, after living in the big house, Fishers Cottage would seem like a rabbit hutch now, wouldn't it?' he teased.

Emma laughed. 'The big house, is that how you've always referred to it?'

Perry paused in thought. 'Yes, actually I have.'

Once again, images of Hamish Deville towering over him on the staircase flashed into mind. He'd never get over the first impression of the house and how apprehensive he'd felt. But, he reasoned, it wasn't the house, it was Bunty's father who had caused that. Hopefully in time he'd learn to like 'the big house', especially as it was his daughter's home now. Which then posed the next quandary for him.

'Emma, I'd like you to invest the money from the sale wisely,' he advised in a serious tone.

'Well, I wasn't thinking of blowing it all,' she joked.

'No, I mean…' He struggled to find the words. He could hardly say, 'keep it safe in case Felix decides to throw you out, or you decide to leave,' could he? But that really was his main worry. He hated to think of his daughter being beholden to anyone. Emma had to have choices, be her own woman. Plus, his daughter was known for being rather impetuous – look how she'd suddenly packed her job in. He also recalled the dreams and ambitions she'd once had for the band. Counselling a secure investment certainly wouldn't do her any harm.

However, his daughter proved to have a touch more sense than he'd given her credit for, and intuition too.

'I know what you're thinking, Dad,' she said, all flippancy gone.

'You do?'

'Yes. You think I could end up on my rear, with no place to go and very little else.'

'I wouldn't put it quite like that,' he calmly objected.

'There's no need to worry, Dad, honestly. I might be head over heels in love, but I'm still me, Emma. Haven't I always been feisty, sticking up for myself?'

He grinned. 'Yes, you have.'

'Well then,' she said, then added, 'and Felix is a decent man, Dad. Why do you always think the worst?' Her voice showed more concern than accusation.

'Because I'm your dad and I worry about you? Because it's my job?'

She smiled, touched by his words. 'Maybe it's time to concentrate on *you*. You and Bunty.'

'Maybe,' he answered.

'OK, well if that's everything, I need to get back to keeping *the big house* running. Bye, Dad.'

'Bye, love.'

He looked at his phone. Emma's face appeared as his background photo. His daughter, who had just announced was 'head over heels in love'. That said it all, didn't it? She had her life to live, and so did he. With a spring in his step and a new feeling of optimism, he collected his belongings and started to load the car. Once done, he locked the front door of Fishers Cottage for the last time and bid a final farewell.

As expected, the news of Jasmine's twin pregnancy spread like wildfire throughout Samphire Bay. After informing their families, Jasmine and Robin were happy for all to know. When Robin told Jack he was in fact about to be father to two babies and not just one, he threw his head back in amusement.

'You don't do things by halves mate, do you?' he'd chuckled.

'I may need more time off though,' warned Robin, wanting to be clear from the start.

'I know,' Jack nodded, 'no worries.'

Together they'd decided to employ a small group of builders. Renovating the warehouse into apartments had been an ambitious project from day one, but neither regretted taking it on. Instead of being overwhelmed by the task, they had done the sensible thing and sought help, and having been in the trade for so long meant they had contacts and knew who to employ.

As predicted, both sets of parents had been thrilled by the news of the twin babies. So much so, Jasmine wondered how excited they were going to be once they were born. Her mum had already reached fever pitch and her fussing had gone into overdrive. It was at this point that Jasmine started envying Felix Paschal living on a peninsula, cut off by the tide. How peaceful it must be, she thought, and how convenient. Visions of being bombarded by future grandparents sprang into her mind, filling her with a turbulent mix of glee and dread. Then again, she more than likely would need a helping hand. Having two newborn babies wasn't going to be easy and at some point Robin would have to return to work. Luckily she would be able to continue working from home, albeit maybe not take as much on, but being a freelance graphic designer meant she was her own boss who could plan her own schedule and workload.

Already they'd designated which would be the nursery room in her cottage. Originally, Jasmine had planned the smaller of the two remaining bedrooms. Now, it was to be the bigger bedroom, allowing space for two cots as well as the rocking chair which Robin had inherited from his grandmother. Also, in order to make room for Robin moving in, they'd had to rearrange Jasmine's bedroom. Moving the king size bed to the opposite wall of the window meant that another wardrobe could be placed beside hers and, as an added bonus, they had splendid views of the bay. Not that either of them envisaged having time to sit in bed admiring it.

'What with two babies and a warehouse to convert, I'm going to be well and truly knackered,' said Robin as he was unpacking his clothes.

'Yep,' Jasmine replied with a grin.

Robin smiled devotedly at her. She was beginning to show. The swell of her abdomen was evident in the denim dungarees she wore. Never had he loved her more. The very thought of this wonderful woman carrying his children filled him with awe. He'd do anything for her, anything for *them*. Which meant he needed to make more money, quick. Yes, he was due to earn a pretty penny once the warehouse renovation was completed, but that was at least a year off, with help. He'd need money well before that. Becoming a father wasn't going to come cheap and, despite Jasmine's good intentions, he didn't really think she'd have the time or energy to continue working.

So, he too had decided to sell his apartment and gain some welcomed cash. The work and finish that had gone into his home was of top quality, the fixtures and fittings all done to a high spec. Plus, having a balcony which gave such stunning views of the sea was also a good selling point. Robin knew full well that it wouldn't take any time at all for his apartment to sell. Samphire Bay was a premium location. People tended to stay once settling there, which meant property very rarely came on the market and was in high demand.

Instead of going through an estate agent, Robin had chosen to put it on the market himself. By advertising in local newspapers, magazines and online, he'd already gained much interest and had arranged a few viewings. A part of him had wished he'd never sold the cottage next door to Jasmine's. He and Jack had renovated that property and at the time had had reservations selling it. It was bigger, as they'd converted the attic space into a loft bedroom with sky-light windows, and now he couldn't help but think that would have made an ideal nursery for his twins. When saying as much to Jasmine, she'd disagreed.

'But I wouldn't have had Bunty for a neighbour.' Then she gave a little laugh. 'You could always renovate the loft here too, in time,' she quickly added at seeing his face.

'Yeah, 'cos I'm gonna have lots of time on my hands, aren't I?' he replied dryly.

'No, I meant when they're,' she pointed to her bump, 'a bit older.'

'Hmm, maybe. The extra room would mean we'd never have to move,' conceded Robin, who refused point blank to even contemplate leaving Samphire Bay. Seeing Jasmine frown, he explained, 'If we had any more children.'

Jasmine's eyes widened. Did he want a house full? Before she could respond, they were interrupted by a knock at the door. She looked out of the window to see Bunty at the back and, opening it, called for her to come inside.

'Door's unlocked, we're upstairs!'

Bunty made her way up and joined them, looked around the bedroom and smiled.

'Me and Perry are about to do the very same,' she said. 'Only I doubt there'll be as much space for his stuff. I've way too many clothes to get rid of my huge wardrobe.'

'Then why not take it out and make your smallest bedroom a dressing room?' suggested Robin.

'What a good idea, Robin,' replied Bunty in glee. 'You don't fancy putting up some shelving and storage space in there, do you, darling?'

At this Jasmine burst into giggles.

'Bunty,' said Robin assertively, 'as lovely as you are, no, I don't.'

'Oh.' Bunty looked crestfallen.

'He's going to be a bit busy,' said Jasmine giving her a playful nudge while rubbing a hand across her bump.

'Yes, I expect so,' Bunty nodded her head. 'A job for Perry then.'

Robin and Jasmine exchanged knowing looks. No doubt Bunty was going to keep Perry on his toes. Did the man really know what he was letting himself in for?

Chapter 29

Filming had finished for the day when Emma took an important telephone call from the police. They wanted to call and speak to her and Felix later in the afternoon. As soon as everyone had left the house, Emma told Felix to expect a visit.

'What news do you think they have for us?' she asked, beginning to feel a little on edge.

'Obviously information about Anika,' replied Felix, knowing it was only a matter of time before the story hit the press. He knew she'd been charged with breaking and entry, as for the violence against Emma, that was undetermined. He assumed that was what the call from the police was about.

They both sat waiting on tenterhooks for the knock on the door. Eventually it came and two officers – who introduced themselves as Detective Inspector Mason and Detective Sergeant Jones – were shown inside. After sitting them in the drawing room, Detective Inspector Mason cleared his throat and began.

'We have come to inform you that Anika Genness has been charged with stalking, breaking and entry and also attempted grievous bodily harm.'

Emma's eyes slid towards Felix, who was staring at the DI motionless. He was busy speculating how all this was going to pan out. He could see it now, Anika arriving at court looking stunning and perfectly composed with a trail of paparazzi behind her, cameras flashing, microphones pushed into her beautiful face. She was used to this kind of attention, but poor Emma, or his mother for that matter, were not – and they'd have to give evidence. A dread filled him.

'When's the trial?' he dully asked.

'There won't be one,' Detective Sergeant Jones replied, her tone and manner straightforward and no-nonsense.

Felix's head shot up abruptly.

'What do you mean?' he asked.

'Anika has pleaded guilty to all charges,' she answered.

'She's pleaded guilty? You mean—'

'Anika has representation and taken the advice given to her,' interrupted DI Mason.

Felix blinked, not quite believing what was being said. Anika had actually taken advice and admitted *everything*?

He frowned. 'But I thought she'd denied harming Emma?' he questioned. Emma too looked gobsmacked at hearing all this. She'd been psyching herself up for the witness box in a packed court room.

'Ms Genness has obviously given the whole incident a great deal of thought and decided this is the best option for her,' said DI Mason.

'You mean for damage limitation,' retorted Felix, resenting the reference of the nightmare they'd had to endure as an 'incident'. But of course, why hadn't he guessed this? Anika was hardly likely to want a trial, with maximum publicity tainting her image. She was the dazzling model who'd been wronged by her ex-boyfriend. Standing trial as a mad stalker, who had broken into his house and attacked his girlfriend with a broken glass bottle, was most definitely not the kind of profile-raising she'd want. So, Anika had done the sensible thing for once in her life and taken the only advice which had been offered to her, to own up and try to keep as tight a lid as possible on it. Still, word was bound to get out but, he acknowledged, nothing like the level of attention a very public trial would bring. He gave a large sigh.

'Does this mean I won't be required to give evidence?' asked Emma, anxious to have it confirmed.

'Yes, you won't be needed in court,' replied DS Jones with a tight smile.

'Oh, good.' Emma sat back with relief.

'And neither will Madam Sinclair,' said DI Mason.

'Right, I'll let my mother know,' Felix replied. There was a slight pause before he spoke again. 'So, what happens next?'

'A plea hearing will be set, followed by the sentence Anika will be given,' DS Jones said.

'She'll still end up behind bars though, right?' asked Emma urgently. The very notion of the crazy bunny boiler coming for her again filled her with terror.

'Undoubtedly,' assured DS Jones, 'especially with her track record.'

'Thank God for that,' said Emma looking at Felix. He gave a shaky smile and reached for her hand.

'It's OK, Emma, she's not going to harm you ever again,' he said gruffly. Nobody would. Not while he had breath in his body, he thought fiercely.

'Well, we'll be off now.' DI Mason stood up. 'Any more developments and we'll be in touch.'

Felix showed the officers out and returned to find Emma still sat stock-still in the drawing room. Once more guilt seeped into him, hating what she'd been subject to. He went over and put his arms round her.

'I'm so, so sorry for all this,' he whispered into her ear.

'But it's not your fault,' she replied, pulling herself back to face him. Her eyes searched his face, willing the self-reproach to leave him. If anything, *he'd* been tortured enough by Anika. The woman had made both their lives a misery. A surge of resilience pierced through her. 'Now listen,' she instructed assertively, 'we are going to forget Anika Genness even exists, do you hear me?'

Felix's mouth twitched. He loved it when she was forceful. 'Yes,' he obediently replied.

'She's well and truly out of our lives.' Emma gave a firm nod.

'Never to return,' agreed Felix.

'Exactly!' cheered Emma.

Felix was smiling, already beginning to feel better.

'Let's drink to that,' he said, getting up and heading towards the drinks cabinet.

'Absolutely,' affirmed Emma joining him.

After pouring them a couple of very strong gin and tonics, the two clinked glasses and each took a hearty gulp. Felix looked at her, filled with admiration at her fortitude.

'Once filming is over, I'm going to take you away on holiday and spoil you rotten,' he told her.

'Oh, yes?' Emma raised an eyebrow, liking the sound of that. 'Anywhere in mind?'

'Somewhere very private and secluded,' he replied, kissing her.

'Hmm.' She was liking it even more.

'Yes, where we'll be totally alone, cut off from the outside world,' he continued between kisses. Then he stopped when Emma burst into giggles. 'What?' he asked, bemused.

'It sounds like here,' she said.

Seeing the irony, he too joined in her laughter.

'Actually, I was thinking of somewhere a little more exotic,' he went on.

'I'll look forward to it.' She gave him a hard hug. 'In the meantime, you've a drama to finish,' she said resolutely, kissing his cheek.

Yes, thought Felix, he did, and when it was all over he'd throw the mother of all parties.

Robin was expecting a viewing that morning. He'd already showed someone round earlier in the week and it had proved promising, as they'd asked for a second look. He re-read the email going over the details of today's viewer. He was unsure if she was single or married, as her title was Dr Tara O'Hara. He smiled at the way her name rhymed. They'd only just exchanged names and email addresses, so he knew nothing more about her.

Dr Tara O'Hara was prompt though, as she rang the bell from the front entrance to his flat.

'It's Dr O'Hara, I've come to view your apartment,' she said through the intercom.

'Great, come on up,' replied Robin, buzzing her in. He stood at the top of the hallway stairs to greet her. 'Hi, I'm Robin.' He held out a hand.

Shaking it, she replied, 'Pleased to meet you.'

She was smartly dressed in a dark trouser suit and green blouse, which matched her emerald eyes perfectly, with a blaze of red hair, cut sharply into a shoulder length bob.

Robin led Tara down the small corridor to his apartment door and showed her inside. Immediately Tara looked impressed with the light shining through from the big picture window, with views of the bay beyond. Luckily, it was a bright, clear morning and the sunshine lifted the place. She was also struck by how empty the flat was. Robin, seeing her brows rise as she scanned over the scant furniture, explained the sparseness.

'I'm actually in the middle of moving out,' he said, 'so most of my stuff's at my girlfriend's.'

'Ah, I see,' she smiled, then continued assessing the room. Robin watched her eyes quickly flicker around, taking everything in. They rested on the open plan kitchen. 'May I?' she asked tipping her head towards it.

'Of course,' he replied. He pointed out the integrated fridge and freezer and told her what appliances he'd be leaving. Tara nodded and seemed content.

Again, she was drawn to the window.

'That's a fantastic view,' she said in amazement.

'I know. Take it from me, you'd never tire of it,' Robin told her.

'Won't you miss it?'

'I'll still have it. My girlfriend's house sits on the edge of the bay. It's an old fisherman's cottage,' he said. Then added with pride, 'We're expecting twins in summer.'

Tara's face lit up. 'Oh, lovely, congratulations.'

'Thanks,' he smiled back. 'It does mean my two bedroomed apartment is hardly going to be big enough for us,' he continued with a chuckle.

'I've just the one son, so it'd be plenty big enough for me,' she grinned.

Robin found it difficult to gauge her age. She looked to be in her late twenties or early thirties and, whilst she'd mentioned having a son, there'd been no mention of any husband yet.

Robin went on to show her the two bedrooms. Tara particularly liked the bedroom with the balcony.

'I'd definitely choose this one,' she said, gazing out onto the small sitting area, 'although I'm sure Calum would object,' she chuckled.

'How old is he?' asked Robin, curious to know.

'Fourteen,' she answered with a bright smile.

Robin was a touch surprised, expecting her son to be much younger. It made trying to guess her age even more difficult, then he stopped trying, realising it wasn't really any of his business.

'Have you always lived in Samphire Bay?' Tara asked.

'No. I moved from north London when I was a teenager, but wouldn't leave here now.'

'Hmm, I can see why. I'm in Lancaster at the moment, where I work.'

'I see,' said Robin, wondering why she wanted to move away.

He took her around the rest of the flat, showing her the various features and answering all her questions – she was incredibly thorough with her inspection and Robin was relieved that she clearly meant business with this viewing.

'I've already sold my house, so I'm ready to move whenever,' she told him.

'Right,' nodded Robin, hopes raising. Was she about to put an offer in?

'And as you've practically moved out and there's no chain, there'd be no delay, would there?' She looked expectantly at him.

'No, not at all,' he agreed.

'Good, well in that case, I'd like to make an offer.'

Robin quickly interjected before she went any further. 'Just to let you know, there's someone coming for a second viewing.'

Tara paused. 'If I offer the asking price, will you take it off the market today?'

'Yes,' replied Robin without hesitation and the two shook hands on the deal. Tara told him she'd put her offer in writing via an email and would give the name of her solicitors. They swapped further details of telephone numbers and addresses.

'Well, I'm sure you'll be happy here,' said Robin as they were parting, 'and feel free to come any time.' Inside, he was glad Tara was buying his flat, she seemed a decent, honest person. He doubted there'd be any trouble with the sale.

'I'd like to show it my son, if that's OK?' replied Tara.

'Of course, just ring when you want.'

'Thanks.' Tara swiftly eyed the apartment one last time, then turned to leave.

Robin was left with a strange sensation. Whilst he was pleased to have sold his home, and for the asking price, he also felt a tinge of sadness to be leaving. This little flat had served him well and he'd grown attached to the place. Still, onwards and upwards, he told himself.

His spirits soon lifted when he arrived at Jasmine's later that day. She'd been delighted to hear about the sale of his apartment.

'That's brilliant!' she exclaimed. 'And for the asking price.'

'I'm not surprised really,' Robin said, knowing how hot the property market was in Samphire Bay. That said, he was glad to be getting his hands on some much-needed cash. Now all his money worries were beginning to vanish. He'd have more than enough to tide them over until the warehouse renovation was complete.

True to form, Tara had put everything in an email as promised and Robin had replied along with the details of his solicitors, so it was full steam ahead. For the first time in a long while, he felt totally relaxed. His life had turned up a notch since learning he was about to become a father – and to two babies at that, whereas he noticed Jasmine had taken everything calmly in her stride, completely unfazed. He looked at her now, concentrating on her laptop screen, busy working away. He smiled at seeing her hand unconsciously rub her swollen abdomen. This time next year they'd be a family of four. He could hardly believe it.

Chapter 30

The cold snap of the early months was replaced by the warmth of April, gently edging its ways into Samphire Bay. Cherry and apple blossoms bloomed into life, tulips added bright spots of colour, while the sweet fragrance from the lily of the valleys filled the air. Sea thrift flowered in white, purple and pink low clumps across the sands.

Nobody was more grateful than Bunty for this. After much planning, preparing and praying, she had been rewarded by the promise of a glorious spring day.

'There, now didn't I tell you?' said Perry as they both checked the weather forecast. 'Our wedding will be bathed in sunshine.' He gave her a quick reassuring squeeze.

'Thank God,' replied Bunty. She'd been on pins for the past week, desperate for the weather to hold out till the weekend. Bunty's plan B was to serve the hog roast under cover, but she much preferred for it to be open on the beach.

Having basically done all she could, Bunty could now relax and just let it happen. Her dress hung in the wardrobe, cream satin ballet pumps tucked neatly underneath. A posy of white roses and gypsophila soaked in water was ready and waiting for the trip down the aisle. Perry's linen suit was hanging, newly pressed too; both outfits side by side, ready for their wearers to be joined in matrimony. The village church stood fully decked out with flowers, freshly polished pews and cleaned stained glass. The church committee wanted the best for their beloved Bunty. She was a popular member and so deserved it.

Emma too was at in a frenzy, waiting for the classic car to collect her. She'd been ready for the past hour, eager to slip into the silk, pale-rose bridesmaid dress. It was a simple, close fitted, long dress with shoulder straps and complimented her figure beautifully.

'You look stunning, Emma,' said Felix as she came down the staircase.

'Thanks. I've actually got butterflies,' she replied, wondering how her dad was bearing up.

'Just enjoy the day,' laughed Felix. He too cut a handsome figure in his navy-blue suit and white pristine shirt, which showed off his olive complexion, inherited from his mother.

The crunch of gravel told them the car had arrived.

'Here goes,' Emma said with a grin. 'See you at the church.'

They exchanged a quick kiss, then off she went.

Perry, meanwhile, was not one bit nervous. He'd waited a long time to marry Bunty, and nothing and nobody was about to ruin his day. He'd even insisted that they arrive at the church together. Well, she didn't have a father to give her away (thank the Lord, or today probably wouldn't even be happening) so in his eyes, Perry didn't see why they shouldn't swan up the aisle hand-in-hand. No, he was making sure that Bunty Deville's hand was locked safely in his the whole of the way.

He'd decorated her vintage Morris Minor with pink and white ribbons and was now opening its passenger door for his bride-to-be. Bunty was elegance personified. The cream dress with delicate layers of tulle and silver sequins looked classy and chic, and the sprig of gypsophila in her hair made her look fairy-like and ethereal. Perry's eyes had widened when he'd first seen her emerge from the bedroom doorway.

'Bunty,' he swallowed, near to tears.

'Now don't go all sentimental on me, Perry Scholar,' she gently chided, but only to stop herself from blubbering. Perry was, always had been, and always would be, her absolute hero; and what a fine figure of a man he looked today. Yes, she thought, he still had it.

Merrily they chugged along, down the coastal path onto the narrow, winding country lanes, past the cobbled square and the village green to the church. Emma stood waiting in the porch archway for them, at fever pitch by now. She waved her bouquet excitedly as they walked to the entrance to join her.

'All set?' she gushed, looking from one to the other.

'Too right,' said Perry.

'Yep, let's do this,' said Bunty.

Emma got in place behind them and, once the organ sang its first few opening notes, they set off up the aisle. The church was packed to the rafters. Practically the whole of Samphire Bay had shuffled into its pews. Heads turned to see the couple, already looking pleased as punch, serenely floating up to the altar to exchange marriage vows. Jasmine's eyes filled upon seeing Bunty. Robin too had to gulp back the emotion. Jack, however, true to form, couldn't help but give Bunty a cheeky wink, which Perry also clocked and smiled to himself.

Felix gave a reading from the bible, full of expression and drama like a real pro. The congregation sat spellbound by his performance. Once the vicar pronounced the couple husband and wife, a great cheer and applause rang out. Rose petals thrown by the congregation fluttered over the newlyweds as they sauntered arm in arm back down the aisle.

'To the beach!' shouted Bunty before getting into the Morris Minor, and threw her posey in the air towards the crowd filtering outside the church. Jasmine caught it, laughing with joy.

'Definitely us next,' whispered Robin closely, making her smile warmly at him. She gently rubbed her ever-growing bump.

Felix and Emma stood together waving the couple off, not realising that most of Samphire Bay were in fact looking at *them*, rather than the bride and groom. The locals were still in awe that someone so famous had come to live among them in their humble village.

Gradually, all made it to the beach, where kettledrums played and champagne was handed out. The couple had been well and truly blessed with the weather for their special day – light, fluffy clouds puttered across the blue sky and the sea was calmly rolling against the shore, small waves occasionally breaking up the flat of the horizon. The hog was roasting well and smelling delicious, and canapes of mini lobster rolls and crab cakes were circulated through the hungry crowd. Perry and Bunty were barefoot in the sand, wrapped in each other's arms, having shots taken by the photographer.

Jasmine and Robin were talking to the vicar when Emma and Felix joined them.

'Hey, fantastic news about the twins!' gushed Emma to Jasmine, giving her a quick hug.

'Thanks,' she smiled, while Robin and Felix nodded and shook hands.

'Yes, wonderful news,' agreed the vicar, then turned to the newlyweds. 'What fantastic pictures they're going to have,' he remarked, gazing across the sunlit bay with its glistening turquoise water.

'They certainly are,' agreed Felix. His affinity to Samphire Bay was growing stronger by the day. Never had he had such connection to a place.

As for Emma, she still had to pinch herself every morning. She'd always regarded Samphire Bay as a romantic, magical spot. To have her dad now living here as well was the icing on the cake, which promptly reminded her...

'Oh, the wedding cake! I almost forgot,' she hissed.

'But I thought they didn't want one?' Felix frowned.

'Yeah, well, watch this,' chuckled Emma.

A little later she was carrying a silver tray containing a huge cake in the shape of a canal boat. The words 'Just Married' appeared down its side.

'Oh, Emma!' cried Perry with delight. 'It's marvellous.'

Bunty laughed and produced a knife. 'Come on, let's cut it.'

Everyone cheered as they jointly clasped the knife handle and plunged it into the cake.

'A bit different to what we're about to board,' said Perry, tilting his head towards it.

'Sorry?' Bunty's brow furrowed in confusion.

'Our honeymoon,' he replied.

'What honeymoon? We haven't planned a honeymoon.'

'*I* have,' stated Perry proudly.

'You have?'

'Yes, Mrs Scholar. You'll be stepping onto a luxury yacht, heading for Saint Tropez.'

'No!' she gasped, hand over mouth in shock.

'Oh yes,' he replied, loving her reaction.

'Oh, Perrywinkle.' She kissed his cheek, then took a moment to simply gaze into his eyes, heart so full of love she could barely contain it.

As the sun shone down, the music played, the drinks flowed and the merriment continued. Everyone partied into the early evening until the tide crept it, the dusk set and a full moon illuminated the sky. Perry and Bunty stood by the shore, its incoming ripples lapping their bare feet.

'Well, we did it, Perry.' Bunty turned to face him.

'Yes, we did.' He held out his hand and together they walked up the beach together, after years of cruel separation, finally as husband and wife.

Chapter 31

The bright spring weather continued and Robin and Jack were keen to finish slating the roof of the warehouse whilst it lasted. They also wanted to get all the new windows installed, thus making the building completely watertight. Once that had been completed, they could start to look at reconfiguring the inside.

Robin, always eager to press on, was pleased with the progress they'd made so far. Jack too was impressed with what they had managed to achieve, especially given the size of the place.

'We'll be able to get rid of the scaffolding by tomorrow,' said Jack, looking up at the front of the warehouse, his hand blocking out the sun.

'That'll save us a fortune,' replied Robin, ever mindful of the cost. They'd had to hire far more scaffolding than they owned, again because of the sheer size it had to cover. Not for the first time, he began to have reservations about taking on such a massive project. It was by far the biggest one they'd ever tackled, but more importantly it was the timing. Never before had he been under such pressure. Not that anyone was pressing him, both Jack and Jasmine kept telling him not to worry; but he was stressing himself. About to become a father to twins whilst still having this ongoing renovation filled him with anxiety. So much so,

Jack was starting to worry about his friend. Seeing his face etched in angst, he nudged him.

'Listen, mate, calm down. Everything's going to work out fine.'

'Will it though? The twins are due in July,' said Robin, scraping his hand through his hair.

'Look, I've put the feelers out, we'll get help, stop worrying.'

Robin nodded, but remained quiet.

'Anyway. There's no rush to finish, is there? You've sold your flat, so there's no money problems.'

'Yeah, you're right,' conceded Robin.

'And you have as much paternity leave as necessary,' assured Jack again.

'Thanks, mate,' replied Robin, blowing out a breath. He suddenly realised how lucky he was to have Jack. He was so fortunate to work with his best friend. He couldn't imagine other business partners being so understanding.

'Right, let's start to get the glazing in,' said Jack, pointing to the sheets of glass waiting to be inserted into the new window frames.

They carefully lifted the first piece lent against the wall. They were using the ground floor room to store all the building equipment, so needed to carry the glass outside. On doing so, Jack tripped on some rubble on the concrete floor and the glass went crashing down. A shard of it landed in the back of his hand, slicing it. Blood poured out as Jack's face twisted in agony.

'Jack!' cried Robin, rushing to see the damage. An ugly, deep incision had been made. He quickly took off his jacket and yanked off his T-shirt, then wrapped it round Jack's hand. 'We need to try and stop the blood flow,' he told him. Then after tying it as tightly as possible, and slinging his jacket back on, he ushered Jack, who was looking extremely pale by now, into the van and headed at breakneck speed to A&E.

'You OK, Jack?' Robin was trying to keep his eyes on the road and him at the same time.

'Yeah, think so,' he replied while wincing in pain.

When they arrived at Lancaster hospital, Robin parked near the A&E department and they both hurried inside. The nurse, on seeing the amount of blood oozing from Jack's hand, immediately took them into a nearby room. After gingerly taking off the blood-drenched T-shirt wrapped round the wound, she declared he'd need stitches. Jack, still white as a ghost, just nodded dumbly.

'Do you want me to stay?' asked Robin.

'No, you go back and lock up,' Jack told him. In their haste to get to the hospital the warehouse had been left un-locked, with all their equipment inside.

'Sure?'

'Yea, I'll be fine, thanks.'

'OK, ring when you're ready to go,' said Robin and left.

The nurse cleaned Jack's hand as best she could before the doctor entered the room. Jack's eyes widened at seeing the very attractive, red-haired woman dressed in royal blue scrubs lean over him to inspect his cut.

'Eww, nasty,' she squinted to get a closer look, while Jack was getting a closer look at her. She had flawless, fair skin, dotted with a sprinkle of freckles across the nose. Her eyes observantly assessed him, two green orbs, dark-ringed, with russet flecks. Jack's pain began to vanish as his attention was diverted to this extraordinary creature before him. 'A few stitches will soon sort this out,' she smiled.

Jack sat motionless staring at her.

'Hmm?' he finally replied, when realising the doctor was waiting for some kind of response from him.

'I said, you'll need it stitched up, but don't worry, I'm pretty handy with a needle and thread,' she grinned.

'Oh, yes, fine. Thanks,' he said, still gazing at her.

The nurse swiftly supplied all the necessary implements and the doctor was soon injecting him with something to dull the pain. A few minutes later she was very strategically sewing the sliced skin back together. Jack observed the concentration in her face. Once finished she looked up at him with another smile.

'There, all done.'

Jack looked down at the neat, tiny row of stitches.

'Thanks.'

'There'll be a scar, but it'll fade in time,' she told him.

'Thanks,' he said again, unable to take his eyes off her, making no attempt to move.

'Try and keep it as clean as possible,' she instructed. At this Jack laughed.

'That could prove tricky, given my trade,' he said dryly.

'What's that?'

'I'm a builder. We – that's my business partner and I – are renovating the warehouse on the quay.'

'Oh, yes, I noticed that had sold,' nodded the doctor.

Having exchanged enough pleasantries, Jack knew it was time to go. No doubt this doctor would be needed for another impending emergency. Would it be inappropriate to ask her out? He noticed she didn't wear a wedding ring. Then as if answering his question her pager bleeped into life and she had to leave rapidly, but not before he clocked her name badge, 'Dr O'Hara'. Jack narrowed his eyes in contemplation. Well, he knew where to find her, didn't he?

Robin had rushed back on site to clear all the broken glass away and lock up. It was no good attempting to do anything by himself. By the time he'd finished his mobile rang.

'Hi, it's me. I'm all stitched up,' said Jack.

'OK, I'll come and fetch you.'

On the drive home they discussed the future of the renovation.

'I'll ring round tonight, try and get some immediate help,' Jack said assertively. Now that he was restricted with his cut hand, time was of the essence.

'Yeah, we need long-term help. If anyone can start, let's keep them on.' Robin looked at Jack's hand. 'You could do to rest that. The last thing you need is it getting infected.'

'The doctor said to keep it clean,' replied Jack.

'Did he say anything else?' asked Robin.

'She,' corrected Jack.

'Sorry, did *she* say anything else?'

'No…' he paused, then decided not to continue.

'What?' said Robin, sensing something was afoot.

'There was definitely an attraction, Rob.'

'What?' chuckled Robin, thinking how typical it was of Jack to come up with something like that, even in such circumstances.

'I felt a real… connection.' Jack looked wistfully into space, making Robin burst into laughter. He smothered it quickly at seeing Jack's look of indignation.

'And… er… did this doctor feel it too?' asked Robin, trying valiantly to keep a straight face.

'Dunno,' shrugged Jack, then added with a sly grin, 'but I know where she works.'

'Ah, I get it. But don't go having another accident mate,' warned Robin.

'Hmm, I'll just have to plan another way to bump into Dr O'Hara,' replied Jack dreamily.

Instantly Robin's ears pricked up. He certainly knew that name, the very buyer of his flat. He opened his mouth to tell him, then closed it, choosing to surprise his mate instead.

'I'm sure you'll meet again,' replied Robin with a knowing smile.

Felix stared in horror at the headline before him. He'd taken to hunting through the tabloids of late, in search of Anika's name. Only it wasn't her name that blazed in bold letters on the screen. It was Mel Nichols. He gulped at reading the article.

> Melvin Nichols, casting director, was found unconscious in his central London flat this morning. It is believed Mr Nichols had taken an overdose. He is currently in a stable condition. His family are devastated by his actions and ask for privacy at this very sad time…

Felix reached for his phone and rang Jennifer, his PA.

'Jennifer, have you heard?' he rasped.

'Yes,' came the cool reply.

'But why did he try to take his own life?' Felix asked gruffly, then added in panic, 'You don't think it was anything to do with my last conversation with him?'

'No. I suspect he couldn't face the shame of being exposed.'

'Who by?' cut in Felix abruptly.

'Rumour has it, he was caught by the chief executive in flagrante with a runner in the dressing room,' replied Jennifer, whose phone had been busy all morning. 'I was just about to ring you.'

Felix took a sharp intake of breath. He closed his eyes in relief. He hated the thought of any potential blood on his hands.

'So,' continued Jennifer in the same chilly tone, 'the old queen was finally ousted.'

'But, to do this?' said Felix incredulously.

'He certainly doesn't get my sympathy vote. Just remember what he was, Felix. And besides, it looks like he's going to make a full recovery.'

'Yes,' nodded Felix. There was an empty, poignant silence.

'And it may not even reach the press, how he abused his power. He could still get away with it.' The scorn in Jennifer's voice was evident.

'Oh, I don't know about that,' replied Felix. 'After this, I'll wager there'll be a few actors ready to spill the beans.'

'Well, let's hope so.'

They said their goodbyes but not before Felix invited her to the end of show party.

As the glorious weather had held out, the TV crew had been able to complete all the outside scenes, leaving the filming ahead of schedule. This had put everyone in high spirits and the much-anticipated knees up was most welcome.

Emma too was elated at hearing the *Lady Scarlett Invest-igates* theme tune, which Laurence Willis had very kindly sent her on a CD. She'd jumped for joy when Felix had blasted it out on surround sound. Her very own track! She, Emma Scholar, was about to sing to the nation. Or, as Felix pointed out, possibly the world, if the rights to the series were sold internationally. This could only open up further doors to a singing career.

As for Felix, he was just plain relieved he'd managed to complete the filming well within time and on budget, which wouldn't go unnoticed at the studio. Hopefully, this would bode well if he wanted another stab at directing. For now though, he relished the time off and the peace and quiet it gave him. And he hadn't forgotten that holiday he promised Emma. They both deserved a much well-earned break. That said, the last few days had been rather hectic, organising the end of show party.

Felix wasn't one to scrimp and had ordered enough booze to sink a ship. Emma had arranged for outside caterers to prepare all the food. She smirked to herself, wondering if, under different circumstances, *she'd* have been the one to sort it out, then giggled, recalling when Polly had called her 'the real lady of the house'. Well, she was now.

Felix and Emma had asked for a 1920s dress code. Each thought it would add a touch of glamour and fun. Bunty had been thrilled when hearing this, claiming it would be just like the 'old days' when her mother had enjoyed the same style at her parties in the Art Deco house. Both she and Perry had been invited, as had Jasmine and Robin.

On Felix's insistence, Emma was to wear the same outfit he'd seen her in for the first time. Emma had sat playing the piano in the hall at Bunty's open house day wearing a gold beaded dress, complete with a crystal chain headpiece.

'You will sing for us, won't you?' Felix asked.

'Maybe,' she shrugged, not wanting to steal the lime-light.

'Go on,' he coaxed, with a winning smile.

'Well, perhaps just the theme tune,' she relented.

'Very apt,' he winked.

Thankfully, the day of the party saw an orange-red sunrise slowly rise up across Samphire Bay. The marbled hall was flood-lit by its glow, as the catering staff hurried about their duties. In keeping with the occasion, they were dressed in black and white waitress uniforms and carried silver trays with flutes of sparkling champagne. A jazz band set up by the piano was playing. The cast and crew had hired two coaches to take and collect them and had arrived bang on time. In they all piled, eager to celebrate. Polly came in character, much to everyone's delight. Suffice to say that nobody mentioned Mel, not even Jennifer when she landed dressed as a flapper girl. Felix grinned as he passed her a glass of fizz.

'You look fab, Jennifer, good sport.'

'I can let my hair down sometimes, you know,' she joked, taking a gulp.

Bunty and Perry arrived with Robin and an ever-expanding Jasmine. Not to be outdone, Jasmine had tailored a maternity dress with tassels and wore a sequined headband, while Robin looked very demure with his sleeked back hair and false moustache.

Everyone had made a huge effort, fully getting into the spirit. Felix looked on from the balcony, his arms round Emma. Had it only been last summer when he'd first stepped foot into this very hall? Little had he known then just how his life was about to change – and all for the better. He glanced at Emma, watching the crowd below dancing to the band music.

'Are you dancing?' he asked, arching an eyebrow. She turned and smiled.

'Are you asking?'

'I'm asking,' he replied.

'I'm dancing,' she grinned, then tip-toed up to kiss him. Never had she been so happy. Coming to Samphire Bay had been the best move she'd ever made.

Together, hand-in-hand, they descended the stairs and joined their guests.

Acknowledgements

I so enjoyed writing this story, filling it with all the things I like; the Art Deco period, a murder mystery and a cast full of colourful characters. I've always loved a good Agatha Christie drama, and the huge white house on the peninsula in Samphire Bay seemed the ideal location to host a 1920s *whodunnit*.

Time flew as my deadline approached, but the timings of the book also had to be clicked into place, which was hugely helped with the feedback and support of those around me. So, big thanks to my editor, Emily Bedford, Alicia Pountney, copyeditor Paris Ferguson and proofreader Marina McCarron. I'd also like to thank the rest of the Canelo team, especially the book cover designer, Diane Meacham, for another brilliant cover.

The very best thing about writing this book involved staying at a marvelous Art Deco hotel in the Lake District, all in the name of research, of course! Wondering round its characterful rooms and listening to Tea Dance music from the roaring twenties, proved a real break from the modern world. I'm often inspired by beautiful period properties and could just imagine Felix Paschal with his cast and crew filming there.

As always, many thanks for all the support and kind words given by family, friends and readers. It's great hearing from you, so do please keep in touch.

Bye for now, until the next book,

Love Sasha x